The Sanguine Door

Genevieve Grey

www.darkstroke.com

Copyright © 2020 by Genevieve Grey
Artwork: Adobe Stock © warmtail
Design: Services for Authors
Editing: darkstroke
All rights reserved.

No part of this book may be used or reproduced in any manner whatsoever without written permission of the author or Crooked Cat/darkstroke except for brief quotations used for promotion or in reviews. This is a work of fiction. Names, characters, and incidents are used fictitiously.

First Dark Edition, darkstroke, Crooked Cat Books 2020

Discover us online:
www.darkstroke.com

Join us on instagram:
www.instagram.com/darkstrokebooks/

Include **#darkstroke** in a photo of yourself holding this book on Instagram and **something nice will happen.**

To Alex,
There is a vampire in this one.

Acknowledgements

This book would not have come to fruition without the support of so many people. The journey has been wrought with self-doubt and challenges, but I am glad to have come out the other side with a story I am proud of. Firstly, I would like to say a massive thank you to the team at darkstroke where my book found its home. I have had so much support and guidance from the team right from the very beginning. Thank you specifically to Laurence, who has answered my hundreds of questions graciously and turned The Sanguine Door into the best possible version.

Thank you to my parents, for always offering words of encouragement and supporting me 110% in everything I have ever attempted. Without you, I would have never had the confidence needed to move my writing from the pages of notebooks to the wider world. To my sister who I love, even though she doesn't read fiction.

To my friends, Bianca and Danielle who have provided endless encouragement and advice. I cherish your friendship more than I can say. Finally, I would like to thank Alex for listening to my stories for hours on end and always asking to hear more. My life is better for having you in it. I love you.

About the Author

Genevieve Grey is a NA fantasy author. In 2016, she graduated with a Bachelor of Laws from Bond University. From there, she found her passion working in criminal law. When she isn't inside a Court room or writing, Genevieve loves to read and play piano.

At age fifteen, Genevieve hand wrote her first novel in a diary and hasn't looked back since. She lives in sunny Sydney, Australia with her handsome German fiancé.

The Sanguine Door

Chapter One

I had always thought a good Monday started with being thrown into a giant heap of garbage.

Rancid trash stood like an insurmountable mountain between us. The smell of rotten meat clung to me like a second skin. I prematurely mourned the loss of my pants, they would be the newest victim of the burn bag. Surprisingly, my target moved like a prancing ballet dancer despite being a goblin. He had managed to artfully avoid the trash, while I was now drenched in fresh garbage juice. The ugly bastard spat blood at me over his shoulder, and I watched as 35,000 credits waddled away and melted into the shadows.

It was slow work pulling myself free from trash mountain. Once I was certain my stomach contents would stay where they belonged, I forced myself to look at the wound. The skin on my shin was ripped to shreds and blood slickened my entire calf. The memory of the goblin's knife like teeth crunching through my tibia shuddered through me.

My eyes closed and I turned my focus inwards, to the black tarry Magic that always laid in wait under my skin. Under my attention, it became fiery and animated. Endorphins dumped straight into my bloodstream in a dizzying rush. It didn't matter that I was behind on rent or that I was about to perform an act of Magic that could have me killed. There was only the intoxicating rush of power and the sharp pewter ring that extended from the tip of my finger. I hadn't used my magic in nearly six months but it still felt more natural than breathing.

There was no pain when I slid the point along my forearm. My skin parted willingly and deep red blood welled to the surface. I moved my arm to let the blood fall into a puddle.

The healing rune was engrained deep in my memory. I traced the complex shape on my thigh using my cooling blood. Power raced through my veins as the rune came alive in a brilliant flash of orange light. It took almost no effort to direct the Magic toward myself. My skin itched horrendously as it knitted together, but when the Magic was done, not even a faint scar remained. My Magic demanded more. The miniscule use of power hadn't been enough. It was *hungry*. Wisps of black, inky smoke leaked from my skin. I squeezed my eyes shut and pushed back. It retreated step by step and by the time I had control, I was drenched in a cold sweat.

The type of Magic I used, Blood Magic, had been outlawed for hundreds of years. If I was caught using it, there would be no trial. I would find myself cut off from my power, imprisoned or if I was really lucky—dead. The hunt against Blood Mages had left a dark stain on history. I stood gingerly, testing out my leg. I tapped the comms charm tucked behind my ear.

Loral picked up immediately. "Arina, are you okay?"

"I'm fine but the bastard ran off. Can you come get me?"

"I'll be there in five."

I disabled the charm and shuffled toward our designated meeting spot. My skin itched with the need to *move*. I wanted to go back after the bounty before he got too far away. The target had been on the loose for four years. No bounty hunter had been able to find him, let along take him in. He had too many friends in high places, and too much money to cover bribes.

Still, the Elect had set a price on his head that was enough to cover my rent for the next three years so it was worth it. Usually, I only busied myself with small jobs. Just enough to cover the cost of living, nothing to draw any attention or acclaim. But when John Smith the goblin had crossed my path, it had been too hard to resist.

I bet on the fact my new identity was secure enough that the small amount of infamy would be of no consequence. Blood Mages were relegated to the history books, and I was happy to leave them there. Loral's beloved, old car bumbled around the corner. I stuck out my thumb as he pulled up to the curb.

"Oh God, Arina. Whose blood is that?" He brought his hand up beside his eye and handed me a towel and a bottle of whisky.

I grinned and greedily swigged at the cheap liquor. Technically it was illegal, but there were no watchers around this part during the day.

"Not mine." I handed the whisky back to Loral and he tucked it inside the compartment under the steering wheel.

I still felt slightly giddy from the use of Magic. It was so close to the surface, even the burn of whisky in my stomach didn't distract me. There was good reason Blood Mages had been culled. The power lust had overwhelmed stronger Mages than me. The power finally retreated once again and left my mind free to ponder more important matters; like how I was going to find the goblin.

I had always been a cocky bitch and more than once it had gotten me in trouble. This was one of those times. I had hesitated on the killing blow because I was so sure I could overpower him and bring him in alive. Now instead of a reduced bounty, I had nothing.

Loral drove further into the outskirts of town, until our dilapidated unit came into view. The grey building stood three stories above the ground and at least half of the windows were broken; including mine. Luckily, magical wards kept anyone out. The front yard was lined with vicious, magically-altered venus flytraps. They snapped at anyone that walked too close. I had once seen my favourite squirrel get eaten by one of the bigger plants.

The trek to the second story was only slightly painful, our building wasn't blessed with a lift. When I finally reached our unit, Loral was at the door waiting impatiently to slam it behind me.

Home sweet home.

Our house was a cluttered wonderland of magical objects and equipment. Various sized beakers and burners were splayed across the kitchen counter. They were filled with different coloured liquids that I didn't dare touch. Loral picked up where he had left off. He poured one beaker into an *actual* cauldron. It must have been a new addition. I would have laughed at him, if Loral wasn't the most talented Potions Mage that I had ever come across. He could and would turn me into a rat for the slight.

Despite his talent, he refused to join a coven. The downside was that he wasn't licensed and relied on back alley shops and private deals to get by. I didn't know the true reason Loral had never joined a coven and likewise he never discussed why I usually only chose poorly paying jobs.

"What's the plan for tonight?" Loral asked.

"I might go out again, see if I can find him at his usual spot."

"Do you need any help?" He raised his brow.

"I'll be fine." We both knew he couldn't cross the border.

I stood from the couch and shuffled toward my bedroom and my glorious shower.

"Be careful!" he shouted after me.

I left Loral to his own devices and wherever he disappeared to when curfew hit. We had a d*on't ask, don't tell* policy that I was grateful for. My room was undisturbed with my clothes still strewn over the floor. I stripped off blood soaked outfit and placed it in the large black bag hanging over the door. It was depressingly full already. For years I had hung it up before every job and burnt the contents when it was finished. There was something about seeing the bag get heavier that gave me strength to continue. It was a visual reminder of what I had already been through.

My shower was too short and made me sour. With money on my mind, I pulled on my clothes and yanked a brush through my hair. On the way out, I grabbed a banana from the bowl and raced out onto the street. I needed to be out of the capital before curfew hit.

My bike was parked around the corner of the building. My anti-theft wards opened when they recognised my touch. I jumped on, and sped toward the border. The dat band on my wrist labeled me as an Elect approved bounty hunter. It meant I was able to cross borders during an active hunt as long as I stuck to curfew. The border to Nexus was only forty-five minutes away. It seemed strange that there was a city so close that was not under the full control of the Elect. The Elect seemed all consuming and infallible when you lived in Ka. Evidence of their rule was everywhere, even in the outskirts of the city where Loral and I lived there were watchers that slipped between the shadows.

As I crossed the invisible border into Nexus my dat band vibrated. Nexus was a relatively small city. It was split straight down the middle. One side was perpetually bathed in light. It housed the wealthy and some of the more important members of the Elect. The glass buildings shone like diamonds under the artificial light. The other side lived in night. The two most powerful vampire covens resided side-by-side in a precarious peace. The architecture was just as stunning, the result of hundreds of years of accumulated wealth. Straight down the centre housed a mix of species. It was close enough to the vampires that the Elect left the area mostly alone. There was a high chance that you could become a vamp's next meal, but that was a risk worth taking for relative freedom.

There were only two areas that had not been consumed by the Elect's omniscient rule, neither of them were safe or cozy.

The bar I was looking for was nestled right in the grey area of Nexus. I drove within the invisible border between light and dark, I knew it well. Most of the street lights had been shot out, and the shadows were filled with the things that went bump in the night. Still, the streets were more comforting here than Ka. After a time, the bar came up on my left. I parked and slipped into the dimly lit dump.

The place smelt of old sweat and spilled beer. Only those who were ready for a fight came to such a fine family establishment. I fit right in. A heavy-set waitress sauntered over to my table at the back of the room.

"What can I get you?" she drawled and sat on her hip.

I couldn't sense any Magic from her, it was odd to see a

human here. I wondered who she belonged to. The vamps? Or maybe some other creature? I ordered and she ambled back to the kitchen. I had bet that the goblin's routine would go unchanged. He was too confident, he had lived free for too many years. Without the healing rune, the injury he had given me would have put me out of commission for a month. He wouldn't bother going somewhere else, not for little old me.

The door opened and I waited with bated breath. I was *strongly* disappointed. Instead of the 5'3 morbidly obese green skinned light of my life, in waltzed a God amongst men.

The man in question put the words tall, dark and dangerous to shame. He had the kind of face that stopped you in your tracks. By his lazy swagger, it was evident that he was used to the sudden pause in a person's expression when they looked his way. The man wore a perfectly tailored suit that clung to his body. He scanned the room until he caught me staring. Blood rushed to my cheeks and the charm around my neck seared the skin under my sweater. I resisted the urge to yank it out. He finished his inspection and strode to the bar. The charm turned cold.

I kept my eyes on the door. Mostly.

The waitress came back with my meal and wine. She slid it in front of me, her eyes glued to her newest customer. The dry meat nearly slid off the plate. I didn't blame her. Finally, the door flung open and I was rewarded for my patience. My bounty shuffled through the door and headed straight for the closest table. He didn't bother looking up, but he seemed to be nursing a bad arm. It was satisfying. I had started to think he wouldn't come after all. The waitress placed his customary gravy slathered roast on his table. It was disgusting watching him eat. The goblin ate as though the food was trying to run from his plate. It made my own meal less palatable. Once he was done, he threw down some silver coins and stood to leave.

It was hard to get your hands on the currency that was used in the off-grid cities. There were no dat bands used here and mine felt tight on my wrist. I should have taken it off, it marked me as other. No wonder Mr. Handsome had stared at me. It was shiny and bulky even under my long sleeves.

The band wasn't Elect issued, but it was the best copy money could buy. I looked like a tourist and tourists got robbed. It didn't sit well. I placed some coin down on the table and turned to follow my target. Before I could reach the door, I was intercepted by a drunken shapeshifter. He grabbed my hand and threw me a lopsided grin. I yanked my arm free and flashed him my own version of a smile; it was closer to a sneer.

"Beat it pal." My voice was kept low, the last thing I needed was a scene.

"What are you drinking? I'll buy you a round." His breath reeked of whisky. He must have had a ridiculous amount of alcohol to get that wasted.

I turned on my heel and moved straight toward the door.

"Hey, bitch. I said I would buy you a drink!"

When he grabbed my wrist again, I resisted the urge to smash my fist into his nose. I dug the point of my ring into his flesh. He howled and I wriggled from his grip.

I raced out into the night but the target had already disappeared.

In the distance there was the telltale golden glow of Fire Magic. My feet pounded the road and I heard the target's distinctive laugh and the glow from another burst of fire. I skidded behind a nearby trashcan. Rubbish was seemingly becoming my natural habitat.

"Hello hunter," the goblin spat, his mouth too full of teeth to fully form the words.

My heart raced. Had he spotted me? I peered out from behind the trash. Standing and throwing Fire Magic at the goblin was the man from the bar. He looked almost bored as the target dodged and weaved away from his attack. The night air was filled with the scent of burnt vanilla. It was a powerful Magic. He wouldn't tire anytime soon. Whoever this man was, he was a force to be reckoned with. My own power flared in response. Anger burned away any hesitation I felt. The bounty was *mine*. The money was *mine*. I snuck closer toward them. Shockingly, the goblin looked even worse in the moonlight. Mr. Handsome hadn't noticed me yet. The target's eyes flicked to me and his face turned savage. I shot him a smug grin.

Surprise.

"You!" he snarled.

Mr. Handsome realised quickly that the goblin was not talking to him and whipped around to face me. Standing this close, I could see the shock in his slate grey eyes. He hesitated for a second too long. I sprinted toward the goblin and leapt onto his back. My daggers slid into my hands and I stabbed down into his large, muscled shoulder. He screamed a sound that shook the stagnant air and tried to hurl me from his back. His skin was too greasy and I slipped right off.

My head smacked into the brick wall. It took me a moment to shake the cobwebs from my mind. In a single movement, I flicked my ring along my forearm.

The backs of my hands were covered in delicate tattoos. They looked decorative, but they had a second purpose. The tattoos formed runes for fire and flames.

Rune Magic was a dying art, mostly because it took such a large amount of Magic to use for little pay off. I swiped a small amount of blood against the tattoos and felt the glorious rush of power surface.

I joined the fray, spraying the goblin with my own flames that sprung forth from the tips of my fingers.

"Step off, he's mine," I hissed toward my makeshift partner.

Before I could get too cocky, the goblin landed another heavy backhand that sent me flying into a building. I cursed. My shoulder exploded in agony and the distinct coppery smell of my blood scented the air. My power seeped through the wound on my temple, looking for death.

Panic tightened my chest.

Magic had dulled the pain, but I couldn't get a hold of it. Smoke leaked from my pores. My hands trembled. The more power that leaked into the air the further my control slipped. The taste of Mr. Handsome's Magic wet my tongue, it was sweet and flowery. I wanted more. My body moved toward him on its own accord.

He lunged at the goblin, sweat lightly coating his body. My tongue traced my lips. *Get a grip!* I reached back and touched the deep wound on my shoulder. Pain radiated in bolts down my arm. It sobered me some and I forced my gaze from the man.

I had used too much power. Between the healing and the fire, I had opened the flood gates too wide. My breath came hard and I braced myself on the wall.

"Looks like you're doing a real stand up job," Mr. Handsome remarked.

Deep gashes now appeared on the goblin's chest and the beast had slowed considerably. I managed to pull myself together enough to stand free from the wall.

"Don't kill him!" I gasped.

"I'm not going to kill him, sunshine."

The goblin was screeching now, a high keening sound. Every vampire and their familiar would be coming to see what the noise was. I didn't feel like being someone's midnight snack. I was still flat against the wall when the goblin started to stalk toward me, aiming to kill off the weakest link first. Mr. Handsome started throwing fireballs with fury but they bounced harmlessly off the thick hide on his back. I gripped my daggers and prepared to toss them into his heart. Before I could let them fly, Mr. Handsome lunged toward the goblin. The goblin brought his giant arm up and smashed him across the chin. My co-conspirator went limp. I felt mildly concerned, until the goblin swung at me again. Adrenaline narrowed my field of vision to the threat in front of me.

I charged the goblin, sliding to my knees as he grabbed at me. My daggers sprung free and I slashed the tendon on the back of his ankles. He collapsed and tried to swing around to grab me. The copious amounts of blood coating my skin made me too slippery and I easily wiggled from his grip. Mr. Handsome was still unconscious. My stomach rolled, I was losing too much blood. It didn't seem like my brightest idea to gamble with my control, but I was out of time.

I gritted my teeth and let my power free. My long plait lifted from my shoulders and I knew my eyes would have bled black. As soon as my Magic was let loose my wounds glued shut. My little goblin friend went as close to white as someone with green skin could.

There was one perk to being a Blood Mage--I was the boogey man.

The goblin froze, a dawning realisation slipping across his features. I felt another rush of power that had nothing to do with Magic. My lips stretched into a grin. The goblin screamed when I pushed from the wall and stalked toward him. He was still frozen when I retrieved my handcuffs from my back pocket and snapped them around his wrists. The Magic retreated from the ends of my hair.

"Sorceress," the Goblin spat with venom in his voice.

The words stoked the rage that burned deep inside my chest. I *hated* the word.

I leaned close, rising up on my toes. "If you don't shut up, I might decide that the price for bringing you in alive isn't worth it."

It would be too easy for me to siphon his life essence. It would take only the smallest of shoves and he would be lying dead at my feet. Goblins didn't have Magic like a Mage, but his essence would be just as satisfying. If the extra power wouldn't throw me straight off the edge into insanity, I would have given in to the hunger. I gagged the goblin and gave him an elbow to the temple for good measure. Mr. Handsome groaned and struggled to untangle himself from the glass bottles and half-eaten food. The trash at least masked the worst of his power.

He got to his feet .

"Thank you for so graciously tying up my bounty, Miss..?"

He towered over me. Under any other circumstance, I wouldn't mind but I was acutely aware of the dat band around my wrist that did not appear on his own.

"Miss—you're welcome. If I hadn't been here he would have made you his dessert."

"If you hadn't distracted me, I would have made quick work of him," he quipped.

I *needed* to taste his Magic for just a moment. I wanted to roll around in it and let it wash through me until he was left with nothing. I took a few hasty steps back, nearly tripping over my feet.

"It was at least a joint effort." He had sheathed his sword and looked at me with his head cocked.

"Sure," I huffed. I was in no mood to argue with him.

What I needed was whisky and unconsciousness.

"I'll organise pickup."

Before I could object, he had activated his comms charm. My head pounded and it took everything I had not to collapse to my knees.

"Jonah, I got someone for you to pick up. The payment is to be claimed by?" he asked.

"Arina Daffodil Bluebell"

He raised an eyebrow. I crossed my arms.

"Arina Daffodil Bluebell," he repeated, as if he didn't believe me. "The target's bound and gagged behind an alley near the Siren's Call, shouldn't be too hard to find. I will report back to the Elect at 0500 tomorrow." He hung up and turned to me.

Monday just kept getting better and better.

"Well, shall we go, *Sorceress*?"

My stomach dropped. I needed to get away from him before I wound up dancing in his blood. It didn't matter how handsome he was, the Elect was not something I wanted to mess with.

"I'm not going anywhere with you. I don't even know your name," I stumbled through my words.

"Luka Highland."

The Angel of Death.

My blood turned cold. Luka Highland was infamous. As the youngest member of the Elect, he carried out their dirty work. The Elect had propagated the idea that his job centered around the protection of its citizens for many years. It hadn't worked. People only dared whisper his name in public and parents told their children that he would come collect them if they misbehaved. I wasn't sure what I expected him to look like, but it wasn't the sharp featured man in front of me.

I had to leave.

Incarceration is a fate worse than death. My mother's voice was frantic in my mind.

"I have to go," I spat out and spun on my heel to leave.

Before I could take two steps, pain shot like a thunderbolt behind my eyes. My hands flew up to my face and my legs crumbled beneath me.

"Are you okay?" Concern laced the Hunter's voice.

What the fuck?

"I'm fine." I pushed myself to my feet and pushed down the road. The Hunter followed a few steps behind. *Loral would know what was wrong with me. Maybe I had been poisoned.*

"You don't look fine. Stop, let me take you to a healer."

I ignored him and somehow made it on to my bike. I didn't look behind me to see where he was. I needed to get far away from Luka Highland. He would bring me only trouble.

Chapter Two

My Magic had begun to settle into a restless vibration deep in my bones the further I got from Nexus. It lapped at my awareness, more powerful than it had ever been in recent memory.

It had to be something in Nexus that set me off. Usually I could bury my Magic deep within my chest and forget its existence. Something had ripped it to the surface. It didn't feel like it would willingly return to the dark tar sliding within my veins. I had never come as close to slipping before.

My sanity returned slowly. I didn't risk slowing down or stopping despite the curfew.

I shuffled into my apartment, grateful that Loral was off on one of his secret rendezvous. I crawled back into my shower and let the water wash over me. When its burn finally matched the burn from my Magic, I dragged myself out and hobbled to the living room. The cabinet looked empty, but it was a clever illusion. I banged on the door twice. Immediately the spell disappeared and revealed half-empty bottles of wine and liquor. Alcohol had been prohibited by the Elect ten years ago. It was illegal to have it and illegal to drink it. *Luckily, Loral and I didn't care too much for the Elect's laws.* I pushed aside the cheaper bottles before I found the one I was after. It had been a gift for my birthday, I didn't know how Loral had gotten his hands on it. I had been saving it for a special occasion.

This seemed as good as time as any.

I ripped out the cork and our worn couch embraced me like an old lover. The amber liquor glowed under the florescent lights. I let the liquid rest in my mouth a moment before swallowing. The sounds from the street below eased my ragged soul. I drunk until half the bottle was empty, and I was pleasantly numb.

I was a snake dressed as a sheep. My physical appearance never raised anyone's suspicions. My body looked almost frail, my face was gentle and youthful. How could people know the deadly power that was barely contained within me? It didn't seem fair. Since arriving in Ka two years ago, I had lived under a strict set of rules.

I couldn't risk sliding further into blood madness.

I hovered my claw ring above my palm, ignoring the screaming protests in the back of my mind. The pull to bathe in power was too strong for me to resist. The alcohol had severed my rational mind from my actions. It was as if someone else was performing the deed. My hands moved to run the razor-sharp edge along my skin. I watched in rapture, as the skin parted and blood welled and spilt from the thin line.

This is the last time. I had promised myself the same thing hundreds of times over. It never seemed to stick.

When the blood splashed on my table, everything was sweeter. The pain from earlier in the night seemed inconsequential, even my run-in with the Elect did not seem important. Three drops of blood rose from the puddle and moved in a slow circle. I alternated between making tiny barbs and harmless bubbles. I grew bored and let the liquid fall back to the coffee table. I felt invincible; all powerful. It was a feeling easy to get used to.

The wound had closed already. I drew blood again, this time from my palm. I let it pool on the glass top in a small puddle. The rune came instinctively. The blood moved easily on the tabletop and I weaved the complex shapes that made up a scrying rune. When it was complete, I took a deep breath and focused on pushing my black smokey power into the shape. The euphoria returned. In the back of my mind I dreaded the guilt that would consume me later. Blood Magic was inherently evil. Every time I accessed it I could feel the stain on my soul spreading. How long would it be until it consumed all of me? Usually the ruby around my neck kept the power dampened to a level that was ignorable, but not tonight.

Tonight I wanted to give in.

In the reflection of the glass I could see my curly hair floating around my head like a halo of hellfire. The whites of my irises were gone, swallowed by black. *Evil.* Bile rose in my throat, but my disgust wasn't enough to stop me. The rune glowed bright against the transparent glass and my consciousness was sucked into the ether.

***

Luka Highland's broad shoulders were hunched over a dingy bar. He wasn't a slave to his Elect's precious rules either—hypocrite. In the reflection of the mirror, I could see him twirl a knife between his deft, ring laden fingers. He watched it with an almost bored expression. His face was cruel and less inviting when not in motion. He had ditched the jacket to reveal black suspenders, and a white cotton shirt with the sleeves pushed up haphazardly to his elbows. The Hunter seemed agitated, and I pushed through the haze to get a closer look. He swallowed the half-full glass of dark liquid like it was water. It seemed he was a man after my own heart.

A thin woman entered the bar and sauntered over to the Hunter. Her pure white hair was cut in a severe bob that ended just above her chin. It contrasted her dark brown skin. Before she could reach him he sheathed the knife and spun on his chair. He stretched his arms along the bar. The smile he unleashed upon the poor girl was heart-stopping.

"Gretchen." He shed the tension he held before, melting into another persona altogether. It was unsettling to see him slip his skin so easily. The beautiful woman hadn't noticed and leaned in to the monster.

Her full lips brushed his ear. "Hunter, the Elect needs you to return immediately. There is an execution tomorrow."

He brushed her off with a wave of his hand. "Leave me be. Gretchen. I won't be their security. I thought you came bearing *better news.*" His voice was gruff and he returned to glowering over his empty drink.

She took the opportunity to saddle up next to him, and fluttered her ridiculously long eyelashes. "You seem tense." She placed a hand on his thigh and squeezed. "Let me take your mind off the Elect tonight. You can return to them tomorrow morning."

She graced him with a small, familiar smile. My power began to wane, the Magic quietened and the haze that allowed me to see things happening in other places started to dissipate. Through the mist I could make out the Hunter springing from his chair and crouching into a fighting stance. His slate grey eyes were all I could see as the room disappeared around him. He stared straight into me. A thin line of smoke trailed from me to him, on instinct I reached along it. Electricity shocked me and I dropped the line. I threw myself from the spell. My breathing was laboured and my lungs hurt, but I was back on my couch. I smeared the blood with shaking hands.

Surely I had been mistaken. He couldn't have sensed me. It was impossible. I was just drunk.

I took a final swig from the bottle. *Stuff it.* I drew a healing rune before I set a match to the remaining blood. Even though I couldn't stand without swaying, I somehow made it to bed where I slept like the dead.

***

The smell of sweat and hard work welcomed me as I slid open the door to the sparring gym. The sound of sweaty supernaturals hitting pads was a salve for my hangover. I dropped my bag into my locker and jogged over to the warmup mats. A few friendly faces murmured hellos. I hadn't been back to the gym in a number of weeks, but it was always the same crowd. I started gently, until the worst of my headache had disappeared. A good workout was just what I needed. My wounds were healed but my mind was still scattered. When my muscles felt loose, I moved to the heavy bag. The wards surrounding the gym buzzed along my skin, but it wasn't an unpleasant feeling. At least they managed to keep my Magic contained. The gym was a purely no Magic zone. Mages were especially prone to neuroticism, fights could spiral in death matches quickly. If it wasn't so expensive, I would have purchased the warding for my house. The bag took my punches until my shoulders burned and knuckles begun to protest.

"Rina!" Jax jogged up to me.

His wife, Erin, wasn't far behind him.

"Hey." I shook out my hands and joined them on the sparring mats.

Erin was statuesque. She stood nearly eye to eye with Jax, which was no easy feat. Her green eyes and tanned skin were striking, especially with her no-nonsense haircut. Jax was built like a truck. He would break your bones if he ever got a hold of you. He had caught me flush with one of his punches one day and broken a number of my ribs. I had made sure never to get hit by him again. Together they made one of the most revered teams of bounty hunters on the Portal. Occasionally I found myself riddled with jealously at their relationship but that was only on bad days. I leant against the wall, happy to watch them warm up and trade blows.

An unfamiliar man jogged over and joined me.

"Ever been five rounds with a wolf?" he asked me, his voice veering too close to sleazy.

"Plenty of times, and I have yet to be impressed."

He pouted at my retort.

"Why don't you go a few rounds with Rina?" Erin dragged Jax off to stand beside me. I stretched out my arms in front of me and cracked my fingers.

"As a warm up, sure." He eyed me.

He was lucky I was unarmed. For that remark I might have held a knife to his throat to see if he pissed his pants.

"Exactly. Rina needs a warm-up before she has a chance with me." Erin was sickly sweet.

The werewolf shrugged and followed me onto the mats. I leant forward, gently stretching out my hamstrings. I needed to work out some of my pent-up energy, and this cocky werewolf was just the right target. It was hard to break a werewolf, they healed too quickly.

"Let's go, Fido," I taunted.

He stalked forward, trying to use his superior size to intimidate me. It didn't work. We circled each other. He was heavy on his feet, a classic brawler. Strong but slow, all I needed to do was stay away from his heavy punches and I would be fine.

Sick of waiting, he thundered toward me; striking out once he was within range. His fist sailed past my head as I weaved out of the way. I had to keep moving. I was outmatched in strength, but my advantage never came from size. Every time he stomped forward with his left foot and threw his right hand I ducked it and landed a swift kick on his leading leg before slipping away. He chased me around the mats like a dog with a chew toy. When he thought I had slowed, he threw a heavy punch. It whistled past my ear. He grunted in frustration. Erin giggled in the background.

"How's the leg?" I teased before sneaking another brutal kick to his inner thigh. He growled, looking more and more wolf like. If it weren't for the wards, he would have shifted. He switched stances and kicked out too fast for me to dodge completely. It brushed my side, but the sting faded fast. I had gotten too confident. He let a feral smile cross his face.

Drop to the floor. Roll clear, stand. Don't let him connect. Draw it out.

I moved without conscious thought. The patterns were the result of spending my formative years in fighting pits. My childhood had been heavy-handed and brutal, but it had given me a killer instinct that couldn't be replicated.

That was behind me. I was legitimate now.

My opponent's movements were growing sloppy and fatigue was kicking in. It was much harder to throw around a heavy-muscled body. I saw my chance and pounced. The next right hook he threw, I darted to the right and returned the blow with a vicious elbow. I was in too close for him to connect another punch, so instead he attempted to grab my middle and take me down. I quickly stabbed out at his knees. He took a few steps backward and I found myself on the front foot. I alternated my attacks between body kicks and head punches and soon my own breathing grew strained. I connected, and he swayed on his feet. I went in for the kill, adrenaline rushing through my veins. Euphoria filled me and nothing else mattered except for the downed opponent in front of me.

"Rina! It's over. He's done." Jax pushed himself between me and the wolf.

I snapped back to reality. The wolf was barely conscious on the ground. I was training, not trying to kill the guy.

"Sorry man, good fight." I stepped beyond Jax and lent a hand to the wolf before pulling him up. He shook his head out, his eye already black.

"You're terrifying." He hobbled over to the wall and squirted some water into his mouth.

He would be fine in fifteen minutes. It was a benefit to being a shifter. Erin pushed herself off the wall and moved toward me.

"All warmed up Pipsqueak?" She teased.

I gestured over to the far side of the arena at the rack of practice swords and daggers. "I'm ready to shake it up, choose your poison."

She skipped over and picked up a long practice sword. I retrieved my old faithful dagger. It was badly weighted and slick with overuse, but I was more comfortable fighting up close. Usually I found myself fighting people who were bigger and stronger. I didn't have the luxury of picking away at them from afar. My tactics involved getting up close and fighting dirty. I had never found any use in honour. Erin circled me, waving her weapon lazily. She would drag this out; try and exhaust me. I shot in fast and hard, mock-slashing at her stomach. She jumped back and slashed down in my direction. I rolled out of range and shot out at the back of her ankles.

I laughed. "Point one for me."

That move had cost me my lungs burned already. I made a mental note—*less laughing more fighting.* Erin was still light footed and looked fresh as a daisy. We struck and parried for the next twenty minutes, seemingly on equal ground. I scored several points in the first fifteen, but as I grew tired, the score became even.

"I told you to lay off the unapproved food Rina," Erin taunted.

I took a moment to catch my breath before running in to strike again. My bare feet slid back on the timber. I brought my daggers up above my head to block one of her downward strikes. The blow reverberated through my bones. My muscles burned with fatigue and I really began to contemplate my current lifestyle. Drinking heavily and skipping meals was not healthy, the stakes were too high for me to be so reckless. My speed was faltering, and she swung faster and faster, pushing her advantage. I had more Magic than her. Even after fighting the wolf I shouldn't have tired so quickly. My back hit the wall. She spun in, dodging my weak thrust and, within a flash, she held the sword to my neck—death blow. Her grin reached her sea green eyes. Erin stepped back. As soon as I had the space I collapsed forward with my hands on my knees. My wretched lungs couldn't draw in oxygen fast enough.

"Match point to me." She looked smug.

"Do you run marathons in your spare time?" I panted. "Hells."

I slunk down the wall and grabbed the nearest water bottle.

"You should come join me some time," Erin said.

She looked ready to go again. I knew I relied too much on my Magic but I hadn't expected just how much. Jax faced his wife with a matching wooden sword in his large hands. They engaged lazily, practicing complicated strikes and parries. I almost felt like crawling out of the sparring space, but it would look pathetic. Instead, I hobbled back to the heavy bag and left them to their swordplay. The next hour was spent throwing useless strikes toward the bag until my muscles refused to obey me. I made my way to the floor, too tired to even collapse dramatically. The ceiling was covered in mould from all the sweat. It made the gym smell musty and familiar.

"Do you have anything exciting on at the moment?" Jax asked, standing over my prone form.

"I captured a bounty yesterday, then I ran into the Elect's Hunter."

Jax let out a low whistle. "The Hunter? How was he?"

I remembered the Hunter's shock, how his cold eyes had bored into my soul as the vision of him dispersed. I shivered, even though the room was sweltering.

"He was… terrifying." I rolled onto my knees, my whole body ached. "And surprisingly good looking."

Erin laughed. "So, just your type then?"

I rolled my eyes. "I wouldn't touch Elect scum if my life depended on it."

Erin scrunched her brow. "Shhh Rina. Even this place isn't safe."

I knew it, but it still made me mad. The Hunter touted the Elect's righteous propaganda; killing those who were the deemed impure or different. Then he went and flouted their sacred rules himself. He was a hypocrite. It was worse than a being a true believer in their rhetoric.

After my workout I strolled toward the centre of Ka. My muscles ached already. I needed to walk now, less tomorrow Loral would have to roll me out of bed. There were still a few hours until curfew. The streets were clean, much cleaner than the grey part of Nexus. Still, the shine couldn't hide the rot underneath. I knew what lay beneath the shiny silver exterior. There was a silent crowd of people gathering ahead. It was unusual to see so many in the streets, especially so close to curfew. It was dangerous. I wandered closer to the mass of bodies. My stomach tweaked as I saw what they gathered around. I had forgotten about the execution.

The square was silver and shiny like everything else, but buckets full of blood had been spilled across it over the years. It loomed over the citizens as a reminder of the Elect's brutality. A skinny boy stood in centre stage. His clothes were torn and he was outrageously thin. A pair of enforcers held him by the scruff of his neck. The boy couldn't have been older than twelve. The crowd began to murmur vile words.

The enforcers were dressed in their customary red suits with masks half covering their faces. Three steel thrones stood at the back of the stage filled with members of the Elect wearing long black robes. The red and black was stark against the brushed steel of the dais. My fist unfurled. The Hunter was not among them.

I pushed through the crowd until I was pressed against the barricade. The boy's eyes were empty and ringed with big, purple circles. Thin, engraved metal encircled his neck. He had been stripped of his Magic. A Mage's Magic was part of their soul, when you took it away they went mad. The boy stared out at the crowd with his hopeless eyes. It didn't look like he'd had the collar on long enough to have the mercy of insanity. It was unsettling to see such despair on a face so young. Even children were not blind to the horrors of the Elect. One of the members stood, his heavy robes falling to the floor. He glided to the stage and silence settled over the crowd. I tried to smooth my features. The boys fear seemed to leak out of him, contaminating every breath I took.

"Welcome." The deep voice carried over the large space. "You have gathered here today to witness justice."

Silence.

"This Blood Mage murdered his own mother. If he is allowed to live, he will slaughter countless people to steal their lives for himself."

Children did not have the requisite constraint to control the violent charm of Blood Magic. When it manifested for the first time, they were lucky if they only killed one or two before being stopped. Without training, a child would succumb to bloodlust through no fault of their own. Public executions were rare enough that they provided entertainment to the masses. I usually made a point to avoid them, but I wouldn't leave this boy alone with these vile people. He deserved to have his last moments witnessed by a kindred spirit.

He was dragged closer to the crowd and brought to his knees.

"Stop!" a hoarse voice screamed.

I spun. The crowd had parted for a middle-aged man with

tears streaming down his face. They scattered away from him, as if his grief was contagious. Immediately a legion of enforcers rained down on him.

"Dad?" a high voice screamed from the stage. Some life had returned to the boys eyes and he struggled fruitlessly against the enforcers. "Dad!" he called out again.

He was not given the chance to respond. The father was cut down by an Enforcer's sword. Red blood spilled from his abdomen and stained the perfectly clean floor. The boy's guttural roar was cut off as he met the same fate. Quiet gasps came from the crowd, there had more excitement than expected. They began to disperse, dodging the large pools of liquid. I pushed against the crowd to the front of the stage. The boy lay in a crumpled heap. The deep gash spanned the whole width of his chest and exposed his pearly ribs. Blood bubbled from the wound even as his chest still rose and fell. His wide eyes frantically shot from one side to the next as if he was still looking for his father. The pool of bright red liquid had dripped down the front of the silver stage and onto the floor. The puddle kept growing until it eventually lapped at my toes.

I stood and watched as he took his last rattling breath, and I stayed until his blood was cold. The walk to my apartment took longer than it should have; I only managed to slip inside just as curfew hit. I didn't bother to undress for bed, instead collapsing onto the mattress and falling into a fitful sleep covered in blood that was not my own.

***

I knew that ground was beneath my feet, only because I was not falling. I knew that I needed to run, because fear pulsed through my veins pushing me away from some unknown threat. My legs burned from exertion and I was exhausted. It seemed like I had been running for hours and I didn't want to run anymore. I had never been prey.

I skidded to a stop and turned on the heel of my boots.

A cold brick-wall pressed against the exposed skin of my

shoulders. It hadn't been there before. I was boxed in. The inky night immediately changed to dawn. The orange and pink sky only illuminated my predicament. There was nowhere left to run.

My pursuer stalked toward me, like a lion about to take down a kill. Despite the light, I couldn't see the face under the hood. The only thing visible was a pair of eyes. They were dark, grey and full of smoke. They were the last ashes on a fire, being tossed into the breeze. I knew them. He lifted his hands to remove the hood. As the morning sun hit his features, his hair shone as red as mine. His chiseled face held a violent promise. The hilt of broadsword in his right hand was adorned with the insignia of the Elect.

He strode toward me, swinging the weapon in lazy half-circles.

I suddenly remembered that even if I held no blade, I was not defenceless. My pewter ring seemed to glint in the morning light. I held it up in front of my face in triumph. I could have kissed it but I sliced the back of my hand instead. The distinctive smell of ash flavoured the air as blood dripped through my fingers and onto the dirt. I couldn't remember the last time I had smelt my power so strongly.

The thought slipped through my mind before I could examine it any further. The power burnt through my body. I relished in the invincibility. It chased away the lingering fear that had been hidden away in the corners of my mind. I was home and whole.

It had been sometime since I had willingly called my Magic forth to attack. A slow smile stretched across my lips. The power continued to grow and I made no efforts to reign it in. It filled me completely until my skin felt like it would burst. When the pressure grew too much, I let it spill from me with a scream. The black tendrils shot with a wild hunger. It continued until my surroundings were coated in black inky smoke.

I would not wind up like that boy, bleeding out on a stage as entertainment.

High, shrill laughter bubbled from my lips. I brought my

hands to my mouth to try and stifle the sound, but it would not cease. Luka Highland would be no more. The Elect would perish and I would finally be free.

My pitiless black gaze turned to the Hunter as he appeared from the smoke. We assessed each other for one cold moment. He quirked his head, examining me closer. For one horrible moment I felt like a butterfly under a pin. Then my Magic turned solid and drilled into his chest. The memory of his blood turned me feral. It had been so potent, it called to me. I needed it as my own. My power buried into his body, but still he remained standing.

Fury spurred me on. My necklace scorched the thin skin of my chest and I ripped it away. The chain broke easily. As it hit the bricks, the red stone shattered into countless pieces. My Magic surged and the ground fell from beneath my feet. My eyes lolled back into my head and my vision went black. There was only Magic. It sparked and burned and I was consumed.

There was no I, only it. I had never felt so alive.

Then there was nothing.

No sliding tar, no burn and no roar. Had I died? Had I finally gone mad? The feeling of loss was so profound that tears cooled my cheeks. My knees hit the pavement and I fell onto my hands. The garnet shards dug into my skin. Tiny cuts opened on my palms and the pain seemed to tether me to the living. I expected the rush of Magic, but it did not come. The pain was just pain.

There was a heavy, unfamiliar weight around my neck and as I sat back onto my heels I was hit with a dawning realisation.

My eyes snapped open.
Collared.

Chapter Three

The last few days with Erin and Jax had been hell. It didn't matter how much I punished my body, I couldn't seem to get rid of the nightmares. They haunted me as soon as I closed my eyes. It was getting too close to nighttime and I had nothing left to do. My hair was stuck to my face with dried sweat, and I reluctantly drunk some tasteless protein shake Erin had given me. I poked at an approved salad with my fork. I could hear her nagging in my ear; *stop stuffing your face with illegal food. Eat some fruit... Maybe if you ate a salad occasionally you might beat me.*

My body was badly bruised from the beating I had received from Jax. I usually won about half the time, but today had been my worst performance to date. Still, it was better to lose to friends than feel the press of cold metal against my throat for real. It had become clear that I relied too heavily on my Magic. I hadn't been practicing nearly enough. It didn't help that the Hunter kept me awake most of the night, and not for the reason I would have liked. Loral kicked open the door. I didn't even flinch, I was so use to his dramatic entrances. He stood in the threshold, his arms laden with brown paper bags dripping grease.

"You're going to have to fix the hole or we are never getting our bond back." I looked back to my salad.

He glanced at the hole in the wall with disinterest. "You look miserable. Have you gotten any sleep at all?" he asked.

I shrugged. I couldn't tell him about my nightmares.

"Did you want to go out?" he asked, setting the food down on the kitchen counter.

"I could have a job tomorrow."

His pearls of laughter echoed through our tiny apartment.

"You've been moping around the apartment for a week. Going out will be good for you."

A night out with Loral sounded like the perfect distraction. It was better than flicking through the channels of approved propaganda.

"Okay, only if we can go to a blood sucker party."

He rolled his eyes. "Fine. I'll made a few calls."

Loral left the room and I opened our cabinet to fish out the booze. When he returned, I had spread out the food and alcohol. He plopped himself down and popped a cork of a clear liquor. It made my eyes water just smelling it. But, I gulped it down and ignored the burn in my esophagus.

"You're a lifesaver," I murmured through mouthfuls of cheesy food.

He took another shot in response. We ate until our stomachs were full and our gaits were slightly wobbly.

I quickly showered and dressed and allowed Loral to fuss over my hair and makeup.

We gossiped about menial things, and I felt myself relax for the first time in weeks. I had gone from bounty to bounty without any rest. It was nice to be doing something fun, the fact that it was illegal made it even better. A silent rebellion. I could almost be reminded of my life before Ka, when I had lived with no restraints.

When we were finally ready to go, Loral fished two invisibility spells out of my purse and handed one to me. I downed the salty tasting liquid and felt it shimmer into place. The spells were expensive, but you couldn't get into the party without one. You wouldn't even be able to see the entrance. It was a handy thing Loral was the most powerful potion Mage I knew. We shrugged on our heavy coats and slipped from the door.

Loral had promised he knew where the party was being hosted and that we would be able to walk the distance. The location of it changed every weekend to avoid detection. Alcohol was banned, along with large congregations of people. Parties had always existed and they always would. It didn't matter if the Elect deemed them unholy. Occasionally the location would be spilled and the party would be raided. I hadn't been arrested yet, and I wanted to keep it that way.

The vamp parties were run by Rammic, a flamboyant vampire with a love of nightlife. He didn't belong to a coven, but nonetheless was one of the most influential vampires living in Ka. There were always a number of men and women hanging off him, hypnotised into a feeder stupor. Their eyes were glazed over and they stared at him with adoration. It gave me the creeps. I couldn't understand the appeal of becoming a feeder. They would give up their lives to be '*looked after*' by a vampire. All you had to do was let them take your blood and they would make sure you never went hungry or cold again. Loral had told me that if you were one of Rammic's feeders you were treated very well. He had amassed a vast amount of wealth over his extremely long life and enjoyed spending it on his pets. It was supposed to be a pleasant exchange but I couldn't ever imagine being imprisoned like that, even if it meant I would likely be safe from the Elect.

"So you never gave me any gossip from your run in with the Hunter. What was he like?" Loral demanded.

"Scary"

"Good thing you kept him away from us." He shoved me playfully, "Oh, don't look so grim."

We arrived in a dimly lit street lined with pretty Elect-approved houses. It seemed hard to believe there was a nightclub hidden in amongst the plain looking buildings. Loral pulled me down the street by the hand until eventually stopping in front of a plain white door. Written at the top of the door in holographic silver were the words 'Witch Hunt.' The magic-laced wards were so thick, I could feel the pulse of sweet orange-flavoured power saturating the air. Any Mage could erect a ward, even a particularly old vampire had enough Magic. If a Mage's will was strong, the better the ward. A lot of people paid to have strong protections on their homes. It seemed like Rammic was no exception.

"What's the code?" I whispered to Loral.

"Macaroni," he sniggered.

His cheeks were flush with booze already. I placed my hand on the door and sent a thread of power into the wards.

Macaroni

They parted and let us through before snapping close behind us. As soon as we were through, the music blasted me. I could feel the bass pulsing through my body. The room was dimly lit. I could barely make out the small dance floor that was surrounded by plush red cushions. In a corner I spotted Rammic. He was sitting in a ridiculous pile of blood red cushions, his feeders surrounding him.

Rammic did not look like anyone I had ever met before. I couldn't imagine being forever trapped in the body of a twenty-five year old. His nose was too long and his lips too plump for his drawn face. In the flashing lights of the clubs, his skin had a waxy translucent hue. His chestnut hair was slicked back artfully and his suit seemed too tight to allow him to lounge as comfortably as he was. The feeders, a mix of men and women, were dressed just as expensively. Their bodies were adorned with precious jewellery. If I looked closer I knew I would have been able to see the twin puncture marks that marred their skin. I made my way to the bar.

Loral smoozed and smiled at almost everyone he passed, it was good for business.

"I'll have two of… whatever that is please." I pointed at a tray of smoking glasses on the counter and passed my coins over.

It went without saying they did not take dat band here. The bartender handed over the drinks. They smelt like cherries and smoke. I handed one over to Loral.

He eyed it sceptically. "You're not dosing me with anything unsavoury are you?"

"Oh no," I say in mock horror. "You've foiled my plan to get you drunk and take you home."

He laughed and dragged me toward the packed dance floor. My dancing was still awkward, despite living with Loral and in Ka for two years. It wasn't that I was bad, I just hated the feeling of the other bodies so close to mine. I could tolerate it only because the air-conditioning was laced. It was easy to get hooked. Eventually the crowd grew too dense and I left Loral to dance. There was a free booth that I shuffled into. A handsome blond-haired man made his way over to me with a drink in his hand. He had a goofy smile and I could see fangs peeking out from his full lips.

He slid into the booth beside me. "I'm Jonathan."

His shaggy hair brushed his eyebrows, framing his telltale black eyes. I felt an easy smile cross my face. It was nice to be captured in the full attention of a vampire.

"Arina," I shouted over the music.

It seemed a second drink had appeared in his hand the next time I blinked. I had barely seen him move. I plucked the drink from his icy fingers.

"Pixie?" he asked.

"Don't you know it's rude to ask?"

He smiled and tapped his nose. "I can usually tell but… you smell so strange."

I took a big gulp from my drink. "Just a Fire Mage."

It was the easiest for me to mimic. Fire was the only type of Magic I could conjure without needing to draw a rune. I still needed blood, but I could easily scratch my palm in an emergency and make it look like an accident. It was one of the reasons I kept my nails so long. I flashed the tattoos on the back of my hands. The black ink spiralled down around my fingers in artful flicks and curls.

"Vampire." He flashed me his fangs as if I hadn't noticed them.

Jonathan took a long draw from his opaque cup. I tried not to think what was in it.

"Where are you from, Arina?" He seemed to savour my name. I liked it.

"Here," I bluffed. "What about you?"

"Ka born and bred, a true traitor then. I'm from Nexus." He shuffled closer to me and brushed against my fingers.

"What coven?"

"Lasombra." The ruling coven in Nexus, the most powerful one in the country.

"You've snuck out for the night?" I teased.

"Promise you won't tell on me?"

The rest of the conversation was light and easy, and I found myself smiling more than I had in some time. After a number of drinks he dragged me back onto the dance floor. When you had a vampire's attention, you felt like the only person in the world. I had enough experience around them that I didn't usually allow myself to get drawn in. Tonight I couldn't find the will power to pull away. I was doing that a lot lately. He had a kind smile and flirted so much it made my cheeks burn. His hands traced down my dress and wound around my lower back. We weren't so dissimilar. His every feature was a trap to take a victims life force. The same could be said about me. The alcohol had made me giddy and stupid. I stretched up on my toes and brushed my lips to his. I felt his sharp fangs nip at my bottom lip. Warmth rose within me. From the corner of my eye I could see Loral giving me a thumbs up. I shooed him away with my free hand.

"I'm about ready to leave," he purred in my ear and a shiver ran down my spine.

Loral danced past me and I plucked the drink from his hand and downed it. I needed it more than him. He laughed at my back as I let Jonathan lead me from the crowd. I seemed to be floating on cloud nine as I left the club. The alcohol, mixed with the dosed air, left me feeling lighter than I had in years. Loral was right, I needed to get out more.

Easy conversation rose between Jonathan and me. The back of his hand brushed mine and he intertwined our fingers. We walked hand in hand down the street, swinging our hands like teenagers. Even though his skin was cold, it was comforting. I couldn't remember the last time someone had touched me in a non-violent way. I was being reckless. The invisibility potion had long since worn off and we were out past curfew. If we were caught, we would be arrested. I couldn't remember why it was a bad thing. Fuck the Elect.

"I'll show you my Magic, if you show me yours." I tried to give him my best seductive eyes. I knew by now Loral's hard work had been ruined. I could feel my hair getting crazier by the second and I was certain my mascara was giving me raccoon eyes.

He flashed his fangs at me and, in a moment, he was gone. Vampire speed was always so impressive. Before I had taken more than a step he returned with a crudely picked bunch of flowers and shrubs. With a low bow he presented them to me, roots and all. Pearls of laughter echoed off the tall buildings surrounding us. It was strange that it came from my mouth.

A scream ripped through the peaceful night. We tensed, the mood suddenly cold.

"Help! Help me!" screamed a female voice.

I raced toward the frightened woman. I could hear Jonathan on my heels. He grabbed my elbow and yanked me down an alley. "Here."

Against a building a man held a trembling woman by the neck. I could see his fangs glitter in the moonlight. The vampire closed them around the woman's neck.

"Stop!" I screamed.

The vampire flicked his feral gaze toward me briefly, paying no attention. He continued gnawing at the woman's flesh. Her screams grew louder.

"What you're doing is against the law. The Elect will come," Jonathon shouted across the alley.

The evil man laughed, a horrible vacant noise. He looked powerful and deranged. It was a dangerous combo.

Rage quickly boiled to the surface. The anger drudged up my Magic along with it, not a tar but a wildfire. The woman would be dead before I could reach her.

Without a second thought I used my ring and slashed my thigh just below my skirt. My eyes flicked black and my power ran into the ends of my hair. The fresh blood the vampire had just ingested called to me. It had Magic in it, Magic I wanted. My smokey power blew from me and drilled into his unsuspecting body.

I forced my power deeper into him and his face twisted in agony. He released his grip and let out a pained scream.

Burn, Burn!

The vampire smoked and withered, collapsing to the ground.

Someone was shouting at me, but I couldn't make the words out over the roar of power. The terrified lady who had slid to the ground was now facing me with wide eyes. She raised an outstretched finger, mouthing inconsolably. Finally her words sounded over the roaring in my ears.

"Sorceress," she hissed. "Sorceress!" The lady scrambled up wall and sprinted away from me, trailing blood.

I felt my hair fall back into place and I spun to face Jonathan. *What have I done?* A swirling sense of dread lodged itself in my gut.

"I'm…I'm a fire Mage," I sputtered. "See?" I showed him the runes on my hands in a feeble attempt to explain.

He brought his hands up in a placating gesture.

"I have no quarrels with an un-collared Blood Mage," he said slowly as if being careful not to spook me.

Vampires had the least amount to fear from Blood Mage's. Still, he looked terrified of me. He began slowly rolling up his sleeve, keeping a close eye on me. I felt like a skittish animal about to bolt, adrenaline pumped through my body. I watched him, not knowing what else to do. When his sleeve was above his elbow, he twisted his arm to show me something. The only thing different was a dead spot in his aura. I grabbed his arm, ignoring his flinch, and brought it closer to my face. In the pale moonlight, I could see in translucent ink a diamond tattooed within a circle. *It was the sign of the rebellion.* I had only heard rumours of the group that claimed to stand against the Elect's draconian rule.

He wouldn't turn me in.

I tore my gaze away from the tattoo to meet his eyes. My pulse pounded in my ears as I gave him a small nod.

"I need to go."

By now the human woman would be arriving at the nearest station to report a Blood Mage terrorising Ka. I sprinted from the alley toward the open street. It was good luck that I was close to home.

The city seemed to close in around me. The tall, glass buildings that I normally tolerated now seemed like a cage from which I needed to flee. Using my power had chased the alcohol from my system and I ran as fast as I could home. I mulled over the symbol on Jonathan's arm, the rebellion was meant to be a myth. The sigil was often painted on to buildings in silent defiance, but I had never thought much of it. The myth was perpetrated by those who were unhappy with their lot in life, the rebellion was meant to be filled with degenerates and the deranged outcasts of society.

The Elect ruled with an iron fist. They remained in control by force alone. Until recently I didn't think there had been any other option. No one dared stand up to them, the prisons were full and the death toll was high. Now they would hunt me.

It was my worst nightmare come to life.

My apartment finally came into view. I sprinted up the stairs and scrambled for the keys. I sent a silent prayer that Loral was still in the club. The Gods must have heard me because the apartment was empty and dark. I legged it to my room and yanked the large black backpack from behind my door, filling the bag methodically.

Leaving was always in the back of my mind. It was only a matter of time before my cover was blown. I knew this place wouldn't be permanent. Still, my chest tightened as I yanked off my heels and jammed my feet into boots. There was a cheap rug on the floor that hid a trap door. I pushed it aside and unlocked the secret compartment. In the small space I had stashed two large bags of cash. I snatched them up and stuffed them into my backpack.

My weapons were next. I snapped sheaths for the daggers on my bare thighs. The rest of my knives went in the backpack. Arina Bluebell was no longer. I cut the dat band from my wrist and smashed it under my boot. The woman's horrified face played in the back of my mind. It hadn't mattered that I had saved her life, she hated me more than the monster who had tried to kill her. I fled the apartment and jumped on my bike before the panic consumed me.

I flew from the city, the frigid wind blowing hard against my face. My helmet had been left behind in my haste. I weaved in and out of the small amount of traffic, the sun would be up soon. I needed to circumvent the cities checkpoint. There was only one area you could slip through unnoticed and only before dawn. Without a dat band I would be untraceable once I passed. The border raced toward me and I slipped through without issue.

The city confines disappeared behind me. There was nothing but old, forgotten roads in front of me. The information had cost me dearly, but it was worth it. By the time Dunlap came into view, the sun was high overhead. My grip finally relaxed on the handlebars. Dunlap had been my home before Ka. I didn't want to return to the city, but it was the only option I had. It was the only place I could hide. On the outskirts of the city there was a run-down motel that looked like it charged per the hour. I pulled up, tucking my bike out of view. It had always amazed me how only a few hours from Ka was a town the Elect had no control of. Dunlap might have been a free city, but it was arguably worse than Ka.

The reception was occupied by a purple-haired werewolf. She chewed loudly on bubble gum. I realised I was still dressed in my slinky dress from the night before. It was a good thing, maybe my appearance would go unremarked upon.

"I need a room for five nights," I said, if I couldn't think of a plan within five days it wouldn't matter anyway.

She gave me the price and I slapped the cash on the counter. No name needed. She threw me a set of keys and mumbled the directions to my room.

Exhaustion weighted at me. The sun was up but I couldn't sleep. There was too much to do, and I couldn't afford to waste time. I quickly dressed and washed the make-up from my face. I took off back toward my bike and drove to the nearest alchemist.

I didn't like how familiar the roads still were to me. I hadn't spent nearly enough time away. The city was always covered in a thick fog and that morning was no different. It was a strange consequence of the heavy Magic use that went on in the city. It seemed to taint the atmosphere. Cold seeped into my bones. I needed to keep moving. My black leather jacket offered little protection against the wind. In the fog, the streets blurred like an old painting. Dunlap's streets were overgrown with weeds and out of control shrub. They covered almost every building and roots buried under the road causing it to crack.

The Elect had no hold here, but they used the black markets and crime as propaganda fuel. If your citizens' only options were to live in the deadly slums of Dunlap, or the Elect's pristine city, it seemed like an easy choice to make. The small shop came into view. I had been here on occasion, their potions were well made. I hoped it was still true.

As soon as I opened the door I was hit with a savage wind gust. It seemed the owner had not sold. The shop had always been windy and so cluttered that glass bottles rested precariously on top of each other. Loral would feel right at home amongst the chaos.

I found the hair potions relatively quickly, there were all manners of colours. I grabbed the most boring looking brown colour and a pair of ceremonial scissors. The store clerk looked at me with a crazed twinkle in her eye. No doubt if I requested a face change spell the news would be whispered all over the streets of Dunlap. It wasn't worth the risk. I smiled sweetly and pulled a few more notes from the roll.

I didn't have the heart to destroy my bike. Instead, I left it unlocked behind the store and made the long walk back to the motel. I kept to the shadows and hoped that no one paid me any attention. It was a fickle wish. There were always people listening and watching in Dunlap, even as the streets looked empty. Ka was overt in their spying, they watched their citizens openly. Dunlap still watched, but they did so from the shadows. A new face would be recognised. I snuck around the back entrance to the motel and into my room.

In the bathroom's toothpaste-stained mirror, I attempted to cover my distinctive locks with the potion. I sat on the faded red bedspread and stared at the comms charm resting in my hand. No one had tried to ring me. I had hoped Loral would call me so I could explain to him why I had left. It was stupid of me to keep it for so long. I swiped my palm with the dagger and wet my tattoos with the blood. The device was engulfed in flames. I let the ash fall between my fingers as the remainder of my carefully constructed life fell to the ground.

I returned to the bathroom and rinsed my hair in the sink. I watched as the dark brown dye circled the drain. When it was washed, I hacked at the length of my hair until it sat above my shoulders. I wrapped it in a scratchy towel so I didn't have to look at it. Finally I allowed myself to crawl into bed. There was more to do, but it could wait until later in the day. It had taken me a whole year of planning to escape Dunlap the first time. After two years, I was just beginning to feel like my unit with Loral could be home. Now I had returned to the dark.

I tossed and turned, unable to find sleep. The woman's face stared back at me with her terrified eyes and trembling finger. Saving her was the stupidest thing I had ever done. Altruism was not in my nature, it never had been. Many times over the years I had stood by and watched while horrors were committed. There was nothing to gain from saving the woman, only things to lose.

The alcohol was to blame. It had made me lose my mind.

After many hours of staring at the ceiling, sleep finally found me. I welcomed the respite.

Chapter Four

The burn of cheap whisky hadn't warmed the cool pit that settled in my stomach, no matter how quickly I had drunk it. I sat huddled in a corner of the dimly lit bar. Luckily for me it was early and mostly empty. My hands trembled slightly around the cool glass and a thin sheen of sweat coated my body. My power slid uneasily under my skin. The hunger had returned. I lifted a hand to rub my necklace. It would be better if the charm was stronger, but dampening charms were almost impossible to obtain. The fact my mother had managed to get one at all was a miracle. I downed my drink and left a few coins on the table.

When I stepped outside, light rain wet me. The miserable weather made the dilapidated houses look even worse. I wasn't fooled. The houses in Dunlap were spelled to look ransacked, but each was almost an impenetrable fortress. Appearances were always deceiving here. Even though I changed my hair, I had no doubt word of my return would spread like a virus through the city. If I stayed too long, my past would surely catch me.

The house looked almost the same as it did the last time I visited. The yard surrounding the skinny green shack was filled with mountains of scrap metal and trash. I took a calming breath. My hand pressed against the cool warding that stretched almost to the edge of the yard. It buzzed under my fingertips with an energy that was as jittery as its owner. Wesley wasn't powerful enough to erect strong wards and he was too paranoid to have someone else perform the work.

For a moment they were visible, then a spider web of cracks emanated from my hand. It crumbled like a wet piece of paper. His alarms started blaring inside the house. I took a leisurely stroll to the front door, taking my time. He would be waiting to set off one of his piddly bombs. My gait shifted into something once familiar. The innocuous persona I had crafted in Ka fell away, and in its place slid something predatory. It was like I had never left the city. I drew blood and spread it across the rune tattooed under my collarbone. The thin shield sprung to life under my attention, it took a lot of energy to sustain. Defensive Magic wasn't natural to me, I rarely used it.

"Wesley my dear, it's me," I spoke in a sing-song voice.

A potion bomb came flying from the upstairs window and rebounded off my shoulder before exploding in the front yard. It looked like Wesley had gotten stronger. I ripped off my hat and glasses trying to see which window the rat was hiding in.

"You know that won't work on me. Come open the door for your dear old friend."

Two more potion bombs flew from the window, each bouncing harmlessly off my shield and exploding in his yard. He would burn his house to the ground if he continued.

"I'll call the Elect," he shouted from behind the door.

He was bluffing and we both knew it.

"I have money Wesley. Just let me in." I hesitated as I reached the front door.

"How much?"

"If you don't let me in, I'll break down your door."

He huffed and opened the door a sliver.

Before he could slam it in my face, I rammed through into his cluttered living room. Wesley was a hoarder. All types of technology took up every space in his tiny house. His spindly arms held a gun at me as I surveyed his living quarters. The weapon was a surprise, he had obtained some powerful friends. Good on him. Guns had been outlawed many years ago by the Elect. They were outrageously expensive on the black market, even more so than dampening charms. Even if you could afford a gun, the metal made your bones ache. You couldn't touch one for long. I had held one once, and vowed to never touch another again. Vamps wouldn't go within fifty meters of them.

"That's no way to welcome an old friend," I drawled.

His face blanched as I gave him a predatory smile. "You're no friend of mine," he spat in my direction.

I moved quickly, hitting the weapon from his unsteady hands and drawing my knife. A thin line of blood appeared where the blade kissed his skin. This close, I could see the sweat on his forehead. His pupils dilated even in the fluorescent lights and he smelt like week old garbage.

"Why don't you take a seat and we can both get what we want?"

He gulped, but nodded. I had tried to be nice to Wesley when we had first met, despite everyone's warnings against him. At the beginning, he had betrayed me to whoever had paid him a visit next. It had nearly gotten me killed on more than one occasion. Wesley shuffled toward the single clear chair, looking back at me every couple of steps. Once he was seated, my knife disappeared back into my jacket.

"I need a new identity, kill the last one. I'll pay you ten grand and give you an extra five to put on the dat band," I said.

That would use up most of my remaining cash stores, but it would be worth it. Wesley was one of the best forgers in the game, when his brain wasn't fogged with illegal potions. He was a junkie, but he made great dat bands and he wouldn't rat me out to the Elect. He had created an identity for me when I had left. I prayed that he was still lucid enough to give me what I needed now.

"Okay." He shivered and looked at me with full blown terror on his face. *Guess my reputation still holds.* "I'll need some new photos."

He ushered me to the other room and I shook out my hair. The room had a green wall with an expensive-looking camera in front of it. It was the cleanest room in the house by far. I stood in front of the camera as he clicked away. After about five minutes I was told the documents would be ready for me to collect that night.

"I'll leave your shit at the Barfly. You can't come here again. Destruction follows you like a curse Imelda."

"That's not my name," I hissed. "If it comes from your mouth again your kneecaps will be a part of my healthy, balanced breakfast." I rested my hand on his cheek and ran my ring gently across his skin. He nodded stiffly.

I left his house, dumping the cash by the door. It wasn't long before I was back at the motel and dumping my things into my backpack. I had laid out a large map on the bed.

When I had left Dunlap, I thought to hide in plain sight. I had run to the very city the Elect commanded. Now it was too dangerous. I had no doubt my face would be on every news blast available. Just another opportunity for Elect propaganda. I was an out of control Blood Mage who had committed murder. It was my luck no one in Dunlap paid any attention to the Elect's most wanted list, probably because half the population was on it.

My options were limited. I could go stay with Lucia, she would help me but her protection would come at a price. I would have to return to the pits. I didn't want to return there but I couldn't hide in Dunlap forever. Eventually the Elect would decide to wade through the slums of the city to find me. *Dammit*, I needed to go underground. I checked the time again, only 6pm. Too early to get the documents.

I returned to the map and searched for my next home.

I couldn't go back on the portal. Bounty hunting was out of the question and I didn't want to return to mercenary work. I had barely escaped with my sanity the first time. My Magic had eaten away at my soul, destroying all the good parts of it. The last two years with Loral had resurrected some of the bits worth saving, but it would be too easy to slide back down into the dark abyss and give in to the tantalising pull of power once again.

I scrunched the map and threw it to the ground. There was no third option for me. I had no good plan for what I would do next. I could sell Joe's potions for some extra cash to tide me over, but it wouldn't last. Besides, I had too many enemies waiting for me to pop back on the radar. I ran the bath to boiling and lowered myself into the steaming water. The tension I had been carrying seeped out into the water.

The feeling chased away the panic that had wormed itself under my breast bone, at least for the moment.

I stayed until the water ran cold. In the fogged mirror I could see the brown of my hair was already starting to look auburn. It curled wildly now that it had no length to weigh it down. I didn't look anything like myself. My beloved dagger went into an stiff sheath strapped to my thigh. The knife and my mother's necklace were the only things I would allow myself to keep.

I placed my distinctive rings into the metal trashcan along with anything else people might have once associated with Arina Bluebell. Before I could change my mind I swiped my blade against my finger pad and set them alight. Without a second glance I left the motel room with my stiff backpack holding the entirety of my life.

The exterior of the Barfly was familiar for all the wrong reasons. A long forgotten feeling of helplessness seeped into my bones and made my knees weak. I hadn't been back here since I had first arrived in the city at 10. It wasn't a place I had ever wanted to visit again. This week had gone from bad to shit.

I was no longer a vulnerable child, I had made sure of that.

I strode into the standalone building without looking back. The bar itself wasn't particularly intimidating, it was the same as all the bars in Dunlap--sticky. Only a few people were scattered around the interior. The night was still young.

"I'm here for Wesley." I leant over the bar and lowered my voice.

A sturdy man eyed me and slid a plain envelope across the counter. I peeked in at the contents. Inside sat a new shiny dat band, the replica looked good enough. There would be no way to test it in Dunlap. I would have to trust Wesley. A scary thought.

"Who would I see if I was after some information?"

The barkeep nodded at a skinny looking boy sitting on the far end of the bar. "That's the spider."

"Thank you." I slid a few notes across the table.

The bar tender gave me a sly smile. "You're not half as mean as Wesley made out." He might reconsider if he knew who I really was.

I slid over to the skinny boy. He looked no older than fifteen. Batting my thick lashes, I leant over toward him.

"Hi, I'm…Lola." An awkward second passed as I thought of a name. Lying use to come so easy. I was out of practice. He seemed unamused by my tactics.

"What do you want to know?"

I dropped the facade. My usual hard expression settled on my features. "I need to know about the rebellion."

"That will cost you." He hadn't looked up from his meal since I had engaged him. He slurped loudly on his soup, his blonde hair hanging limply over his eyes.

"What do you want?" I grabbed for my dwindling bag of coins.

"Not money. I trade in secrets." His voice was rough with age, a strange juxtaposition to his unmarred skin.

"I have money." Sweat beaded at the nape of my neck. He giggled, a child-like sound, and pushed his empty bowl away.

"I don't need money. I want to know your secrets." Clouded, unseeing eyes turned to face me. I stumbled back. He was no child.

"I don't have any secrets." My voice was strained. He nodded and turned back toward the bar.

"Everyone has secrets, girl, but I will settle for your name."

I leant close to his ear. He smelt of soap and lavender. "A."

"*The baby-faced killer.*" He flashed his crooked smile. "It is one of your names, but it is not your *true* name."

Names had power, but I was out of options.

"Imelda." The word burned as they left my lips.

It had been many years since I had uttered the words now I had heard it twice in one day. He showed a small satisfied smile as he peered into nothingness. I didn't like it.

"I also want to know about the bounty for the Blood Mage in the Elect." I peered over my shoulder to ensure no one was listening.

"That will be extra."

"Fine," I snapped. "What other secrets do you want from me?"

"Who ordered the hit on Samson James?"

The words stunned me. The job was so long ago and I had worked hard to blot it from my memory. It gave me the final push needed to leave for good. Fuzzy bloody memories turned crystal clear in my mind. The job had sent a message and cemented my reputation once and for all.

"You want me to break my oath?" My voice was strained and I closed my eyes to try and forget the bloodlust that had once roared within me.

"Yes."

"You will tell me everything I wish to know." I meant it to sound threatening, but desperation leaked from my pores.

"Of course."

I no longer lived by the code. The secret held little importance to me. My life was forfeit anyway. Still, it hurt to say the name.

"It was Alpha Giovanni himself."

"I see." He was positively smug now. He turned to face me with a grin.

I was too long out of the loop. The information was probably worth more than I had bargained for it.

"You wish to know about the Bounty for the free Blood Mage in Ka?"

I nodded. His voice had taken on a hushed tone and I struggled to listen over the noise of the bar.

"What is the price?" My heart hammered in my chest.

"One million credits." An icy shiver ran down my spine. "Although the bounty is not open on the Portal yet."

I had a few days more if my details weren't public.

"Why?"

"The Elect has decided to send their Hunter. I heard he knows her, that they had worked together before."

No.

I struggled to regain my composure. The Hunter had seen

me, he knew what I looked like. How had they discovered my identity so fast? Someone had given me up. Was it Loral, or Erin? The list was short. It was hard to imagine any of my friends forsaking me. I banished the thoughts, they would only slow me down. It didn't matter now, the only thing that mattered was getting out of Dunlap alive.

"The rebellion, where do I find it?" My words were clipped.

"Galway."

"How do I find them?" My frustration had turned to anger and my voice was as sharp as my knife. He seemed to ponder for a moment, I wanted to throttle him.

"They are having a meeting in four night's time, in the old library of the broken city."

That was the best I was going to get. It would have to be enough.

I muttered my thanks and slipped from the bar. My new band was too shiny on my wrist. I found a transport and paid him with the rest of my cash. When we pulled up at the bus stop I scrunched the piece of paper with two words handwritten on it.

Lilith Johnson.

Another name. It was hard to keep track of them all.

The departure board was crude, there were not many buses leaving the city. Galway was a big city on the sea, it had once been a shifter run city before the Elect had overtaken it. It was picturesque, a city to showcase the benefits of Elect rule. It was hard to imagine they would find much support among the people who had once lived there. The bus station was mostly empty and well outside the confines of Dunlap. This was the first of the Elect's checkpoints. If I couldn't pass here, I was screwed. The woman behind the counter looked bored as she stared off into the distance.

I prayed that Wesley had done a good enough job on my dat band. There was a very high chance that his brain was too fried to perform any good fraud.

"I would like to be on the next bus to Galway."

"Twenty five credits." I lifted my arm into the scanning

area. It blinked green twice.

"Thank you very much, Lilith. Please enjoy your trip with us." The sarcasm dripped from her voice. I doubted very much I would enjoy the trip.

The next bus to Galway wasn't leaving until the next morning. A few weary travellers were perched on the rows of chairs with bags and blankets. I found a place out of the way to sit down. I watched the stop with an exhausting intensity. The Hunter was after me. It wouldn't be long until they gathered a crowd to watch my head be separated from my shoulders. The hands racing around the clock face wasn't helping my rising panic. I paced the dirty linoleum and tried desperately to think of ways to escape my upcoming demise.

When the bus arrived it was empty. I squashed myself in one of the last rows. The journey would take about eight hours and I couldn't remember the last meal I had eaten. My stomach grumbled in protest. The squeal of the breaks pulling away was interrupted by a pounding on the door. The driver reluctantly stopped and a man stumbled into the bus out of breath. I eyed him.

His eyes and hair were light, as if he spent a lot of time outdoors. He was clean shaven and looked much too pure to be from Dunlap. The glares the rest of the patrons gave him, indicated they thought the same. I sunk lower into my chair and closed my eyes pretending to be asleep. Through slit eyes, I watched him toss his bag on the seat across from mine and sit down in the aisle row, seemingly unbothered by the looks from the other passengers.

Finally, the bus continued.

He was causing far too much noise trying to make himself comfortable and I dropped my sleeping charade to openly glare at him as he rustled loudly with a bag of noisy food. The sun had barely risen.

"Want some?" He held the bag out over the aisle toward me. My stomach growled loudly. I shook my head. He shrugged and placed them beside him. As he bent over his backpack to retrieve more noisy food, I reached over and snatched the packet from beside him and slunk back into my corner. He laughed at me, which was better than any alternative. The driver had turned up the radio to mask the obnoxious eating sounds. I crushed the packet in my fist. Even the propaganda over the radio was preferable to his munching.

He sat with his back against the window and faced me.

"I'm Judas." I closed my eyes again, "The bus rides going to be awfully long with no one to talk to."

His pestering knew no end.

"My name is Lilith."

I said with my eyes still closed. Hopefully if he realised how boring I was, he would leave me alone.

"Lilith, what brings you away from the beautiful city of Dunlap?"

His sunny demeanour didn't belong here, amongst the downtrodden and mean.

"I needed a change in scenery."

He scoffed, like there was a joke I wasn't clued in on. My eyes itched from the day old make up and the hunger pangs in my stomach had only increased.

"I haven't seen you around the city, what part are you from?"

"I'm not from Dunlap, just passing through."

We continued the conversation in mostly the same way, he asked me questions and I gave vague answers with no follow up. Eventually the lack of sleep got to me, and I couldn't bother to speak anymore. I fell into a light, uneventful sleep.

When I woke, the roads seemed to become less bumpy and better maintained. There would be no stopping until we got to the city.

"So, what do you do for work?" He obviously wanted to make small talk. I couldn't think of a convincing lie, so I continued to stare out the window. The desert outside was dry and bare. It was so different to the wet, lush lands of Dunlap. It was almost like all the Magic had been sucked from the place. No one could live out here.

He continued despite me. "I sell antique magical goods."

"You mean curses?" No wonder he lived in Dunlap.

"Gods no, the Magic is drained from the objects before they are sold at my shop. I'm actually on the hunt for a new object now."

Silence. I realised he was waiting for me to continue the conversation, "What object?"

"An old coin from Galway. It supposedly gave the bearer good luck."

I scoffed, there was no luck in this world. The rest of the journey I sat in relative silence whilst Judas was happy to chatter with only minimal prompting required from my end. The mindless stories kept the worst of the panic at bay and I found myself almost enjoying them.

The smell of the briny ocean blew through the bus before I could see it. I plastered my face to the window desperate for a peak at a place I had only read about. When it finally came into view; The deep blue water seemed to extend forever. Planes of sand stretched down the coast line as far as I could see.

"First time seeing the ocean?"

I nodded, unable to look away. The humidity was stifling and I was sweating through my shirt. I didn't mind the rapid change in temperature, it was better than the cold. The bus pulled up at the pristine station just outside town, the streets were bare and the only thing in the vicinity was the ocean. It was exhilarating.

I strode from the bus, desperate to feel the sand under my bare feet. There had been so much uncertainty in the last few days, it had left me balancing on a knife edge. The vastness of the ocean made me feel insignificant, and I relished in the anonymity. When I reached the line where the grass and the sand met, I kicked off my boots. My hands sunk into the hot sand. I sat in the dying sun, and let it warm me. I felt lighter, some of the stress from the last few days washed away with the tide. Judas sat down next to me. He looked like a puppy basking in the sun.

"Have you ever been swimming?"

He was already undressing, "No. Are we allowed?"

"You scared an Enforcer's going to come get us?" He

teased.

The bus had pulled up far from the city centre and the handful of occupants had dispersed. I hadn't seen where they had gone. I needed a way to distract myself from my Magic that didn't involve getting wasted, maybe I could let it seep into the water. Before I could feel embarrassed, I pulled off my pants and ran into the water. The water tickled at my toes as I admired the setting sun. I waded deeper, the coolness took away the worst of the burning. My mind was blissfully clear for the first time all week. I would not give in to my Magic today. The thought was a small comfort.

The waves were gentle as they lapped at my waist. My head bobbed under and I licked the salty water from my lips. Judas eventually joined me, his golden skin reflecting the last rays of the sun.

"I didn't know you were going to take off like that," His eyes crinkled in genuine amusement.

I admired him as he stood, eyes closed facing the horizon — a small smile across his face. The sun was glorious, he looked like he belonged there. How freeing it must be to have a place where you felt at home.

After a time, we reluctantly left the water and moved back to shore. The sand stuck to my wet feet but I didn't mind.

"You've never been to Galway before?"

"I've seen photos, it seems beautiful," I had postcards. Jax had once told me he was from Galway, but had migrated to Ka when he was a child.

"It's different now."

"Why?"

He gave me a tight grimace. We wandered from the beach and toward the city. The colourful aged timber buildings which had once lined the shore were no more. We hadn't reached the checkpoint yet, but the buildings were all cold, silver monstrosities. It was a replica of Ka. The soul of the city had been sucked out. There was no buzz of people mulling around, the streets were empty. I struggled to compare the pictures from my memories to what was in front of me. Maybe the rebellion had found their sympathises here.

The checkpoint came up quickly. Two Elect Rangers patrolled either side of the scanners. This would be the real test for my band, not some shoddy bus stop outside of Dunlap. Every Elect city had a similar checkpoint. You were required to sign in when you entered and sign out when you left. There were ways to get around the checkpoints, but your datband wouldn't work unless you had been scanned into the database. If you were stupid enough to use it without signing in, you would quickly be surrounded and carted away.

Judas waved his wrist over the scanner. He walked through the gate. On a screen above our heads flashed the words.

Welcome Judas Kareni.

Attempting to calm my breathing, I did the same. The scanner flashed green and relief crashed into me.

Welcome Lilith Johnson.

We weaved through the desolate city and finally arrived in the supposed centre. Everything looked new and unused, I had yet to see a single shifter. The streets were filled with Elect enforcers who were heavily armed and weaved slowly through the buildings. I pulled my hat low over my face. Perhaps it hadn't been wise for me to come here, it was only a matter of time before I was discovered.

"I thought this was a shifter city?" I whispered.

He eyed me for a moment before taking my elbow and ushering me into an alley. I almost drew my knife but he held a finger to my lips.

"You mustn't ask questions here."

"What are you talking about? I just want to know where all the people are?"

Judas shushed me frantically, his eyes scanning frantically, "Be careful who you ask questions too. If you speak out against the Elect, the punishment is death. There is no freedom to speak here like in Dunlap."

He eyed me as if I was crazy. Perhaps I had been too careless with my words. I gave a stiff nod. Before I could take more than a few steps, Judas retook my elbow. His grip was gentle and I had to stop myself from violently rejecting the contact. He led me quickly from me the city centre. The buildings became more broken down. There was a stark line between the Elect buildings and the original city. The roads had turned to dirt and the houses were no better than mud shacks. The people here were starving. I smoothed my face. This was where all the shifters had gone. They looked starved.

"What happened?" My voice was careful.

"This is where the shifters who objected to the Elect's rule live. The Elect has been merciful."

This didn't look like mercy.

"Do you know where the old library is?"

He looked at me, puzzled.

"Why?"

"I've read about it, I want to visit"

"It's through there." He pointed past a ground of hungry looking people. "It's the only original building still standing."

We weaved back through the poverty to the city centre. It was lavish in comparison. We reached the hotel Judas was staying at, it seemed like as good as place as any. I swiped my dat band at the entrance and paid for two nights accommodation. My room number flashed on the scanner.

Judas insisted on walking me to my room. We stood awkwardly at the door for a moment. He seemed to want to tell me something.

"You must not go to the old library."

My ears pricked in interest. I schooled my features into ones of nonchalance.

"Why?"

"Because, it's dangerous."

Why would it be dangerous? I scanned the hall for any enforcers, none were in ear shot.

"What do you know of the rebellion?" I kept my voice hushed. I tested my luck. It seemed too big a coincidence that he was telling me to avoid the place where they were meeting.

"Nothing." His words were too quick. He was a bad liar.

"I want to join." The conviction in my voice was

surprising. "They murdered my parents." I let my voice break at the end, flash some vulnerability, let him think of me as weak.

"There's a meeting at the old library in three days. I can't tell you any more."

I already knew that. I needed more.

"What time?"

"Is this why you're in Galway?"

"Yes, I was looking for you." I desperately needed his trust. *Stay hidden in plain sight.*

"The meeting is just after midnight."

We stood for a moment more before he strode silently toward the elevators. Had I made a mistake? This might have been the second stupid thing I had done in as many days.

Chapter Five

The hotel sat nestled against the sand. It was plainly furnished and the water wouldn't run past lukewarm. No one had given me a second glance. Of course, to people who hadn't seen me in person, I looked nothing like the runaway Blood Mage with bright orange hair. My fine features were hidden under a barrage of brown curls. My distinctive rings had been destroyed. I looked like a foreigner, only because I was well-fed. The cool ocean breeze drifted gently across my face from the open window on the balcony. Kneeling, I scratched a rune into the wooden floor. the symbol for precognition was powerful, it was one I had only studied but never performed. Now that it was drawn, I hoped I had enough Magic to activate it.

I tried to focus myself as I closed my palm around the blade, coaxing my Magic awake. Blood fell to the floor, soaking the rune. The raging fire burning inside me exploded into a noxious vapour. Gentle wasn't my style. The words to activate the Magic tumbled from my lips, my voice taking on a strange timbre.

Ostende mihi futura, praeterita mihi. Ostende mihi rerum volo video vidi.

I wish to see anyone who would do me harm.

Concentrating on that thought alone, I gritted my teeth and willed my power into the blood. Sweat beaded at the back of my neck as I forced my will. The rune shimmered but did not flare to life. I grunted in exhaustion as I pushed more Magic into the markings. The future didn't like to reveal itself to anyone but the Gods. Finally I was rewarded. It came to life in a bright flash of light. I fell back. The room disappeared and my vision went black.

Dark figures crept in the moonlight, covered by shadows.

Their faces were obscured as they rushed through the unfamiliar streets. One after another flashed before me. All were blurry figures, some of them familiar. I spotted a few bounty hunters that I had considered friends. Had they betrayed me? The flashing images made me nauseated. I came back to myself, trembling with my cheek pressed against the wood. The only consolation was that I didn't see Loral's face among the group, or even Jax and Erin. I pushed myself back to my knees and blew out an unsteady breath. My head pounded with the beginnings of backlash.

I utilised as much power as I dared to burn the remnants of the blood. At least no one would attack me tonight. From what I understood, the clearer the image, the closer it was to fruition. I was safe enough.

I slipped soundlessly from my room. The cold night air felt nice on my raw skin. I wandered aimlessly through the streets, but I couldn't shake the feeling that I was being watched.

It's just a side effect of using so much Magic.

It had made me twitchy. My control was hopeless, I suddenly missed my parents. They could have taught me so much. If I'd had their tutelage, I could have lived a normal life. They had done it, despite being cursed. They had been happy. I kept to the shadows. The streets emptied and I was left alone with my turbulent thoughts.

The run-down exterior of the Barfly, with its wooden sign hanging crooked over the entrance, wouldn't leave my mind. It had been a mistake to return there. I should have insisted Wesley pick another spot. I could almost feel the freezing fingers of the Ice Mage trail down my spine. His teeth had been cracked, and his eyes yellow as they drunk me in. His hot breath had sent goosebumps down my neck and I had instinctively known he was dangerous despite my age. He had taken the last of my innocence, but had paid for it in blood. I yanked myself back to the present. The emotions had been suppressed for so long that I had forgotten their potency. I shoved my trembling hands in my pockets. My skin felt unclean.

Like an alarm system, my power began to race through my

veins. I spun on my heel looking for the threat but the streets were empty. A skinny black cat with green intelligent eyes hunted me from behind a crate. My eyes closed and I wiped my sweaty hands on my jeans.

Pfft, an evil Blood Mage scared by a cat. If Loral had seen me jump, he would have never let me live it down. I bent onto my knees and started to scratch behind his ears.

"Hey little guy, what are you doing out?" I cooed. The adrenaline had settled once I realised the threat was only furry. The cat brushed up against me, purring loudly. "Who do you belong to?" I lifted the shiny black collar searching for a name.

"Me." A voice emerged from the shadows.

I jumped up and crouched, hand on my knife. The Hunter emerged from the shadows. How long had he been following me? I had forgotten how astonishingly tall he was. Before I could turn and flee, his strong hands gripped my biceps. I heaved at the feel of his palms against my skin. In a panic, I wriggled uselessly against his grip forgetting all my training. There was nothing tactical or smart about my frantic escape attempts.

"Don't move or you'll feel the fiery wrath of the Elect." His hands warmed in warning.

My skin blistered at the contact and the pain brought me back to myself. I was not a helpless child anymore and he was not an Ice Mage. The sweet smell of his burnt vanilla power filled my lungs. I tilted my head and met his cold, stony eyes. "Do you rehearse that line in the mirror?"

He chuckled, his lip quirking at the corner.

"A Blood Mage is powerless without *blood.* Shall we see who's a faster draw?" His hands burned hotter, scorching my skin. The pain made it hard to think.

Concentrate!

I blocked it from my mind. I could make another go at my knife and try and strike him before he burned me to a crisp. I couldn't draw enough blood for a meaningful attack by biting my tongue, it was just as likely I would spiral out of control. I wouldn't risk it yet.

I didn't like my chances. The Hunter was the youngest

member on the Elect for a reason.

"What do you want *Hunter*?" I spat.

It was hard to imagine a situation where I ended up on top, especially with his iron grip circling my biceps ready to watch me burn. I could sense his Magic circling, just waiting for his command.

"You need to come with me, *Sorceress*. The Elect will save you before you fall further into madness."

A bubble of laughter escaped from my lips. He wanted me to go *willingly* to the Elect. Did he think I was an idiot? I couldn't contain my giggles. He looked as if I had slapped him but his hands went cold. If I went with him now, I would spend the rest of my life in a cage, drugged and drained of power.

"I would rather die than be imprisoned by you."

The giddiness quickly soured into raging anger. I had witnessed the Elect's murderous wrath first hand. There was no mercy.

A finger of his power licked beneath my ear and my eyes closed involuntarily. My own bitter Magic rose up to meet it. Instead of pushing the power back down, I coaxed it forward. The flood gate opened and warmth filled my body. The cat hissed at me. I felt my hair drift from my shoulders as power permeated my every atom.

I pressed my chest to the Hunter and flashed open my blackened eyes. He took a sharp breath. I used his distraction to bring my knee up hard in between his legs and yanked myself from his grip.

Run.

I took off down the road. My feet pounding the pavement as I desperately tried to put distance between us. The Hunter recovered quickly from my low blow and I could already hear his footsteps catching behind me.

Mid step, I yanked my blade from its hilt. I couldn't spare the attention to watch. I gripped the blade and pulled it across my palm.

I jammed my dagger back in its sheath and used the blood to ignite the shield rune beneath my collar bone. I concentrated on the rune and felt it click to life just before one of the Hunter's fireballs came hurtling past me. The streets all looked the same as I weaved through the city aimlessly. The Hunter seemed like the type of man who would not want to share the glory. I didn't think the Enforcer's would come to assist him. I concentrated hard on pouring power into the spell. The blood flowed from the wound in my hand. I could feel my body weakening from the loss already. The leaking blood would give the Hunter a trail right to me. My shield stalled and another fireball singed the ends of my hair.

Shit, shit.

My shield spluttered once more before finally dying out.

The further I ran, the more remote the area became. It was too late to turn back. There was nowhere else to run. I stopped dead in my tracks and whirled to face my enemy. An uneasy sense of deja vu settled over me. I half expected a cold brick wall to appear at my back. As soon as the Hunter was close, he slowed to a jog and my power flared in warning.

His stupid sugary Magic was driving me to the edge. I had even less control than normal. Instead of risking my flimsy control, I activated the fire runes on the back of my hands. I flung a fireball in the Hunter's direction. He returned fire. One after the other, we dodged and weaved the other's attacks. Rage swelled inside of me, impossible to ignore.

Kill him, burn him.
The Elect must pay. They made you what you are.
Dodge, roll, burn.
He's my enemy.
Kill. Burn. Destroy. Give in…

Suddenly I was standing over him. The Hunter was on his knees and I held his throat. My Magic drilled into him, power pouring in tendrils seeking only to kill. I could feel the satisfied smile on my face. It would be so easy to suck out his Magic and take his life. It had been too long since I had felt another's life force dwindle under my will. His eyes met mine, unafraid. Only a crease in his brow indicated that he felt any pain.

Unsatisfied, I poured more power into him. My only goal

was to see his face twist in agony. A pained screamed finally escaped his lips and his hands flew up to grip his head. The sound of his agony filled me with a sick joy. The Hunter fell back onto the pavement.

He must pay.

In the moonlight I caught a glimpse of my reflection. My eyes were as black as the darkest pits of hell and my teeth were bared in a snarl. I could see the power rippling beneath my milky skin even in the puddle.

What was I doing? I didn't want to be a killer anymore.

The thought snapped me back to myself. I attempted to get my Magic under control. As I reigned it in, my power begun to lash out at me in revenge. I was totally helpless against its wrath. I whimpered, my body screaming in protest. The Hunter sat up slowly, his eyes shining.

Everything within me screamed for death, his or mine. I crumbled to my knees. The fire licked at the inside of my skin.

Tears streamed down my face but they did nothing to cool the burning. It wouldn't have surprised me if when I opened my eyes, I was left without flesh. The pull of power was overwhelming, I desperately screamed out for the release. If I gave in now, all would be lost. I would not retain my sanity against the overwhelming torrent.

"Collar me," I spat between clenched teeth. This was a battle I could not win. "Please."

There was an eerie click, then everything was cold and I was finally at peace.

When I awoke it was as if I had never lived.

I felt impossibly light. The burden of power had been lifted and replaced with peaceful emptiness. Before everything had been felt over the thick padding of Magic, now it was gone.

When I finally opened my eyes even the peeling ceiling seemed to captivate me. I was grateful the curtains were drawn and that I wasn't exposed to the sunlight, it would have been blinding. The break from the Magic was so freeing. Slowly the wonderment wore off and I realised what had happened. I wiggled to sit up and saw my once-beautifully-manicured nails had been cut to the quick. I growled.

Where was I?

The Hunter stared at me from across the room. He was sitting, straight-backed, on a wooden chair. He wore new clothes and looked freshly showered. His hair was a burnt amber colour in the light, his skin flushed like he had just been on a run. He stared at me with eyes that were a melted platinum. Now that I didn't scream for his death, it was hard to ignore his looming presence.

We stayed in silence.

Memories from the night before swirled in my brain. I had been everything I had sworn that I wasn't. My time of being a cold-blooded killer was behind me. I had given that up when I left Dunlap.

"We'll be travelling to Elect headquarters at dusk."

"Why not get a pick-up service?"

He let out a barking laugh that made goosebumps rise on my arms. "Good one."

"What time is it?"

"7pm."

I had slept the whole day.

"Who made your dat band? It's a very good fake."

It was my time to laugh. As much as I hated Wesley, I wasn't going to rat him out.

"What will you do with me?"

"You'll be placed in a facility for Blood Mages."

"A prison."

He shrugged. Grisly tales of what happened at the prisons leaked into dimly lit bars. I had tried for many years to find more information but no one would talk. If a child was discovered to be a Blood Mage, they became wards of the state or they were executed in the streets — dependent on the message they wanted to send. Children would be dropped off at Ka and then never be seen or heard from again. No one would ask after them. Blood Mages were evil. It didn't matter what happened to them in the prisons, only that they couldn't be a danger to society. Blood Mage ability wasn't normally hereditary. It popped up randomly and you wouldn't know about it until a child got mad or killed someone in a tantrum. My mother always said that imprisonment was a fate worse than death. Escape was my only option. I would send the Hunter a bouquet of apology flowers when I was at a safe distance. Not even Lucia would offer me safety now, the rebellion was my only option.

I took the chance to sleep, the bed was better than any I had slept on in years.

"Get up."

There was a weight on my chest and I peeked through my lashes to discover a black cat staring down at me. Its green eyes startled my sleep-addled brain. I sat up, the Magic handcuff burning into my skin. The cat jumped off in a huff. The empty sensation which had initially given me peace now began to gnaw at me like an itchy sweater. I rubbed the heel of my hand against my chest.

The cat purred happily in the Hunter's arms as he stroked behind its ears. The clock on the bedside table read 4:30am. Of course, he already looked showered and dressed. I wondered if he had slept at all.

"I need to shower." My voice was still thick with sleep. I was never a morning person. Captivity hadn't changed that. He flicked his wrist and the bonds trapping my hand dissipated. *Only the best for the Hunter*. I cradled my arm, shaking out the pins and needles.

Jumping from the bed, I walked to the tiny bathroom — no windows. The Hunter hesitated in the doorway, half inside the bathroom. His hulking form took up too much room. I was already feeling claustrophobic.

"Are you going to watch me undress?" I sneered.

A twitch under his eye was the only response I got. A familiar bag flicked from his hand and landed at my feet.

"I've taken your potions and weapons."

With that, he slammed the door. How had he discovered where I was staying? I quickly rifled through my bag to discover only fabric. He had been thorough. I was weaponless, but at least I had clean underwear. I unwrapped the crude bandage from around my hand. The stupid thing hadn't healed. My hand stung wickedly under the water. Ironic that the only injury I had was self-inflicted. Blood coloured the pool at my feet. It swirled down the drain but held no draw for me.

There was nothing but the sound of running water.

Don't think about it. Don't think of anything.

When I was sufficiently calm, I wrapped a hand towel around the injury and wiggled into fresh jeans and a singlet. In the foggy mirror, my hair was now distinctly red. The cheap potion was barely hanging on. I examined the thin ring of metal at my throat. It could almost be a necklace. In my nightmares it had been an unsightly, bulky thing. It was unbelievable how such a tiny piece of jewellery could render me useless. I was on the back foot, but I had gotten by without using Magic before. I emerged from the tiny bathroom and ran into the Hunter's hard chest. He snatched my bag back. His breath caught and he gently lifted my injured hand. He inspected my crude bandage with distain.

Without warning, he yanked me back to the bedroom. My nerves were frayed and my head swimming from blood loss.

"This is worse than I thought." His voice was gruff when he unwrapped the towel.

I drew back, half expecting a blow. When it didn't come, I relaxed. He held my hand to the light. The cut ran straight across my palm and was red and angry-looking.

"I know a healing rune if you'll just uncollar me for a—"

"—No."

It had been worth a shot.

"Fine. Let me bleed to death." I ripped my hand from his grip and wrapped it back in the towel, ignoring the sting.

"Don't be so dramatic." He eyed me for a moment before flicking his wrist. Magical bonds immediately encircled both my hands. The Hunter went to his things on the chair and took a moment to search.

He was right thinking I would attack him the moment he turned his back. No one had ever accused me of having honour. He retrieved first-aid supplies and sat on the bed next to me.

Healing potions wouldn't work on me without my Magic. It would be like drinking stale bath water. I was still cuffed as he unwrapped the towel and placed it on his lap. He didn't flinch at the blood. It was surprising. Most of the population believed a Sorcerer's blood was disgusting. Maybe he didn't believe all the Elect's propaganda. I didn't know if that made him better or worse.

The Hunter studied the wound carefully, turning my hand to see how far it extended. Once satisfied, he slathered the cut in an ointment and retrieved fresh bandages. His fingers were gentle and the balm blissfully cooling as he wrapped the wound. His cat had joined us on the bed and watched as his master bandaged me.

"What's your cat's name?"

"Pickles." He was matter of fact, focused on securing the bandage.

"He's cute." His green eyes were smarter than the average tabby and I swore the cat sneered in my direction. When he finished, my hand felt much better.

"We have to leave now." He gently grabbed me by the bicep and led me outside the motel. My heart pounded in my chest. I didn't want to go to the Elect. His car was right by the door and I was roughly guided into the passenger seat, he immediately locked the door. The Hunter slid into the driver's seat of the shiny black Jeep, the cat followed. I awkwardly did my seatbelt up, it was a challenge with my hands cuffed together.

"Can you un-cuff me? I'm not going to attack you when we're driving." He peered over at me. I felt uncomfortable under the weight of his stare.

With a flick of his wrist I was released. I stretched out, and Pickles decided my lap was the best place to sit. He padded around in a circle before nestling in for the drive.

The silence was deafening.

I reached my hand out to turn on the radio and was promptly swatted away. The Hunter looked perfectly at peace with the silence. Maybe he preferred it over the drivel that was on the radio. Whilst stopped at a traffic light he reached over and took the cat from me.

"He was comfortable where he was," I said.

He scoffed. Rude bastard.

"I have a proposition." I turned in my seat and leant toward his stern features. My confidence was a bluff. He could char me like a BBQ before I could squeal and we both knew it.

"You're not in a position to negotiate."

"I can help you infiltrate the rebellion." He raised an eyebrow at me. "And in return, I expect the Elect to show me leniency."

There was the little fact that I didn't actually know where the rebellion was, but I could find that out easily enough. His poker face was perfect. His lip didn't even twitch.

"The rebellion is a pipe dream. They are no threat to the Elect."

I remembered his face of disgust when I had first performed the locating rune. The Ice Mage had come to him with word of the rebellion. They were moving against the Elect. I knew they were terrified of an uprising, no matter how small. They thrived on absolute control and wouldn't tolerate anything less.

"The murmurs of rebellion grow stronger. It would be better to silence them before they turn to shouts. I can help you do that."

He turned to me now, his eyes squinting.

"What would you want in exchange?"

"My freedom."

"That's a steep price." His gaze returned to the road, poker-face firmly back in place. "I will speak with the rest of the Elect."

"You must do it now. They are having a meeting tonight."

He pulled over the car, his grey eyes set in a challenge. "What's to stop me torturing the information from you and going myself?"

I swallowed down the lump which had risen in my throat.

"Firstly you couldn't get it out of me. Plus, I'm your perfect cover. No one suspects a Mage that was collared by the Elect and seeking revenge."

He thought it over for a second before leaving the car. My blood pressure continued to rise when he locked the door. It was just me and Pickles. Time seemed to move more slowly. Through the window I watched the Hunter pace. His brow was creased and he seemed annoyed as he spoke into his comms charm. It was a pity I couldn't lip-read. After what felt like hours, he unlocked the car and hopped back into the driver's seat.

"The rest of the Elect will agree to the following terms. You will assist me in infiltrating the rebellion. You will gain your freedom, if and *only* if the rebellion is completely dismantled. You will also remain collared." He let me stew in silence for a moment. He didn't seem happy.

The deal was better than I had expected. I stuck out my hand and he gave it one firm pump.

"We need to make an oath."

I kept my fake bravado but underneath felt uneasy. A deal made on oath could not be broken, lest both parties suffer the consequence of a painful death. It wasn't something people did often. It was usually as a show of commitment to a partner, a grand gesture of love.

"Fine with me. You'll have to do the spell alone." I gestured to the collar.

"I have enough power." He seemed offended that I had insinuated otherwise.

"Okay, so I will try my best to dismantle the rebellion and, in return, I will earn my freedom."

"Hilarious." He stared at me dead pan, "The phrasing will be, at my direction, we will completely dismantle the rebellion and any additional missions the Elect see fit. Once completed in full, the Elect will pardon you from one count of murder."

"You might as well lock me up right now. I will only agree to dismantling the rebellion completely. If we fail, I may be taken into custody by the Elect. If we succeed, I will be granted immunity from all persecution and my status as a

Blood Mage removed."

He looked at me for a moment and seemed to consider his options.

"At my discretion, I can take you into custody."

He didn't say anything about me having to go willingly. "We have a deal."

He did not allow me another handshake. The Hunter retrieved a shiny dagger from his waist band and leant over me to open the glove box. He retrieved a notepad and pen and begun scribbling variations in the original tongue. He was too slow. I had lots of practice in the old language, it was how the more complex runes were activated.

"I'm faster." I gestured for him to hand me the pen and paper.

"Forgive me if I don't trust you."

"You can check it."

He didn't hand me the notepad, instead he continued scribbling. Fine, I didn't need paper.

"Ibi erit pactum an perdere in rebellionem concitarunt. Et est plena libertas concessa est. Vos can be taken vincula sunt in quolibet tempore."

The words spilled from my mouth. I didn't get to show off my language skills very frequently. He glared at me and continued writing. After what felt like forever, he had come to the same conclusion that I had. The Hunter turned to me and took my injured hand with his. He unwrapped the bandage and set it aside before taking the knife and shallowly slicing my other palm. He did the same for his own hands before hiding the dagger and clasping our hands together. I flinched at the sting in my wounded hand but kept my gaze steady on his.

We began the incantation, the words filling the inside of the car. I could see the strain on his features as he took on the weight of the oath by himself. Energy sizzled between us and the air took on a different pressure.

"It's done."

I had made a deal with the devil. Now I just needed to stay alive long enough to see it through.

Chapter Six

"Go back to Galway. The meeting is there." He swung the car around and we drove in silence back to the motel.

A sense of dread had filled the space my Magic use to inhabit. It was an unwelcome feeling. We returned to the Elect approved hotel in the centre of the city. I spent the day locked inside alone with only my traitorous thoughts. He returned my fake dat band to me before leaving our room.

The Hunter's wards were pulsing with power. There was no way I could get out. Still I had to try. The carpet had nearly worn down where I had paced the tiny room. I had spent many hours trying unsuccessfully to break the complex Magic. Without my power I was next to useless. He had returned to the room late at night with dinner. My stomach was in knots, nausea rolled violently through me. The food sat heavy in my stomach. I could feel the sweat beading on my forehead and goosebumps rose under my skin.

For a brief moment I thought I might have been dying.

I stumbled over to the sink and splashed my face with cold water. When I looked in to the mirror, my eyes were wide and terror-filled.

Get a hold of yourself.

The cold metal around my neck was suddenly suffocating. My blood pounded in my ears and my heart thudded in my chest. The tingling in my skin made me scratch at my arms. I couldn't have this thing on me any longer. My now blunt nails clawed at my neck, pulling uselessly and leaving deep scratches that pearled with blood.

Hadn't I dreamt of this? My Magic being quietened forever, being controlled by something other than power? In my childhood I had often lay in bed dreaming about life where I had been born a boring Fire Mage.

I retched but nothing came up.

What had I done?

I had been foolish to think the Elect would be satisfied with the disbandment of the rebellion. They would slaughter everyone that had even contemplated standing against them. I squashed the thoughts immediately. Imprisonment was a fate worse than death.

Get a grip! You made an oath.

I stared in the mirror. When I was certain I wouldn't melt into a puddle of tears, I marched out of the grey bathroom and sat at the table. I cleared my throat and attempted to slow my breathing. He mercifully didn't mention the self-inflicted wounds that were on my neck. His face was a mask of indifference. I schooled my features to match.

"Where are you from?" His casual voice broke the terse silence. I stared at him.

"What?"

"Well, *Lilith,* you're my friend. Isn't that why I'm helping you? We should know information about each other." His silvery eyes judged me for being slow.

"Oh. Of course. I was born in the grey side of Nexus." He nodded, unsurprised.

"I was born in Ka. I've lived there my whole life. How old are you?"

"22." It was like an awkward job interview.

"I'm 25. What are your parents' names?"

I cringed and turned to look out the small window. It wasn't like they were infamous criminals, but it felt private. I didn't want to make friends.

"All you need to know is that I'm a bounty hunter and a *Fire Mage,* like you." I crossed my arms, wincing as I pulled at the bandage on my hand. "The rest you can make up for all I care."

"How's your hand feeling?" He reached over the couch as if to touch me, but pulled back at the last moment.

"Fine."

"Let me look." He tugged at my sleeve until I relented and placed my hand in his lap.

He unwrapped the bandage and I turned away. I didn't want to see the blood.

"Why aren't you covered in scars from casting?" He went to his back pack and retrieved more ointment.

"When I draw upon my power it usually heals me if the cut is shallow. I also know a few healing runes."

"So you practice Rune Magic as well?"

I shrugged. My parents had drilled the patterns into me since childhood. I had known the basics before I had learnt the alphabet.

"It takes a lot of power to cast Runes," he noted.

I didn't need a reminder of my lost Magic. His touch felt nice as he smeared my hand with the cream. I hated it.

"Thank you," I muttered. Thanking the Hunter wasn't a good habit to get in to. I sunk into the hard chair and closed my eyes.

"What does it feel like?" I opened one eye and raised an eyebrow.

"It hurts."

"You know what I meant."

"So the Hunter wants to know how it feels to use Blood Magic? That sounds treasonous to me."

"Forget I said anything." He rose and stomped to the other side of the room.

No one had ever asked me about my power before.

"It's… euphoric." I rubbed my chest, aware of the icy feeling that had been slowly building since I first awoke.

The Hunter asked no more questions.

I rolled onto my side and huddled against the arm of the couch, hopeful that I would be able to get some rest. I should have stretched out on the bed, but it felt wrong with my enemy watching on. The Hunter roused me from my light sleep. He seemed to trust me enough not to keep me cuffed. Not like I could betray him anyway. Not with the oath holding us both in place.

We drove past the city and came to the poverty struck place Judas had shown me. We reached the old library. The carpark was empty and the moon was obscured by clouds.

Before I could walk toward the building, the Hunter stopped me. He threw me against the jeep, using his body as a barricade.

What the hell?

I struggled to breathe under his substantial weight. He fished something out of his pocket and held it in front of my face. It was a round potion capsule, shiny and red.

"What's that?" I tried to pretend he wasn't pressing his arm across my throat. Fear filled my veins as his gaze turned predatory. It seemed he wasn't able to suppress the monster for long. A sinister smile crossed his face. He had shed the lamb skin and revealed the wolf underneath.

I was an idiot for thinking him harmless.

"It's a paralysis potion," he said out the side of his mouth.

"Okay." I lifted my chin and tried to look bored. My bravado was ruined by my shaking hands.

Paralysis potions were very rare and very expensive. Only two potion Mages in the world could create them and their power didn't come cheap. The charms were like heat-seeking missiles, they caused the victim to be under the control of the wielder until they decided otherwise. I had only heard stories about the horrific psychological effects they had on their victims. The things people were forced to do. It wasn't something I ever wanted to experience.

"Don't underestimate me, sorceress. I didn't get to my position by accident." I shivered even though the weather was balmy and his body was hot against mine.

"I really hate that name," I mumbled, my voice sounding pathetic.

"If you betray me, I'll make sure you live to regret it. Oath be damned." The Hunter had been serene so far, but I had no doubt underneath the icy exterior was cruelty. He knew when to let it peak out.

I found myself nodding as he dragged me toward the dark building.

The door was unlocked and we let ourselves in. I shoved my trembling hands into my jean pockets. Judas's lithe figure lent against a column. When he saw me, his face lit up with a breathtaking smile.

"Lilith!" He marched toward me, taking no notice of the Hunter standing beside me. "You came. I couldn't find you at the motel and I got worried."

I found myself reciprocating the easy grin. With Judas around, the terror was easier to control. "Of course. Judas, this is my dear friend. I went to find him, I hope it's okay I brought him along."

"I'm Noah." The Hunter didn't miss a beat.

Judas assessed him, his light eyes scanning his features as if he knew who he was.

"I need your help, Judas." I softened my voice, drawing his attention to me. Crocodile tears swelled in my eyes. "I wasn't truthful to you on the bus. The Elect is hunting me for a crime I didn't commit. They collared me, Judas."

His eyes widened in shock. I thumbed the thin metal around my neck, pulling it from my shirt.

"I didn't see this before."

I blushed a deep red as I fumbled with an excuse. The Hunter saved me. "She usually keeps it glamoured. We've been searching for ways to get it off."

Judas nodded solemnly. "Of course. No wonder you were so reserved when we first met."

We trailed after Judas as he weaved through the empty rooms. The Hunter and I were herded into a small room with a desk. Judas gave me a small smile and stood at the back of the room. The Hunter and I sat side by side on the plastic chairs. I was hyperaware of his body next to mine. I needed to find a way to get that potion from him.

"Let me do the talking," the Hunter whispered in my ear.

Arrogant asshole.

After we had stewed for some time, the door opened. A short, balding man entered the room. I couldn't look away. He was captivating. Immediately I knew he was a leader. Armies would follow him and lay down their lives at his command. He smiled in my direction and a warmth flooded me. I was blanketed with a sense of confidence. I could shake it off, but I didn't want to. The assuredness filled the empty cavern in my chest.

"Welcome. I'm Joseph. What are your names?" His gravelly voice filled the small room.

"Lilith." My voice was reedy in comparison.

"Noah," the Hunter followed.

Joseph held out his hand and we placed our ID bands into his palm.

"Judas has said you want to join us."

I nodded.

"I have known them for a long time Joseph, they can be trusted," Judas said. I turned to face him, studying him.

"Thank you Judas." Joseph set his calm gaze on me and took my hands in his. "Why do you wish to join our cause child?"

"The Elect murdered my parents when I was a child. They collared me and took away my Magic." The hatred in my voice was palpable.

He nodded solemnly. "The Elect has taken much from you."

He reached toward the Hunter and did the same. Anxiety built within me. If the Hunter stuffed this up I didn't know what would happen.

"I made an oath to free her and I intend to follow through." His voice was so sure.

I almost believed him.

"You speak the truth. You're welcome to join us. We have a number of rules which you must promise to adhere too. Secrecy is paramount to our survival. Since you already know Judas, you will be stationed within his cell. We do not disclose our last names. You will not know anyone outside your cell. What are your skills? Everyone is useful here."

"We were bounty hunters. I am a Fire Mage and so is Lilith." He shifted in his seat. "…Before she was collared."

He was good.

"Excellent. The compound you will be stationed in needs more fighters. I will be travelling with you tonight. We will introduce you to everyone tomorrow morning."

He stood from his chair. "Come, you must be tired. It is

late. I do not believe many others will join us tonight."

We stood to follow. "We have bags in the car," the Hunter advised.

Joseph brushed him off. "Go get them. We'll be here."

The Hunter strode off and returned with both our duffel bags.

"What about pickles?" I asked, creening my head to try and find my new furry friend.

"I sent him back home."

I pouted. We were led to a car. Judas was standing outside. When he saw me, he wrapped me in a tight hug. I stiffened and frantically wriggled out.

"You made it."

"Sure did, buddy." I punched him lightly in the shoulder. He looked down at me like I had grown an extra head. I jumped back in case he got any more sudden urges to hug me.

"You guys have to wear these." He held out some blindfolds.

The Hunter and I were seated in the back row and Joseph took the front seat. If there were others, they had left long ago. I wondered why they had waited so late. Judas's idle chatter filled the darkness. It was fortunate that he liked to talk so much. The Hunter seemed to be about as much as a conversationalist as I was.

It took a few hours for us to come to a dirt road. I wondered if the Hunter was taking a peak from under his blindfold. The road was bumpy and I jostled in the backseat. I threw my hand out to steady myself, the Hunter had the same idea and our fingers met. He hissed and ripped his hand from mine while muttering an apology. I swallowed my retort.

"We're nearly here," Judas murmured from the front seat.

The car rolled to a stop and I heard Judas and Joseph slide out of the car. My door opened and a warm hand grasped mine. This one didn't pull away. The touch was uncomfortable to me, but I didn't want to telegraph the fact that I was an outsider, so I smiled gratefully in the direction I thought the face was. I gingerly climbed from the car, careful not to hit my head.

"Watch your step." Judas led me around, his hand gentle on my lower back.

I heard the Hunter stumble in the gravel. I hoped he fell on his blindfolded ass. We were finally led inside and down a steep staircase. I tripped on the last step and felt a strong arm wrap around my waist, saving my face from a meeting with the ground.

"You can take them off now." Joseph's calm voice filled the small space.

The air pressure had changed and there was a considerable chill to the room. Judas let my hand go and I rubbed my arms for warmth. When my eyes finally adjusted to the dark, Judas switched the lights on and I realised how small the corridor was. If I reached out with both hands I could touch the sides. Turning, I looked longingly up the stairwell. It didn't seem as if we would be seeing sky anytime soon. I should have savoured the moon longer.

"How are you feeling, Lilith?" Joseph sounded genuinely concerned.

"I'm fine. Just tired."

"Of course. Judas, please show them to a room. We double-up here. We don't have much space. Tomorrow I will introduce you to the group."

I gave him a closed-lip smile. Joseph turned and strode down a long corridor. The thought of sharing a room with the Hunter wasn't appealing. There would be no peace. We were ushered into a small room filled only with a double mattress and a single drop light in the centre. Judas flicked the light on. He delivered an extra blanket and our bags before reluctantly leaving us.

The walls were bare dirt and the entrance was covered only by a flimsy white curtain. I stood on the brink of something I couldn't describe. The weight of it pressed down on my shoulders and I struggled to take another step forward. It was too much and not enough at the same time. Any joy inside of me was swallowed by the dark thing.

"I'll take the floor." The Hunter interrupted my train of thought and pulled a pillow off the bed. I finally moved forward and crawled on to the mattress. Exhaustion overcame me and I wrapped myself in the scratchy blanket. The Hunter must have found the light switch because suddenly the room was black and sleep took me.

It felt strange to wake in the dark; I lay on my back for a long period of time before the Hunter flicked on the lights and loomed over me. It didn't look like he had slept much.

He held up my bag. "There's a shower through there. You go first."

I snatched my bag. The bathroom was tiny and dark. There was no light and no door. A shower and toilet were jammed into the small space. Thankfully there was no mirror. I got dressed into my last change of clean clothes and hung my shower washed garments over the toilet to dry. I shuffled back to the tiny bedroom and sat on the mattress. The tiny cracks running down the wall seemed to demand full attention. My body started tingling and the edges of my vision begun to go grey. Dark clouds of fog rolled through my brain dampening any emotions until I felt nothing. I was looking through the haze of plastic that had been washed too many times.

"Arina." The Hunter held me by the shoulders, his face close to mine. Translucent droplets of water slid slowly down his bare chest. They caught the yellow light, sparkling like amber. If I looked hard enough I could see the whole room reflected back at me.

The thin tether that held me to this earth was cut and I felt my awareness flee. "Arina."

I was shaken roughly. The movement caused the water from his dark hair to find a path down his face. Droplets hit my face. His hair fell just short of his eyes, his grey eyes.

"Snap out of it."

There was a small bead of water at the end of his dark lashes. It looked like it would fall at any moment, his eyes.... his eyes.

"Arina!"

Why was I looking at his eyes? The room suddenly seemed much louder, like the water had cleared from my ears.

"What?" I snapped.

I shook my head, trying to disperse the thick fog. The Hunter took a step back from me. The fear drained from his features and the indifferent mask returned.

"Your hand. It's not healing."

I held my arm up to the light, the wound was suddenly painful. At some point I had unwrapped it. Blood ran freely down my forearm and onto the floor. The cut was fresh, when it should have been healed already. The edges were angry and infected. I looked up at the Hunter in alarm. Panic bubbled within me, my heart pounding in my chest. Infections were not for Mages. It was a human aliment. Questions raced through my mind.

What had happened? Was this a taste of the horror that people spoke of when they whispered about collars?

The Hunter sprang into action, scrounging up more bandages before wrapping and cleaning my hand. The blood still seeped, he pressed a cloth to the cut trying to stem the flood. His brow creased with worry.

"It's okay. It's just bleeding from the hot water." I didn't know who I was trying to comfort.

When the blood slowed he left me to go and get dressed. How long had I been sitting in the wet singlet? It was cold, even in the stagnant air. Neither of us bothered to speak again. I didn't want to think about how the collar was affecting me already. The initially pleasant feeling of emptiness had now begun to suck my soul from my body.

We sat in silence until someone came and retrieved us. A teenage girl who had not yet grown into her body stood meekly in our threshold. She ushered us down the skinny hall. We walked quickly in single file. The Hunter nearly had to duck his head to avoid the roof. Eventually the passage opened into an oval-shaped room. There was a small kitchen on one side and three long picnic tables on the other. On top were bowls of fruit and bread.

Joseph was standing at the head of the tables. The group was larger than I expected, about fifty people of all species sat around the tables.

He paused when we entered. "Please join us."

The Hunter and I squeezed onto the end of a table. As soon as we were seated, he began.

"I know you're all restless for war. But fast change is undone quickly. The saviours become the new oppressors, and the cycle continues. We must be smarter. True revolution, the kind that sticks, the kind that makes the world safe and fair takes time. The rebellion stands for equality. We want a society in which all species stand together and govern as one. The Mage Elect has ruled with oppression for too long. Their reign will soon come to an end."

His words were hypnotic. I could envisage his world. It was a world of freedom without death. People would no longer be persecuted for simply existing. With Joseph at the helm it all seemed possible. Someone cheered, and then someone else. Soon shouts and calls of support broke out, rising in volume.

"We are in negotiations with the Vampire King and a number of Alphas."

More cheers from the group.

"We must stay strong. We are at a crucial juncture. True rebellion never dies!"

"True rebellion never dies!" the crowd parroted back.

There was an energy in the room and it was intoxicating. I stole a glance at the Hunter, his jaw was set and his eyes narrowed. I wondered what he thought of this. This was the Elect's worst nightmare. They thrived on fear, not hope.

"We are joined by two new members today. Lilith and Noah, please stand."

I stood. Silence fell over the crowd. I looked at their faces, they were filled with so much hope and I was here to crush it.

"Please make them feel welcome."

Applause broke out.

"I will be leaving this morning, I won't be returning for some time. I will have direct contact with Loral and Sylvia. Please listen to them in the coming months."

With that he was seated and lively conversation broke out.

People reached over each other to get to the food. My stomach rumbled and I snatched up a piece of bread along with an apple.

A plump middle-aged woman with a warm smile turned toward me. "Welcome Lilith. It's so nice to have a new face around here."

I couldn't return the sentiment. Instead, I shoved the apple in my mouth. Before I could slip back into my room, Judas bounced over to me, a lopsided grin on his face.

"Morning Lilith."

"Good morning."

"Joseph asked me to introduce you two to everyone. Also, we have a doctor who said he is certain he can break the enchantment on your collar."

A few shocked gasps came from the people around us. My glare had paralysed tougher men than Judas, but he seemed oblivious. Instead, he took my hand and seemed to want to parade me in front of the crowd like a show dog.

I planted my feet. "Let everyone enjoy their breakfast."

"Rina?"

A familiar voice made me swing around. Loral was standing in the threshold of the door. I was too shocked to move. He ran toward me and wrapped me in a tight hug.

"What the hell did you do to your hair?"

I shook my head and buried it in his cotton shirt. Of course that was the first thing he would say. He was okay. The joy was short lived. I looked into his eyes. He needed to get out of here. If he stayed he would die with everyone else.

"How do you know Lilith?" The Hunter emphasised my pseudonym.

Loral shot me a look.

"We were roommates. Who are you?" Loral accused.

"This is my old friend, Noah." I gave Loral an easy grin.

"You've never told me about him."

I forced an unsteady laugh. "Well, you can see why."

"Just like you to try and keep a man like this all to yourself," Loral teased.

He turned his friendly smile to the Hunter. "Where are you

from, Noah?"

Loral's voice was kind now, his guard down. He trusted me.

"Ka," Luka answered. "I was a private bounty hunter."

The lies flowed from his mouth as easily as they did mine. From the corner of my eye I could see Judas in an intense conversation with an older gentlemen. They hurried toward me.

"How long has it been on you?" the dark-haired, older man demanded. I assumed they meant the collar and not the life-sucking leech that was my companion.

"Four days." Only four days.

"How did they put it on?"

"I was on the run. They found me and collared me. But I managed to escape with Noah's help." I looked at him and tried to school my features into something resembling gratitude. It wasn't easy.

"We have to get it off as soon as possible. Come with me." The older gentlemen dragged me from the busy room. I was grateful to be away from the crowd.

The Hunter and Loral followed as I was dragged down another skinny corridor, breakfast forgotten. The conversation died behind me.

"Davis is our healer," Loral added as I was ushered into a small office.

There was a table covered with books and loose papers. I sunk into a comfortable armchair and Loral stood awkwardly near the door with the Hunter. The healer pushed his glasses up his nose and inspected the ring around my neck. Concern laced his kind features.

"Collaring is the worst kind of torture for a Mage. I'm surprised you are so calm."

He was kind to ignore the ugly scratches that surrounded my new piece of jewellery.

"This is a strong one. I've never seen inscriptions such as these." He sat back, pondering. "It will take me a while to figure out the incantation to unlock it, but it must be removed as quickly as possible."

"What's going to happen to me?" The need for information burned within. It was foul mimicry of my lost Magic.

"Mages are irrevocably intertwined with their power. When it is taken away…" the healer's face turned grave. "It has serious side effects."

"Like?" Loral prompted.

"Is your Magic powerful?"

"Yes," Loral answered for me.

When the Healer looked to me for confirmation, I nodded.

"If your Magic was weaker, it would only affect your mind. But if you have half as much power as your companion, your body will fare just as badly."

I spun to look at the Hunter, his face was unchanged. *Did he know?*

Loral's eyes were wide and he was gnawing at his nails. "More, she has more power than him."

I didn't know how my friend knew this secret about me.

"I'm going to die." My voice was small. How long did I have?

"We won't let you die. I'll find a way to remove it, I promise you," The healer put a warm hand over mine.

"Thank you."

He snapped photos of the ring and sent me on my way. I couldn't stand to go back out to the dining room, not even hungry as I was. I wanted to go back to the bedroom and think, but the winding corridors were disorientating. Loral took me by my elbow.

"I need to speak to Lilith. Go down that corridor and turn left and then left again. You'll be back in the kitchen."

The Hunter eyed me and then left us in peace. It was good to be out of his presence. Loral took me further down into the depths of the compound. I wondered how big it was.

We finally stopped in front of a door. Loral ushered me in. "I was so worried about you."

"I'm sorry. I'm so sorry." My voice wouldn't seem to go above a whisper. I hadn't realised how much I had relied on him. My friend had been placed in the firing line because of me. It was also a relief to know he hadn't been the one to betray me.

"Are you okay?" He looked into my eyes. There was only concern shining through.

I nodded, not trusting my voice.

"What happened?" His voice was fervent.

Did he know what I was?

"I'm a Blood Mage." Bitter regret dripped from my words.

"I know." My gaze snapped to his. "I know. I've known for ages, silly girl." He took my hands. "You could fool others with that stupid Fire Mage story, but not me. I know you."

"But why didn't you…?"

I was lost for words. He knew? Why hadn't he said anything to me? All this time I had done my Magic in hiding, thinking I was keeping my secret.

"I didn't want you to run away. You're not as scary as you think."

I blinked rapidly, gratitude threatened to overwhelm me. I wanted Loral to yell and shout at me and call me all sorts of horrible names. It would have been easier.

"The Elect collared me, but I managed to escape. Noah helped me." I forced the story through my lips. "I've worked with him on some jobs before, he's a good guy."

I stuttered through the last part. Loral needed to trust me completely. There could be no doubt about my loyalty if I wanted to live.

"I just wish you would have introduced us sooner." He laughed with forced levity. He didn't mention the collar again. Maybe he saw how precariously I sat on the edge of sanity.

"So, can I fix your hair?"

The distraction was welcome. He could do whatever he wanted to my hair as long as he kept talking.

"Loral, there's a massive bounty on my head," I said.

"No one would dare stand against Joseph, if he deemed you worthy to join our cause you will not be betrayed."

I turned toward him. "No one can know what I am. They'll

turn on me."

"Arina, we have a Blood Mage living here already. No one here thinks she's evil."

"She isn't a murderer."

"You're not a murderer." He rolled his eyes. "Now, undo your hair."

If he knew of my past in Dunlap, he might have viewed me differently. I was too tired to argue. Instead, I did as he asked and unfastened my damp pony tail. He splashed the potion on my hair and brushed it through gently. We sat and he told me how he had escaped Ka.

Loral had left the house once he had seen that there was a Blood Mage on the loose. He had assumed the *'red headed psycho'* was me and had fled to the safe house before enforcer's had come knocking. I rinsed my hair in the sink. Loral had a mirror in his bathroom. My hair was almost back to its natural colour. I couldn't help but smile as I ran my fingers through the ends. Loral brandished a pair of scissors. He started snipping away, fixing my uneven cut job. When he was done, my hair was sitting just above my collar bones.

"You're the best."

"I'll do it again soon. We can get it back to your natural colour. I have to meet with Joseph before he leaves. I'll give you a few days to settle in and then you can join us. I could use your help here."

Loral hooked his arm through mine and we made our way down the corridor. There was a weight pressing on my chest that had nothing to do with the collar. I couldn't bring myself to meet Loral's eyes.

Chapter Seven

The next few weeks passed quickly as I settled into a routine. I was grateful that my room was far from the central areas. It cut down on the small talk.

Judas had shown me around in the first few days. The compound was fully self-sustaining and everyone had a role to play. After breakfast we would spend a couple of hours tending to the fields. The work was not made for me. The fields were lined with heat lamps. It was a sad substitute for the sun. The plants didn't seem to mind as much as I did. The fields were surprisingly large. Rows of lush vegetables and fruit had been planted meticulously; courtesy of Judas and the other Earth Mages.

I had never thought of gardening as a particularly manly thing until I saw Judas out there with his shirt clinging to his sweat, and mud on his boots. It was extraordinary to see him where he belonged. The plants flourished under his careful touch.

"Lilith, that's too much water," he admonished.

I quickly realised that I had been pouring on the same spot for some time. Judas came over to where I had drowned the seeds and fussed over the dirt. When he finally rose, he gently took my hand and traced the fire runes. I guessed it was to get me away from the plants more than anything.

"How did you find out you were a Fire Mage?"

Uncomfortable with the contact, I pulled away and continued down the worn dirt path watering the freshly planted seeds as I went. "I had a book in school and set it alight accidentally."

It was almost true. Someone had snatched it from me and I had lost my temper and nearly killed the poor girl. "You were young?"

"Yes, very. When did you discover you had an affinity with Earth Magic?"

"I was old, about sixteen. It was in a Magic class."

I hadn't been to school since my had parents died. It was easy to forget that everyone else had trained their Magic in a classroom. My classrooms involved less playtime and more beatings.

"Come over here," he said.

Judas crouched in the dirt. A small white daisy sat alone amongst the potatoes. *How had it gotten down here?* He hovered his hands over it and it grew as high as my knees.

"It's beautiful," I said.

"Go grab one of those pots."

I did as he asked and collected one of the plastic pots from the edge of the fields. He took it from my hand and filled it with dirt. Judas gently uprooted the small daisy and placed it in the container before handing it to me.

"You have to water it every day, but it should have enough Magic to survive for a few months."

"Thank you," I grabbed the pot from his hands and cradled the small flower. If it could survive underground, so could I.

He brushed a stray tendril of hair from my face, "How are you feeling?"

I looked around seeing who else was in the fields. At some point everyone had left, we were alone. It made me more uncomfortable than I cared to admit.

"I'm okay."

"Are you sure? You seem distant today."

"I'm fine. I promise." I gave him a grin. It wasn't a conversation I wanted to continue. I was all too aware of my failing health, I didn't want to dwell on it for any longer than necessary. My bones ached from the small amount of physical labour.

"Well, then I think we're done here." He wiped his hands on his pants and looked over his work. He beamed with pride. We washed our hands in the sinks by the entrance and moved through the bare corridors of the compound.

The compound walls still threatened to close in on me. I

wasn't used to being in such small confines. I dreamed of being on the hunt again, the adrenaline pulsing through my veins and the open road in front of me. When I was after a target I felt absolute certainty in myself. I wasn't used to this feeling of insecurity. I needed a distraction.

"Do you have any plans?" I hoped Judas wasn't busy. If I had to sit in my room again I would go mad.

"No plans this afternoon."

"Is there anywhere to train?"

He looked at me, puzzled. "I don't fight."

I had never met anyone that couldn't fight. It was what I had always done in my spare time. I didn't have any other hobbies. Even Loral could get himself out of a sticky situation if he needed to. It only seemed to highlight the disparity between us. He was all things light and good and I… wasn't.

"We could watch a movie," he suggested.

"Sure."

I followed him into the large living area. There were a number of couches and beanbags laid out in the room surrounding a small television. It was usually a popular area, however this morning it was just Judas and me.

He knelt in front of the television and fiddled with the remote.

"What did you want to watch?"

I shrugged. "I don't mind."

The tv blared to life, the scratchy sound filled the room. I collapsed onto a faded pink couch and Judas sat next to me. The movie wasn't enough to keep me entertained and my mind began to wander. The emptiness pressed on my consciousness and the now familiar anxiety began to build within me.

"I'm leaving for another mission soon," Judas said.

"How soon?"

"In the next few days." He leant back, his arms folding behind his head.

"Back to Dunlap?" I asked.

He shot me a cheeky smile, the skin under his eyes crinkling. "You know I can't tell you."

Judas's smile turned to a frown as he inspected me closely. I turned my eyes to the screen and tried to ignore his worried glances. If he would just stop looking at me I would be fine. I bit my tongue to stop from shouting at him.

Without saying a word, he gently took my uninjured hand. "We'll get the collar off soon."

"It's fine. I'm fine Judas." I stood pulling my hand from his. My voice was sharper than I intended, I tried to soften it. "I need to train."

He looked at me the concern so thick on his face it made me sick. I fled the room like a coward.

I spent most of my time in the gym area. There were a couple of people living in the compound that were skilled fighters. It felt familiar to watch them train.

I could almost imagine I was back in the gym with Jax and Erin. If I turned around, they would be sitting in the corner with easy smiles on their faces. Erin would complain that I wasn't eating enough salad and Jax would give her an indulgent smile. The gym was empty, the red dirt walls were lined with well-used practice swords and mirrors. It was the only room I had found where I could breathe freely. As a result, I often lingered there. I could tell most of the group was uncomfortable around me, so I usually trained when no one was there. I didn't want to telegraph the fact I was a threat. I knew the Hunter trained as well, but I had yet to see him. We had been avoiding each other quite successfully. I laid down in the centre of the mats, staring up at the ceiling. The yellow light flickered.

Before my life had been undone, I had never cared much for the sunlight. From the age of eleven, my waking hours had been opposite to most of the world. The moon had been my confidant and I had always preferred the darkness. Now I longed for nothing more than the summer breeze on my face. I would even take the sunburn if it meant I could feel the suns rays on my body. Maybe it was all the time I had been spending around Judas. His Earth Magic was rubbing off.

Moping didn't suit me.

Sitting up, I begun gently stretching my tight muscles. I

warmed up before taking out my frustrations on the heavy bag. The longer my injured hand was stuck by my side, the more trapped I felt. Eventually my frustrations bubbled up and spilt into my actions. I was stuck like mouse in a cage, just waiting to die. The burning pain was easy to ignore as I threw all my weight behind the flurry of punches.

My body was covered in sweat, and I thought of nothing else but my aching lungs and burning shoulders. With the endorphins rushing through me, I could almost forget the cold metal pressed against my windpipe. When I gained the courage to look down, the wound on my hand had reopened and blood had begun to seep from my bandage and trickled down my fingers onto the red dirt.

"Stupid," I muttered and cradled my hand so blood didn't spill onto the mat. The brief moments of clarity hadn't been worth it. I rushed out of the room looking for the healer, his office was relatively easy to find in the maze of corridors. He was scribbling into a note book when I entered. He barely looked up.

"Davis." The bloody bandage was cradled to my chest. He pushed his chunky glasses up his nose and ushered me over to him.

"How did you do this?"

He snapped on some gloves and began unwrapping the soaked bandage. I didn't want to look.

"It's old but because of the collar it hasn't healed. I just opened it back up."

He nodded. "Okay, come sit up here and I'll see what we can do." I was led to the bed in the tiny ensuite. There were draws of medical supplies and a bright overhead light. The doctor sat on a rolling stool and brought the draws closer. The strong smell of antiseptic filled my nose. I sucked in a sharp breath as he splashed the disinfectant over my hand. It hurt like hell. I had been avoided the doctor for just that reason. He looked at me apologetically and grabbed my hand back where I had pulled it away. A healing rune would have been so much easier.

"I'm going to stitch it up. I wish you'd let me do it earlier."

I didn't want to look when he gave me a human numbing agent and I definitely didn't want to look as he stitched the wound. All my bravado disappeared as soon as healers got involved. I had secretly tried to chug down Loral's best healing potions, but the cut still hadn't scabbed over.

It felt like ants were crawling under my skin.

"All finished."

I thanked him and rushed out the door, unable to stand the smell any longer. I shuffled through the corridors, making my way slowly back to the room. I needed a shower to soothe my sore muscles. Training could only calm me for so long. There didn't seem to be a solution for my restlessness. I couldn't destroy the rebellion faster than the collar would destroy me.

In the tiny room the Hunter and I shared, the lumpy mattress on the floor was made to within an inch of its life, courtesy of my roommate. Even the crude stack of pillows we took turns sleeping on looked presentable. He had made us a rudimentary closet and both our clothes were folded and organised against the front wall. The fact he had touched my clothes creeped me out. I didn't want to imagine him touching my lacy underwear. It looked like we had settled in for the long haul.

If I'll be alive for the long haul…

I banished the thought. I had gone through too much to die now.

Still, it was easy to huddle on the floor of the shower, close my eyes and pretend the world didn't exist for a little while.

"Lilith?" the Hunter called out tentatively, breaking my trance, "Are you okay?"

So many names and none of them felt like they belonged to me. I turned off the water and wrapped myself in a giant towel.

"I'm fine." I threw on my only pair of track pants and one of my thin singlets. I only had what I managed to grab from my apartment. Loral had to give me some of his clothes to sleep in. The Hunter stood in the threshold.

"Your hair."

"Loral dyed it again," I rubbed the wet curls with my towel and sat on the bed. He had finally got it back to its natural colour.

"It looks …nice"

I almost choked on my tongue. The compliment sounded like it held razors as it came out of his mouth. The Hunter sat on the bed beside me and we waited in awkward silence until I couldn't stand hearing the leaky tap drip anymore.

The collar had made me neurotic.

We had barely spoken three words to each other since we arrived. I needed to get this over with. I was tired of being trapped underground.

"What are we going to do?" I turned to face him, crossing my legs. We were sitting much too close. I tried not to telegraph my discomfort. I couldn't seem to bring back my easy confidence.

"We gain the groups trust. A few people are still uneasy with our presence." He didn't look up from the book he had picked up from the bedside table.

Disappointment made my lip curl slightly. This was going to take much too long. The longer I got to know these people, the more it would hurt to help the Elect destroy them.

"The Doctor stitched my hand." I felt a strange, desperate need for personal interaction. I was going stir crazy avoiding everyone.

It felt like I hadn't spoken more than five words to anybody except Judas. During my time in Dunlap, I would spend months without interaction. Now I couldn't stand even a few days.

Over the last few weeks the Hunter had morphed back into the lamb. He was charismatic when he wanted to be, and all the women swooned over him. He acted like he was oblivious, but I wasn't dumb. He didn't bother to keep up the charade around me.

"There's another Blood Mage that usually lives here," I blurted out. I'm not sure why I hadn't told him earlier. "Everyone likes her."

I sounded like a teenager trying to persuade her parents to

like a new boyfriend. *Pathetic*.

"I know. You should meet her, perhaps gain some information."

I nodded slowly.

"When did you find out you were a Blood Mage?" He turned a page, but I could hear the interest veiled behind feigned nonchalance.

I paused, contemplating how much to tell him. "I was five. My parents were Blood Mages."

"That's unusual?"

"Very." I wanted to tell him more about them. Strangely he was the only person I held no secrets for. "My parents were murdered by enforcers when I was ten." My voice was steady, as if I was reading a recipe or instructions. The violence that bathed my life after their deaths had allowed me to gain some distance.

He finally looked back up from his page, *almost* sympathetic. The flash was gone as quick as it came.

"I'm sorry." His voice was low. I had expected him to refute my claim. I didn't know whether it was better or worse that he hadn't defended their actions.

"They slaughtered them. My parents never used their power to hurt people. They didn't even use Magic to fight back when they came. The enforcers eviscerated them. If I wasn't hiding in the pantry, they would have killed me too."

No one knew this story. I had buried the memory deep and had not consciously thought of it since. Sometimes my mother's haunted green eyes popped up in my nightmares, but usually I was good at blocking the memory of her out. The Hunter rested a hand on my shoulder. I stared at him hard.

His hand slid back to his side.

Loral appeared in our doorway at just the right time. He eyed the Hunter and me approvingly. "Let's eat."

I followed him out into the kitchen. I was desperate to forget the heavy conversation and my mother's pleading emerald eyes. I could have used a bottle of liquor.

Chapter Eight

The dining room was filled with easy conversation and boisterous laughter that continued through the meal. We both needed to gain favour. A small group of people were leaving to get supplies in the morning. The Hunter had volunteered, but Loral insisted that it was too dangerous to leave me here alone in my *'current state'*. He didn't like to talk about my lack of Magic or impending death and I found that it suited me just fine.

The next morning I was disappointed to learn Judas had left. I hadn't even had a chance to say goodbye, he had slipped out before breakfast. I had half expected him to leave a note, but our last interaction had ended frostily. The thought of gardening wasn't as appealing without his easy smile and stories of adventure.

Instead, I mumbled to Joanne that I was feeling ill and shuffled back to my room. The emptiness in my chest paired with the cold mattress didn't make for a relaxing environment. My eyes closed, but I couldn't sleep.

"Arina," the Hunter barked from the threshold. He never called me Lilith when we were alone. I peeled open one eye.

"I know you're not asleep. Did you want to train?"

I yanked the blankets and shot up from the bed. It sounded like the perfect distraction. "Fine."

The training area was empty, everyone was busying themselves with morning chores. It was the only perk of being collared, I seemed to be exempt from any chores I didn't want to do. It seemed the Hunter was also excused. I took the centre of the room and begun stretching. My muscles ached from overuse, but at least my hand was feeling slightly better. Dissociation nagged at the edges of my consciousness. I needed to be moving, less it take over again.

The Hunter stood to one side, hands clasped behind his back. Stalking toward the weapons rack, I grabbed a staff and threw one at him. His eyebrow quirked as he snatched it out of the air.

"I've never seen you use a staff before."

I thought I had seen him skulking around the training room. *Stalker.*

"I'll have the advantage then."

There was no more talking.

I thrusted toward his mid-section and he batted me away. Frustrated, I feinted the same thrust before swinging the staff toward his head. The Hunter jumped back out of the way just in time. He rolled his shoulders and relaxed into a more comfortable stance. We began trading blows, our staff meeting over and over. My limbs felt as if they were moving through jelly.

There was no time to think. One wrong move would cost me. The loud smacks that echoed around the room were interrupted only by the sound of my heavy breathing. The Hunter struck out at me from above, leaning over to force me to carry his substantial weight. My muscles twitched under the force of his much larger body. The only strain I could see from him was a slight tightening of his eyes. With a yell, I flung myself backwards scrambling out of his way. My back hit the mats. I had hoped he would stumble off balance, but his step didn't falter as he stalked me down. I braced for his downward strike.

Instead, he reached his hand out toward me and pulled me up.

"Let's go again." He sat back into his preferred stance.

Our dance restarted. I hadn't noticed it at first, but the asshole was pulling his strikes. He had the opportunity to hit me multiple times over. He seemed to misjudge the distance or allow me time to block. After another strike went suspiciously wide. I threw down my staff. He immediately straightened.

"Stop going easy on me," I shouted.

"I'm not."

"So you're just bad?"

He winced at my words. It was the only reaction I had seen from him in days.

"If I'm slow enough to be caught, don't pull your strike."

"You're not at full strength. I don't want to hurt you."

The bonehead was so confident in his ability to beat me. "That's my decision to make. Don't pull your strikes," I enunciated clearly, spitting the words at him.

"Your funeral." His face returned to the infuriatingly calm facade.

The Hunter threw my staff at me and we began again. He did as I asked. It was satisfying to see the surprise on his face when I caught him right in the ribs. Fire filled his eyes and he struck back, hitting me just above my knee. The pain chased away the fog in my brain. We continued, only stopping when I couldn't continue. The Hunter stayed even as I left.

My smile came easier than usual as I dragged my battered body down to the healer's office. Distraction was good.

He didn't look up when I entered his tiny office.

"I have another book on runes for you. It's an old one."

"Thank you. Are you any closer on the incantation?"

He looked up from his work, his eyes filled with a sadness that betrayed his words. "You'll be the first to know."

I nodded and scooped up the battered book, my muscles aching already, "How are you feeling?"

Davis looked me up and down, assessing with his clinical gaze. Nothing would slip past him so I shrugged instead, not trusting my words. Davis stood up and begun riffling through his cabinets. He finally retrieved a small vial of green liquid. "It'll help with the pain."

"Healing potions don't work." He knew this.

"It's not a potion." He gave me an indulgent smile. "It's human medicine."

I didn't question how he had gotten a hold of it. Instead, I slipped it into my back pocket. Before he could press further on my condition, I gave him my thanks and left.

I strode through the corridors, the hum from the generators

set my teeth on edge. The compound could survive cut off completely from the outside world, the fields of crops could survive with Magic and there were underground springs that water could be filtered from. Because the Elect was still unaware of the location, there was a few luxuries allowed. But soon enough, Elect enforcers would rain down on the place, knowing every intimate detail curtesy of me.

Some of the residents still shot me glances as I passed them. They didn't trust me, rightfully so. I was a reluctant spy. Still, I had been shown nothing but kindness. If I was a better person I would have come clean and refused to lead them to their deaths.

The only thing in my favour was that Loral had been so busy organising the next move that I hadn't seen him much. It would have been easier for me if Loral was out of the picture. I could have almost pretended that he wasn't involved. It had surprised me how deeply entrenched he was in the movement. It was where he had run off too all those nights.

I finally reached my room and sat on the floor, not wanting to dirty the bed with my sweat. The Hunter was no doubt still training, more machine than man.

Suddenly Loral burst into my room and ushered me out. "Stella's finally back. She wants to talk to you."

Stella was the other Blood Mage in the Compound. She had been out on an extended excursion. Originally it seemed exciting to meet another, but now dread filled me. The only other Blood Mages I knew were my parents, and they had been good.

It was likely she could sense what I was, even through the collar. The reward money lingered in the back of my mind. It seemed too big of an enticement to me. I couldn't trust Loral when he told me no one would betray me. You could take the million credits and live a cushy life without a worry from the Elect. The risk was too high. If I was caught, I would be carted off and tortured for the rest of my very short life.

"Let me shower before meeting her," I said.

When I was clean and dressed I reluctantly followed him

to the dining room where a young woman sat with her back to me. Her limbs were long and lean, the muscles of her shoulder tensed as she ate loudly. Her long, black hair fell straight down her back. An otherworldly presence hung about her. I could sense her power as soon as I entered the room, it smelt like cinnamon and smoke. She looked fragile, but her power told me otherwise.

It surprised me that I was still able to sense her power. If someone had enough Magic, it was easy to sense their magical signature. The skill hadn't been taken away along with the rest of my power. Perhaps it had less to do with my Magic and more to do with my inherent birthright as a Mage.

The Hunter's Magic was distinctive, his power smelt like burnt vanilla, and the sweetness overwhelmed almost everything. Loral's was more subtle. I could only sense him when he was performing greater works. His Magic smelt of fresh spring air and apples, the smell had permeated our apartment. It had taken me a while to realise what it was.

Loral cleared his throat. I had zoned out again.

"Stella, this is Lilith. I told you about her." I had never seen Loral look so uncomfortable before. He stood a good distance from the girl.

"The collared Mage." She whirled to face us, her eyes a deep brown. I felt captivated under her gaze. "Leave us."

Loral shot me an unapologetic smile before slipping out of the room. Her power was oppressive and I felt the need to wiggle out from under it. Is this what it felt to be around me? No wonder I had trouble making friends. Even if other Mages couldn't sense what I was, did I subconsciously make people uncomfortable under the weight of my Magic?

We stared at each other from across the table. Without warning, Stella grabbed my injured hand and inspected it. Her brow creased.

"This will keep getting worse until the collar is removed. It is very dangerous to have your Magic suppressed for this long. Have you had any episodes of dissociation?"

My teeth ground together and I gave her a slight nod. Her brow creased. I ignored her. There were more important things to talk about.

"You're a Blood Mage?" I asked.

"Yes."

"Are you terrified of losing control?" It was the one question I needed to know. Did she live with the same fear that I did? She seemed so composed, so in command. In comparison, I felt like a frantic mess. Ever since I had met the Hunter, everything had been turned loose. I was balancing on the knife-edge of control. One push and I would be sent over the edge into insanity.

"I'm not scared of my own power. It's my power." She laughed as if I was asking the most absurd thing she had ever heard. I suddenly envied this woman.

"I'm a Blood Mage too."

"I know."

She gestured to the space next to her and I took it. Some of her calm energy washed over me and the weight of the collar didn't feel so heavy.

"How long have you known what you were?"

"I was a teenager. Before then I didn't think I had any Magic," she giggled. No doubt it seemed absurd now, with the amount of Magic she now held at her finger tips.

"What happened?"

"I was out running when I tripped and scraped my knee. I knew immediately. I couldn't tell my parents, so I left." The sadness that twinged her voice was obvious.

I felt like I should say something, but the words were stuck in my throat. She continued, smiling, her emotions changing so fast it was difficult to follow.

"They were both Earth Mages. We had the most beautiful gardens in Micador."

I hadn't been to the city, but it was now held tightly under the rule of the Elect and all the gardens destroyed. She babbled about stories from her childhood. They were all happy memories. It was as if the fleeting sadness I had seen was a figment of my imagination.

Suddenly she paused. "Good night my sister." She turned and sauntered from of the dining room. I sat, slack-jawed, alone at the table. I hadn't gotten a word in. Had I done something to offend her? I contemplated following her out into the living room but didn't want to embarrass myself.

Seeing Stella had left me in a foul mood. I could almost feel my tumultuous Magic rolling under my skin. It seemed I was the only one who struggled so much with control. As I stormed back to the bedroom, I saw the Hunter lounging on the bed. His long body was stretched out languidly on the mattress and he held a worn book in his hands. He looked at me over the top of the pages, his slate grey eyes seemed to turn to molten mercury as he drunk me in. This man was the root of my problems. I wanted to do nothing more than blast him with Magic and watch that smugness drain from his eyes. It wasn't even his turn to sleep on the mattress.

He was like a lion laying in the grass, waiting for his prey. Men like him had always leered, as if I were a meal to be devoured. They found out sooner rather than later that I was poison. When I met his gaze, he didn't avert his eyes. He met my anger head-on. Why would he turn away? His giant ego suffocated the room. The Hunter had never once second guessed himself. He had never felt panicked insecurity.

I hooked my thumbs in the waistband of my pants. The zip was deafening in the tiny cave-like room. I peeled the leather from my body. He shifted on the bed. It was satisfying to see how he watched me. There was power in seduction, it was how a lot of my targets had ended up dead. Men never seemed to be able to think once your shirt came off. I stepped out of my pants.

There was a hunger in his eyes as I sauntered toward him. He dropped the book as I straddled his waist. The Hunter stiffened when I leaned toward him, my hot breath on his neck. Gently, I trailed my finger behind his ear and down his neck until my hand rested on the middle of his breast bone. Goose bumps rose on his bare skin.

"What I wouldn't give to have my Magic back," I whispered in his ear, and I pressed my palm down in a silent threat. "Or even a knife."

He pulled back to look at me, a sly smile on his face. "The

oath would kill you too." His voice was low and husky.

"I might decide that it's worth it."

The comment earned me a toothy grin, I pushed off him with a snarl and went to the bathroom to sit under the hot water. When I returned, with my skin pink the Hunter had disappeared and I was alone.

I was reckless and petty, but it felt good to claw back even a tiny bit of control. The bed was free and remade, I pulled the blankets up to my chin and fell asleep with a satisfied grin.

***

I emptied my mind, my only thoughts of the practiced flow of movement. The wooden sword was heavy in my hands and sweat ran down my back. I practiced thrusting, striking and parrying. Without my power, it felt like I was carrying bags of sand around my ankles. But if I stopped training, I knew the black hole in the centre of my chest would consume me.

Two water Mages, Anthony and Levi, were sparring in the middle of the room. I had seen them train most days. Anthony often gave me a meek smile when he entered, but we hadn't spoken at any great length. They were both too young to have seen any real combat, but their technique seemed sound. Maybe they would let me practice with them. I was bored of training by myself. The Hunter trained with me when he felt like it, but I wouldn't go seek him out. When they stopped between rounds, I wandered over.

"Hey, can I join with you guys?" I tried to keep my voice friendly but failed.

They looked at each other and then at me, puzzled. It was almost comical. "But you're collared." Anthony seemed perplexed.

"It's fine. I'm used to it."

"We don't want to hurt you." Anthony pushed himself to his feet. He wasn't particularly intimidating.

"Trust me. You won't hurt me." I tried to reassure the pair. "Ever used practice swords?"

Anthony shrugged and went to pick up a broadsword from

the wall. He shifted the hefty weight between his hands. I stood in the middle of the mat, facing the boy. He looked uncomfortable standing across from me. I needed to remind myself I was here to make friends. I couldn't hurt them.

We circled for a few moments.

He struck out lazily and I swatted his sword away. He hadn't put any real effort behind the blow. Anthony lunged slowly toward me again. Even impaired as I was, I had enough time to kick his sword hand. The blow caused him to release his grip and the blade went scattering to the ground.

"Move faster," I commanded. I allowed him to pick up his weapon again, if it had been anyone else I would have pressed my advantage. He begun to strike me with more vigour. Still, his attacks were easy to block. They had no violent intent behind them.

"Stop going easy," I complained, as I stopped an overhead downward strike.

He should have been able to overpower me with his size. But I hadn't even needed to use technique. I was getting by on my measly strength alone. Eventually I grew bored of blocking and begun striking back. Over and over my weapon kissed his neck. If he ever had to fight for his life he would be grossly underprepared. When I had seen him sparring earlier, they both looked fast and proficient. He thought me weaker than him. It would be his mistake.

Every time he missed a block I begun to whack him with the sword just hard enough to get his attention. Every time the sword hit him he would flinch. No doubt his midsection was covered in red welts. Eventually he got the hint and picked up the pace. He was soon out of breath. I lowered my weapon.

"I can go again," I gestured to Levi, dropping my sword. "Hand to hand?"

He stepped onto the mats with me.

"You can hit me," I reminded him.

His hands were heavy, but at the last second he hesitated. They weren't used to training with women. Instead of hitting him, I swept him down to the mat over and over. The fifth time I straddled his chest I hesitated before getting up.

"Have you never grappled before?"

"I have," he muttered defensively and wiggled out from under me.

I lunged in again. Before I heaved his weight back onto the mat, I stopped.

"I'm tricking you here, see? When I grab your arm, you can't step toward me like that."

I grabbed his arm above his elbow and pulled. On cue, he stepped toward me with his back leg. Expertly, I ducked to the ground and tucked the crook of my knee around his ankle. Levi lost his balance and fell straight onto his butt.

"Now you know what I'm doing, try and break out of it."

We stood again. I grabbed his arm and he twisted my wrist until I lost my grip.

I grinned. "Better,"

We threw more combinations back and forth. Every time he would throw a punch, I would dodge to my right. Eventually he stepped toward me and ended his combination with a left blow trying to catch me. I executed the same motion as before, using his weight against him. He fell hard.

"Ooof. I did it again"

I helped haul him up. "You'll get better."

My chest hurt so I let them go a round by themselves. The boys were much rougher with each other, neither one could get the upper hand for very long. When they grew tired, they sat beside me, sweat dripping from their noses.

When the Hunter strode in, Anthony jumped up, suddenly full of energy again. Their eyes lit up. It was clear they worshiped him.

"Hey, Noah."

He looked over with an easy smile. "Hey, Tony. Are you guys sparring?"

Tony? He was on nickname basis. What the hell?

"Yeah, we were sparring with Lilith too," Levi chimed in.

"I'm surprised you're not more beat up." He looked at me, mischief in his eyes.

"She doesn't hit very hard," Levi tweeted, looking smug.

My eyes narrowed, that little twerp. I hadn't wanted to whoop his ass, but now he was asking for it.

"Why don't you lift up your shirt?" I raised a brow.

The Hunter laughed, the booming sound filling the small room.

"Well how about I give you boys some real competition?"

Asshole.

They nodded eagerly, a lot more excited to spar with him than with me. If only they knew who he really was.

"I'll go first." Anthony stood in the middle of the room and jumped around on the balls of his feet. I relaxed back onto my hands. This would be good.

The Hunter was meaner than me. So much for making friends. He wasn't striking at full strength, but wasn't giving the boy love taps like I had. Anthony was mercilessly picked apart. He had no answers to the Hunter's complicated technique. After falling to his knees, Anthony tapped his hand hard against the mat. He had signalled his defeat.

The Hunter stood over him. "You can't tap in real life."

I thought for a second he would continue but instead he held out a hand and helped Anthony to his feet. He crawled next to me and I shot him a smug smile. Levi didn't hesitate in jumping up, even though he had just watched his friend get beat up. Ever the asshole, the Hunter didn't wait for him to get ready. Like a viper, he struck out before the boy could prepare. It was something to see. His technique was flawless and no doubt the result of years of grueling training.

Some people looked uncomfortable within their bodies, but the Hunter was not one of those people. It was clear in the way he moved that he had absolute surety in the way his body would respond. Every step was taken with unarguable confidence. When Levi couldn't run anymore, he covered his face and cowered on the ground. The Hunter let him up and he stumbled over to sit beside his wounded friend.

The Hunter looked at me expectedly. With a groan I stood and shook out the remaining tightness in my muscles. He was too arrogant for his own good.

"Ready to stop picking on children?" I teased, picking up

my practice sword once again. He grabbed the other one and sunk into his stance.

We began.

Our movements were almost identical. He was slightly faster, and I found myself on the back foot. Every block or strike was just a millisecond behind. The force reverberated through my bones. It was lucky for me that the blades weren't real.

We moved through complicated combinations. He didn't bother using his size advantage against me, but focused instead on pushing himself faster.

After rolling out of the way of a downward spike, I realised my breathing was too strained. When I tried to get up, the blood rushed from my head. I sat back awkwardly on my side trying to hide my disorientation. The world had turned static.

"I'm done," I huffed out after a moment.

"Are you okay?" The Hunter dropped his sword and rushed toward me.

I brushed him off. "Just tired."

I rolled onto my back, spreading out my arms. Before being collared, I had been in the best shape of my life. Now it felt like I had never run a day in my life. The Hunter brought me a water bottle. My muscles shook under the meagre weight.

The two boys took the opportunity to slink out of the room.

"See ya tomorrow," Levi managed to shout out before they both hobbled off to get some healing potions.

"Keep going." I pushed the Hunter away. "I'll be fine in a moment."

His concern was worse than Judas's. I dragged my heavy body toward the side of the room and sat with my back against the wall. He stared at me a moment before nodding.

I was grateful when he turned his attention to the heavy bag. His blows reverberated through the room. He hit it so hard that I thought it would break off the chain. After a few minutes he was slick with sweat, his black shirt clung to his body. He peeled it off and threw it to the side. Without the shirt I could see the mass of scars that decorated his back. It was like a work of art. I wanted to run my hands over every scar and hear what he had done to the people who caused them. I surpassed a groan.

He's the enemy. Death wrapped in a pretty package—nothing more.

The lack of Magic was turning me crazy. When he was training, the careful, controlled facade seemed to fade and his feral nature came out. When he exhausted himself he turned to me. His curly hair hung over his eyebrows and he raked his fingers through the lengths.

"Enjoy the show?"

I fought the blush that threatened to colour my cheeks. Instead I wiped all emotion from my face and shrugged listlessly. I wouldn't feed his ego.

"You're done?"

"For now."

When we walked back to our shared room, Luka didn't put his shirt back on. It was payback. He liked watching me squirm just as much as I enjoyed watching him.

Chapter Nine

After incessant begging, Loral had finally broke and told me Judas was getting back later in the afternoon. As a result, I was sitting in the dining room waiting for him.

The Hunter and I had fallen into an easy routine. We would train in the morning before breakfast, and after lunch time we would hold an informal class. It had started with Levi and Anthony, but then the word had spread and now we had about ten wannabe students.

I had skipped morning training with the Hunter today, my body was too sore. I almost regretted telling him not to pull his punches. The last few days had been hell, but I had too much pride to ask him to dial it down now. No matter how hard I trained, I was getting worse.

Don't think about it.

I felt silly waiting in the kitchen. My hair was brushed and I had even managed to find some make up from Sylvia. It was too late to wipe it off now. The book of runes the healer had lent me lay on the table, forgotten. The teachings inside were all ancient, the newer ones much simpler, and had wider applications. Still, it was good knowledge.

I waited for what felt like forever when finally Judas's familiar figure bounded through the entrance to the kitchen. I jumped up. His warm smile lit up the room and his blonde hair was damp and hung over his eyebrows. It must have been raining outside. I had never wanted to stand in the rain more.

I would have to persuade Loral to let me go on a mission, collar or not.

When he saw me, he immediately dropped his bag and wrapped me in a tight hug. His thick arms wrapped around my waist and my feet lifted off the ground. I just managed to stop myself from flinching at the contact.

The compound was lonely. There was only so much reading and training to do. Judas would have stories from the outside, I couldn't wait to hear them.

"Welcome back," I said when he put me down, his smile reaching his eyes. "How was the outside world?"

"Wet. It didn't stop raining. I barely got to see the sun." He fake pouted.

"Do I get to know what you did?"

"Nope, but I did get you a present." He unzipped his backpack and brought out a bag to hand to me.

I wasn't one for ceremony. I dug into the bag and pulled out tracksuit pants and workout gear. He looked embarrassed, his golden skin flushing pink.

"I heard you complaining to Loral about not having any clothes to wear. There's something else in there also." I smiled at his thoughtfulness.

In the bottom of the bag there was a small box. I ripped it open. Inside was an inscribed gold coin hanging from a thin chain. I picked it up and let it dangle in the kitchen light. Ice shot me like a dagger to my heart, it could have been one-hundred degrees outside and my insides would still be frozen. My mouth forced itself into a smile as I looked at the golden chain.

"What is it?" I didn't understand the engraving, but the longer I looked the more the writing seemed to writhe in the light.

"It's the Coin of Galway. I thought you could use some luck." He took it from my hands and fastened it around my wrist.

"The one you told me about on the bus." My voice was hollow. "Is it really lucky?" I dangled it up in front of my face.

"Very much so. Do you like it?"

The bracelet was beautiful. No one had ever given me a gift like it.

"I do." My voice was warmer than usual. My eyes stung

with something that felt like tears.

He beamed.

Judas glossed over his time on the outside and instead entertained me with stories of his near death expeditions in his life before the rebellion. It was crazy to me, the lengths he went to for some dusty old antiques. He was a firm believer that the historical Magic the artefacts held needed to be protected. It didn't hurt they were worth a pretty penny. I barely had to prompt him. The stories flowed one after the other. If I focused on Judas, I could ignore the screaming in the back of my mind, It demanded to know how I could willingly trade my life for his. The guilt was louder than usual.

Before I knew it, people had started to file in for dinner. Stella sat wiggled in beside me. Judas stood suddenly.

"I'm tired from my journey."

I looked at him, puzzled. He had seemed fine ten minutes ago.

"You're not eating?"

"No. I'll speak to you tomorrow." He knelt down and kissed my cheek before leaving the dining room. I watched him go.

"You're looking worse today, Lilith. Very gaunt. I hope Davis gets that collar off soon." Stella pulled me from my thoughts.

I gave her a closed mouth grimace. Stella was too honest. It was a refreshing change, except when she told me how shitty I looked. The mascara wasn't fooling anyone.

"Thank you, Stella, It's my new look."

The Hunter took Judas's seat and shot me daggers. "It doesn't suit you."

He had no sense of humour. I was the one dying. Dinner was soup and I struggled to stomach the watery substance. Stella was right, I hadn't been able to eat much the last week and my clothes were getting baggy. I didn't want my new look to become permanent. When dinner was finished, I helped Sylvia clean up.

She passed me dishes to dry. I didn't mind the repetitive

movements.

"Is that bracelet new? It's beautiful."

"It is. Judas got it for me."

She lowered her voice, leaning close to me. "You must be careful with him, Lilith."

I shot her a puzzled look. Judas was as harmless as a fly. Maybe one of her daughters had a crush on him.

"I'm fine, thank you, Sylvie."

She nodded, looking unconvinced. We finished the dishes in silence.

When I returned to my room, I couldn't shake the uneasy feeling in my stomach. The Hunter was sitting on the mattress, head in a book, his knuckles bruised and bloodied. He must have skipped cleaning up to go snooping around again. I got into the soft tracksuit Judas had brought me. I didn't bother to cover up. There wasn't much to see anymore. The nagging pain had gotten worse. I turned back around to search for the medicine the doctor had given me. Ignoring the Hunter's worried look, I finally found the vial. The tiny cork was hard to get out with my shaking hands but I finally managed it. I let a drop fall onto my tongue. The gnawing pain eased some and I fell into bed beside him. I should have asked what would happen if I died before we could complete our mission. There was a million questions I should have asked, instead I stayed silent.

The collar was taking its toll. The healer's medicine had taken the edge off, but the ache felt like a part of me now. The tiredness I felt could not be remedied with sleep.

"What's that for?" the Hunter asked, placing his book down. I was glad he hadn't asked me how I felt.

"Pain."

He gently picked up the medicine. The tiny vial looked strange in his hand. It was the first time I had given in and drunk some.

"I thought healing potions don't work."

"It's not a healing potion. It's human medicine." He inspected the contents, uncorking the lid, and sniffing before pulling a face and handing it back to me.

"Did Judas give you that?" His voice was even as he grabbed my wrist, the golden bracelet hanging loosely from my bones. I snatched my hand back.

"Yes."

"You've clearly caught his attention."

"I wasn't doing it on purpose," I snapped.

The Hunter gave me an indulgent smile. "I'm sure you could get valuable information from him."

"What are you suggesting?" I crossed my arms over my chest and narrowed my eyes.

"I'm suggesting you exploit his clear infatuation with you," he said the words like I was an idiot. "You're weak, you need saving."

"I don't and I'm not weak."

"I know that but Judas does not. Let him feel like a hero."

I turned away from him unwilling to hear anything else he had to say.

Chapter Ten

Luka

Dinner with Micah and Salone had given Luka much to think about. He had been taught from a young age that the werewolves were an uncivilised group, filled with hatred and desperate for war. The majority of their history was bathed in the blood. The pair had shaken that belief. They had explained that the devastating wars and the yearning the packs felt for peace. He could see now the manipulation. The Elect would throw their support behind an Alpha that they could control. Once that ceased to be the case, a new challenger rose to the top job. A stable hierarchy was never allowed to remain for long, and the packs were plagued with infighting.

As he sat brooding over this new revelation, Arina entered the room and cleared her throat. Her face was carefully blank, but he could tell from the slight tension in her shoulders that she was uncomfortable around him, even after so many weeks.

"I'll take the floor tonight," her low voice offered.

They had come to an informal agreement that they would take the mattress on alternating nights. She had slept on the bed for the last two. He guessed she was feeling guilty.

"No, it's fine. I don't sleep much anyway." He rose, unwilling to startle her. She had been extra jumpy the last week, her nails bitten down to stubs once again. He doubted she even noticed. She seemed almost in and out of consciousness. Judas had constantly shot her worried glances when he thought she was not looking. If he was being honest with himself, she looked close to death. The jokes she had made about it were frighteningly close to the truth.

Her bony shoulders shrugged. She ignored him and sat down on the floor anyway. Luka was scared the lumpy pillow bed might leave her bruised. She needed to stop exercising. He couldn't spar with her anymore. It was too dangerous.

"It's fair."

It was hard to remind himself that she was his prisoner, at least until they dismantled the rebellion. It wasn't wise to live in such close quarters to an enemy for so long. It was only natural to develop some empathy towards them. Luka was particularly at risk of it, his superiors had always criticised his softness. He turned the light off and lay on top of the covers. They needed more information. They had been excluded from any tactical meetings and he guessed that it was her doing. She was sabotaging them, even as it killed her.

Tomorrow he would enlist them on the next mission. They still had no idea how the rebels were being funded, or what their next move was. If they found the source of the money it would be easy enough to disband them. Destroy the source of their income and then cut off the snake's head.

The young woman that first showed them to the group, Valerie, had been a wealth of information. Luke knew he was abusing her teenage infatuation. It was almost too easy. She lapped up the attention and spilled secrets. She had told him how each cell worked in dizzying detail. She liked to listen. It was clear that Joshua was the orchestrator of the whole thing, even if he tried to advertise to the world that each cell was decentralised. No doubt he had a carefully laid-out plan. Without him the movement was just a group of disgruntled citizens.

They wouldn't all even need to die.

He shifted his gaze to the girl. As frail as she was, Arina had impressed him with her training. He had sparred with her full-tilt and she had never complained, only yelled when she thought he was holding back. Even without her Magic she would be a terror to fight. She was like a vicious terrier.

When they lay in companionable silence, it was easy to forget how close she had come to killing him. Her Magic had been overwhelming. Luka had never felt such uncontrolled power before. He had been enraptured by it, until she had used it to nearly kill him. Luka had underestimated her and nearly lost his life because of it. It would never happen again.

She was always a threat.

The question of why she hadn't just killed him often plagued his thoughts, especially late at night. Her problems would have been sorted, no bounty hunter would dare come after her if she had defeated the infamous Hunter. She could have lived her life somewhere in a shady town without the Elect's interference. They would have claimed her captured, but would have left her alone for fear of further embarrassment.

Arina started up her nightly routine of tossing and turning. Her mumbling pulled him from his thoughts. He sat and watched her intently. *What was going through her head?* She had agreed to dismantle the rebellion in exchange for her freedom. It was no easy feat. Surely she had recognised the risks. He almost admired her guts. Still, she had not deluded herself into thinking the Elect would spare any of her new friends. He often questioned if she felt any guilt, then wondered the same about himself.

It was more likely she was plotting against him. Her motives were obscure since she did not seem to care for money or status. She had only asked for her freedom, he did not understand her. After hours of the thoughts rolling around in his brain, he pulled his boots back on and decided to go hunting for information. Luka needed to know if she planned to betray their bargain.

It was almost a nightly routine at this point. There had been nothing to find as yet. He moved through the compound silently. When he was halfway to the healer's office he felt something he shouldn't have—Arina's power. The light floral scent overwhelmed his senses. It was as strong as when it had drilled into his chest.

A frantic scream cut through the silence. Luka started running. Their room was out of the way, hopefully no one else would have heard the noise. When he flicked on the light she was sitting up, viciously pawing at the collar. Her neck was marred with deep scratches and blood stained her grey sweatshirt. She hadn't noticed him come in. Luka bent down to her level and tried to pry her hands from around her neck. She was unexpectedly strong.

It took all his strength to yank them from around her own neck. Her hands were freezing and clammy.

"Arina," he said softly, trying not to spook her further.

He called her name again and again but still she stared blankly ahead, a horrified look on her face. Her eyes had been alight with fire when they had first met. Now it was as they had been doused with icy water. It made the green look paler, almost grey. Silent tears begun to fall down her lightly-freckled cheeks. Her power had fallen silent again and he wondered what horrors engulfed her mind. Her mouth moved, muttering frantically. Luka leant toward her, trying to hear what she was saying. It sounded like half-mangled incantations. Violent shudders begun to rack her body and he frantically pulled a blanket around her shoulders. Luka pressed her arms to her side to try and stop her from clawing at her skin. Arina screamed again, a horrible gurgling sound. He covered her mouth with a palm.

"Shhh. It's okay. You're okay, Arina. You're safe." He awkwardly drew her small frame onto his lap, avoiding looking into her lifeless eyes.

As gently as he could manage, he lifted her from his lap and used the sheets to tie her hands by her side. Luka sprinted from the room, desperately searching for help. When he finally found Loral's bedroom, he didn't bother knocking. He burst in out of breath. Loral sat up in his bed, startled.

"Arina."

That was all her friend needed to hear. He flew up and ran toward their room. When they arrived she was sitting as Luka had left her. At least the screaming had stopped. Still, her face was wet with tears and she had started to treble violently. In the light it was clear how skeletal her face had become. Arina's shoulders stuck out in sharp angles, even in the thick sweater Judas had bought her. It had only been eight weeks since the collar had been put around her neck, but she looked like she had been subject to the torture for much longer.

Luka had watched as she pushed the food around on her plate, and he hadn't done anything about it. Loral dropped to his knees and moved toward her. Surely he saw it as well. She was dying.

"Arina?" He shook her gently, still she chanted. "Snap out of it!"

He turned to Luka, the rage on his face clear. *Did he know it was Luka's fault?*

"Do you know what she is saying?" Luka stayed in the threshold.

"I don't speak the old tongue." He begun stroking her curly hair too fast to be comforting. "She doesn't deserve this."

Loral's eyes shone with an intensity that sung to the amount he cared for her. There was nothing more to add. It felt wrong to watch as she was stuck in the horror of her own mind. Luka was finding it hard to convince himself he was still in the right.

"We have to get it off," Loral moaned. Silent sobs racked her body to hammer his point.

The week before, Luka had cornered the healer and demanded he tell him more about the collar. Davis had explained in horrifying detail what would happen to her. When you collared a Mage, you suffocated a part of their soul. They were less of a person because of it.

The idea that the fire that run through his veins could be snuffed out horrified him. It seemed an unjust punishment for her crimes. Any other Mage would have been hailed as a hero for saving a helpless woman. Even as she had turned her terrifying Magic toward him, he did not think she deserved a death such as this.

Luka begun pacing the small room.

"Arina, come back to me," Loral cooed.

The despair was suffocating. The emotion wasn't familiar. Luka turned from the room and found his way back to the healer's office. His desk was filled with workings for the incantation needed to free her. It took complex math to remove a collar. He had to decipher the runes and discover the unique formula to reverse them. He was so close. Luka hesitated before picking up his pen and scribbled some corrections in the doctors handwriting. It was not enough to complete the incantation, but it was enough to help.

She couldn't help the Elect if she was dead. The Elect must remain in power. That was the only thing that mattered and the rebellion threaten that. Without Arina, he couldn't fulfil the mission.

The rebellion must fall. Luka was confident that she wouldn't risk death by betraying him.

He needed to clear his mind. Luka ran toward the gym and spent an ungodly amount of time smashing into the heavy bag until his knuckles bled. Every time he slowed, treasonous thoughts invaded his brain. Arina was a super weapon and he would set her free. The image of her haunted face bombarded him in response. He had done that to her. Her wrath would have been preferable.

Thwack, thwack, thwack. The heavy bag took the punches without complaint.

When he was done, Luka went back to the bedroom. Arina and Loral were gone. He spent more time than usual cleaning their small space. He picked up one of her discarded shirts and couldn't stand it any longer. He left the room to hover around the outskirts of the compound. Eventually Sylvie sought him out to say that they had moved Arina to the healer's office. Apparently she was the same. When he finally surfaced in the kitchen, everyone looked towards him with pity. It made him feel ill and he fled to the gym once again. Luka was in half a mind to remove the collar himself, but he couldn't commit the last act of treason against the Elect.

"Luka?" a gentle voice rasped from the entryway.

The Hunter whirled around and saw Arina leaning against the door frame. It was the first time she had said his name. It sounded strange coming from her lips. Arina looked restless, like her bones itched. She stood scratching at her arms and tugging the hem of her sweater. The urge to pull her into his arms and smooth the crease between her brows was shocking.

"You're back." His voice was steady, despite how he felt.

"Yes."

They stood at either end of the room. The icy silence stretched out between them.

"Food is ready. I just came to get you."

Luka nodded and her sharp eyes tracked him as he crossed the room. Her fiery hair stuck out in crazy angles, curling wildly. It was surprising that Loral hadn't fussed over her. Perhaps he was too tired. Luka couldn't help but stare as she led him down the corridor. She reeked of coffee, the lack of sleep dawned on him. The exhaustion seemed to catch him as soon as he saw her well.

They arrived to eat, only Judas and Sylvia were sitting around the table. When they had first arrived at the compound, Sylvia had been cold to them both. Now she doted on Arina. It was easy to see the way people gravitated toward her, despite her aversion to most company. Judas's eyes lit up like a child's when she entered the room. These people were in the palm of her hand, but she didn't seem aware of the devotion she inspired.

Sylvia placed a cup of hot coffee in front of Arina. Luka had to get his own.

Judas stood and begun cooking for her.

"I think it's just us today," he called over from the small kitchen. "How do eggs sound?" He laughed at his own joke.

His overly-sunny disposition set Luka's teeth on edge. He ate in silence to avoid saying something he would regret. His mood was rotten from lack of sleep. The trio chatted easily, but Luka had little interest in small talk. He didn't have the will to pretend today. The dark circles under Arina's eyes were the only thing he could look at. Her layered jumpers had been a feeble attempt to disguise the bones jutting out from her body.

What would give out first, her body or her mind?

As if hearing his thoughts, she stared at him with her haunted green eyes. Luka stood up, his knees pushing back the seat. All eyes turned to him. He stumbled into their bedroom and retched uselessly into the toilet. The only things that came up were bile and dark coffee. When he finally composed himself he returned to the healer's office. Davis was working furiously, scribbling away at his notes. Luka sat down opposite him. There was only one thing he could do.

"How close are you?" There was desperation in his voice, "She's dying."

He needed her alive to fulfil the oath.

The healer finally looked up; a smile crinkling his eyes. "Close. So close."

"Let me help." He looked skeptical. "I'm good at puzzles."

He passed the paper he was working on. Luka read the incantation out loud, pausing where the errors were.

"This doesn't sound right," he added.

The doctor's eyes lit up and he snatched the paper from Luka's hands.

"That's it! That's it." He scribbled the correct change and sprinted from his chair. Luka rushed after him as he ran toward the kitchen.

"Lilith! I've got it!" he yelled as he ran down the hall. Arina, Judas and Sylvia fell silent.

The Healer keeled over to catch his breath. "I've got it. I know how to unlock it!"

Arina's eyes met his and filled with fear. Did she believe that the oath would kill her? Luka had thought it through well enough. They could get around the oath if a force outside their own removed the collar. Helping the process hadn't killed him yet.

"Come to the infirmary. We'll take it off right away."

"That's fantastic news!" Judas beamed, grabbing her hands.

"Yes, great news." Her smile was weak, "Just let me go get Loral. I'll meet you guys there."

Luka followed Arina out. No one seemed to notice how pale she had become. They rushed after the healer toward the infirmary. Arina hurried down the corridor, ignoring Luka following her. She wasn't going toward Loral's room. She was going toward her own.

"Arina, what are you doing?" Luka's voice was hushed.

"Don't call me that. People are awake," she hissed.

She tore into their room like a hurricane, picking up her belongings.

"Stop. What are you doing?" Luka grabbed her shoulder. She flinched. He dropped his hand immediately.

"Leaving. You know we can't let them take the collar off. Take me to the Elect. We can infiltrate another cell." Her eyes were pleading.

"No."

"The deal was that I stayed collared."

"You're getting the collar off."

Her jaw clenched. "You know that's not possible! I'm dangerous, take me back!" She got in his face, shoving at his chest. "We made an oath! It's about to be broken. You have to take me to the Elect"

"The oath was that you were to be taken to the Elect at my discretion. I'm not taking you back there."

She opened her mouth to argue back and he grabbed her by the shoulders. "You'll die if it isn't taken off today. You can't complete the oath if you're dead."

She didn't say anything for a long time. He was scared she had slipped back into one of her episodes before she finally nodded. Arina let Luka lead her from the room and back toward the infirmary. A small crowd had gathered to see the feat of Magic. Loral was already waiting as she came in, someone else had brought him.

Arina toyed with the ruby stone around her neck as she sat on the gurney, silent. Not even Loral or Judas were gifted a smile. Luka hovered behind her. She grabbed the collar of his shirt and brought his ear to her lips.

"Promise me you won't let me lose control."

He stared into her eyes for half a second before nodding. He could grant her that.

"Are you ready, Lilith?" Davis looked giddy, paper in his hand. The room was tense as he begun the incantation. He spoke it flawlessly, the words flowing from his lips. Her eyes locked straight ahead as he spoke the last word. The collar fell away into ash.

The sweet scent of Arina's power filled the room, blanketing it in a heavy fog. She gripped Luka's hand, digging her blunt nails into his palm. It was intoxicating, her golden glittering Magic unfurled, spreading from her chest.

She was all orange and gold, like the sun. It was impossible look away.

Arina finally exhaled, the colour returning to her cheeks.

Cheers sounded in the room and Loral ran up and wrapped her in a hug. Judas was next in line, he lifted her off the gurney. Her small hand still gripped Luka's. An alien feeling tightened his chest. He watched closely for any sign that she was losing control. Her eyes were tight but they hadn't changed colour. Her skin was no longer clammy and pale, instead healthy colour had returned.

Luka knew he shouldn't have been able to see her Magic. He doubted anyone else in the room could see it. Still, it soaked the room around him in a wondrous, glittering show. It was how he had tracked her to Galway, the glittering strands seemed to trail her where she went. They called to him, coaxing him closer to her and brushing against his bare skin.

"Thank you." Arina bowed her head to the healer. Luka hadn't heard what she had been saying but there was palpable emotion in her eyes. She cleared her throat.

"I need to come clean about something,"

Luka stood straighter and shot her a worried look. Loral had a smug smile in the corner. Would they turn on him? Had she found a way to break the bargain without being killed? Before he could snatch her, she spoke.

"I have lived my life in fear for too long." She wiped her hands on her track pants, looking down at the floor. "I'm sorry for lying to you all. I'm not a Fire Mage as I claimed when I first arrived."

None of the small crowd looked confused. Arina seemed uncertain, the words stuck in her throat, until Stella stepped forward.

"Lilith is a Blood Mage, like me."

The majority of the group didn't raise a brow. It was easy to see Loral had been telling everyone behind her back. Judas was the only one to take a small step back. His face crumbled. Luka didn't like it, he sneered at the man.

"Let's celebrate!" Loral intervened before Arina could see his reaction.

Arina seemed oblivious enough. She looked up and recaptured his hand. Luka found he didn't mind the contact. The group surrounded and congratulated her. Eventually they made their way to the dining hall. Everyone cheered when Loral pulled out some old bottles of champagne, passing around the cups.

"True Rebellion never dies!" Sylvie yelled over the boisterous crowd.

"True Rebellion never dies," Luka found himself parroting back with the group. The words felt new in his mouth. He snatched two cups from Loral and filled them to the brim. He needed a drink. It had been a long, sober eight weeks. Luka handed a cup toward Arina. Her return smile was forced. He could see her eyes scan the room for the one person who wasn't there.

Chapter Eleven

I swirled the wine around the cup. My skin felt so fragile, like it would tear at the slightest touch, and my Magic would pour out. Without the collar, my lungs felt like they could expand again. The weights that had seemed to hold down my limbs had disappeared. I felt better than I had in weeks, but my body was still weak. It would take a while for me to gain back the muscle I had lost.

The dining hall was louder than usual. It seemed my freedom was a victory against the Elect itself. Most of the compound had joined in on our impromptu celebration.

My shiny gold charm flashed in the yellow hanging lights. I covered in with my sleeve. Judas hadn't come. He had escaped the room as soon as my collar was removed. I downed my liquid courage and stood. The Hunter caught my gaze, his brow quirked.

"I'm going to find Judas," I answered.

He gave me a curt nod and I excused myself from the room. The festivities continued without me and I weaved through the narrow corridors of my new home. I brushed my fingers against the pock-marked wall, the dust gathering on my fingertips.

My Magic buzzed under my skin. Still, I worried that if I let it fester too long it would billow out of control. I rounded the last corner to Judas's room and brushed my hands on my pants. Enough waiting.

"Judas?" I called out.

Silence.

Shadows moved under the door.

"I'm…"

My hands were sweaty and I picked at the dry skin

surrounding my nails. The apology was stuck in my throat. "I…ah. I shouldn't have told you I was a Fire Mage."

"I'm busy, Lilith." His usually lively voice sounded flat.

I turned on my heel and strode back toward the dining room, stuffing the uncomfortable emotions down. If I went to sulk in my room, Loral would come get me and demand to know what was wrong. I deserved Judas's hate. I had lied to him and couldn't even muster an apology.

When I returned to the kitchen there was a smile on my face. It felt unsteady, but it would hold. Loral had amassed a group around him. He was generous with the wine and his animated motions had captured his audience. I couldn't hear the story he was telling but, knowing Loral, it would be a good one. He had a gift with people.

The Hunter sat on the fringe of the group looking particularly sullen. He didn't bother with the charismatic facade and everyone was already too drunk to notice the shift. It was hard to understand who the real Hunter was; one moment he was happy to be the centre of attention, the next he blended into the background. It was probably why he was so good at his job. I sunk next to him on the bench, dragging a full bottle of wine toward us. I refilled my cup first before topping up his. He looked like he needed the drink.

He leant over and whispered in my ear. "I think the story's about you."

I groaned, downing the sickly sweet liquid. I was grateful that he didn't ask me what happened with Judas. We were far enough away that I couldn't hear the details of Loral's story, but I did hear his bad impression of me. He had a fake scowl on his face—pouting and looking particularly miserable. The crowd erupted in howling laughter.

Luka tried to hide a grin as he topped up my drink. "How are you feeling?"

"In control." I sipped on my wine rather than skull it like I had wanted to.

Loral started up another story. I recognised it. He loved to tell it after a few drinks. I found myself smiling.

It was when we barely knew each other and I had barreled

into our apartment, demanding he help with a death potion. He thought I was after revenge and abruptly laughed once he realised I was talking about poisoning a plant. My heart twisted and I stood from the table.

If Luka and I succeeded, Loral would not be around to tell his stories. It took all my concentration not to retch.

"I'm going to kill them all. They will rue the day they ever crossed me!" my friend roared in a mock imitation of me. "It was a squirrel!"

The crowd broke out in laughter. Loral flicked his eyes to me. I tried to shoot him a placating smile but my cheek twitched.

I'm tired, I mouthed. He dipped his head and returned his attention to the group. The joy followed me as I left the dining hall.

I paused in the threshold of our room. It was stupidly clean. The Hunter had been on a rampage. I yanked the quilt loose and plopped down on the bed.

I needed a drink.

Like he had read my mind, the Hunter appeared in the threshold of the room holding two bottles of wine. There were deep purple bags under his eyes. I hadn't noticed how exhausted he looked earlier.

"What did you do to the bed?" he asked.

"Unless you brought that wine for me, get out."

Two mugs magically appeared in his other palm. I shuffled so my back was against the wall. The Hunter crossed his legs under him and begun pouring.

He handed me a pale green mug "I've been meaning to ask. What did you do after we caught that bounty?"

I nearly spat out the wine. "I went home."

"Did you know who I was?" He watched me over the lip of his cup.

"If I'd known, I would have run the other way a lot faster."

Surely he knew that running into a member from the Elect hadn't been on my to do list.

"If I recall, you did flee on a motorbike."

I finished my drink. This wasn't a conversation I wanted

to have. I didn't bother to hide the fact that I was ignoring his question. Instead, I refilled both our mugs.

"I saw you that night," he mentioned too casually.

"I may have been doing some drunk scrying." I grimaced. "I'm not very good."

He laughed too loudly for the small room. The sound was warm and replaced the cold atmosphere. He must have been more drunk than I thought.

"I think the problem was you were too good," he quipped.

"You weren't meant to be able to see me. I must have done it wrong."

"What did you see?" He lifted a sharp brow.

"I was surprised to see you partaking in rebel activities," I indicated to the half-finished bottle of wine.

"What did you think you were going to do, report me?" His cheeks were flushed.

"I also saw a Mage trying to take you to bed." I regretted my words as soon as they left my mouth. It wasn't like me to speak so openly. I half expected him to end our conversation.

Instead, he topped up my cup.

"Yes, Gretchen! She thought I'd lost my mind when I bolted without a word."

"Could you see me?"

"Not at first. I thought someone was following me. Then you just appeared, sitting on the floor looking up at me."

"Did you know what I was?" No wonder he thought he had gone mad.

"Your eyes were black. I had some idea."

"That's what it looks like when I use my power."

"But not runes?"

"Only when they are complex."

We sat in comfortable silence for a moment. The alcohol buzzed in my veins, amplifying my Magic. I reached for the bottle, the Hunter had the same idea and our fingers met. His touch was surprisingly hot, as if his Magic was as close to the surface as mine. Goosebumps rose on the nape of my neck.

I peeked through my lashes to meet his molten eyes. He flexed his fingers and wrapped them around the neck of the bottle. I snatched my hand away.

"How did you stay hidden in Ka?"

"I took small money jobs, but I wasn't there for long."

I drowned my misery with wine. If I hadn't gone after that Goblin then perhaps none of this would have happened.

"Can you tell me about the squirrel?"

I shot him a glare, expecting him to be mocking, but there wasn't a hint of teasing in his voice.

"I moved into the apartment before Loral, and the place was a mess. Trash everywhere. Living among all this mess was this baby little squirrel. It was the first thing I ever cared for. Eventually, when he healed enough, I set him free. I used to see him around the apartment. Then, one day, when I was walking home, one of the giant venus flytraps had him in its mouth." I shifted my weight on the bed. The room was feeling slightly off kilter, but it didn't distract me from my story. "I didn't have my knives so I run into the apartment all frantic. At this point Loral had never seen me so much as crack a smile, so he thought something truly horrific had happened. I kept telling him that they hurt Harry and that I was vowing my revenge."

"What happened to Harry?"

"He was fine, but I killed a whole bunch of those awful plants."

"A fair punishment."

He almost made me believe that a one-woman-crusade against plantkind would have been justified. The bedroom was freezing, the dirt walls seemed to emanate cold. The collar had taken away all my natural defences to the elements. Luka, on the other hand, seemed to radiate heat. I was bundled in sweatshirts and he still only wore a t-shirt. It was one of the perks of being a legitimate Fire Mage. I shuffled closer to him, wanting to be in the orbit of his warmth.

Mercifully he didn't say anything when I pressed my shoulder against his. The heat from his body washed over me and the worst of my shivering stopped. Luka took my hands in his and tried to warm them.

"You're freezing."

"You're hot," I quipped, my words melding together.

A broad smile lit up his face. It reached his eyes. The hard silver of his iris's had turned into molten mercury, and the harsh lines of his face softened. "You think so?"

"Don't let it go to your head."

His ego was big enough. I pulled away and laid back on the bed, my joints popping and cracking as I stretched out.

Luka stared at me. "Didn't you get the bed last night?"

"I did."

Luka laughed and moved to turn off the light. He laid down on the stack of pillows on the floor. "Good night, Arina."

"That's not my real name." I closed my eyes, feeling better than I had in weeks.

"Is it Lilith?" he asked.

I scoffed.

He didn't push further, and I drifted into a dreamless sleep.

The next morning, Stella yanked Luka and me from bed, and pushed us into a room to practice Magic. We had been going for a number of hours and my headache had only barely subsided.

Stella sat across from me, a frown marring her features.

"Your Magic is out of control. Get a handle on it please," she said through gritted teeth.

The humming in my veins was so freeing that for a moment I didn't want to stop. The black smoke blanketed the room, ferreting into the crevices of the wall. I took a deep breath and reigned in my power. My body vibrated with it, the Magic didn't like to be controlled. Stella nodded, the lines on her face smoothing.

"Blood Magic is the sanguine door. With just a splash you can access the roads that stretch like veins through all living things. It is the power of life and the power of death. All of the living can be touched through the door. You must first find the right roads," Stella said. The story was vaguely familiar, like I might have heard it from my mother. "Good.

Now draw it into a ball. It is a pathway. Nothing else."

I tried to do as she asked, but my Magic felt slippery. It had always been a sludgy liquid, but since meeting Luka it had turned into a smoke. It wasn't something solid I could hold onto. I persisted until my power felt like a misshapen beachball.

"Tighter," she demanded.

I was drenched with sweat by the time Stella was happy with my performance.

"Now, focus on drawing the Magic down your arm and pool it in your palm."

I closed my eyes and she ran her fingernail down my bicep. I released a tiny tendril of power. I could feel the black smoke travelling through my veins. I shivered in anticipation. A stinging sensation slashed at my palm, I felt my Magic flare and scrambled to get a hold of it.

"Stella!" I opened my eyes and saw blood pooled on my palm.

"Concentrate! Your Magic is everywhere. There's no way you'll be able to perform any sort of rune like this."

I closed my eyes and took a shuddering breath. I felt the power pool reluctantly in my open hand.

"Good. Now try and hover it."

I was well-practiced with this trick. I let my blood hover above my palm in little spheres. It worked much better when I was drunk. I had told Stella as much, but she had merely snorted.

"We're not performing a party trick here. You need to actually use your power."

I did as she asked. As soon as I allowed more Magic to flow down my arm, my hold on it broke, and it exploded from me. Stella threw a shield up to protect herself. I was panting. The power backlash would hit me hard later. Blood ran down through Stella's fingers and onto the ground. She could weave runes without the physical shape. She could cast almost instantaneously. It seemed impossible. The concept was entirely foreign. I couldn't handle my Magic with any type of finesse. Without a physical rune to focus it, the power seemed to be set on kill mode.

"Sorry."

She stood, brushing herself. "Again."

I followed her direction. This time I got a hold of my Magic a little easier and the ball was wound a little tighter. I let a tendril trail down my arm and pool in my open palm. The wound had already closed and Stella re-slashed it. She enjoyed the wince of pain it elicited from me. It was nice healing so quickly once again. I let the power rise from my palm.

"Good…Good. The power is not sentient, Lilith. Remember that. It's neutral. You bend it to *your* will."

The name caught me off-guard, another small betrayal. I opened my eyes suddenly disgusted. As soon as I lost concentration, my power exploded and I was flung back against the wall.

The wind was forced from my lungs and I slumped to the floor. As much as Stella said otherwise, I knew my power and it was not neutral. It was darkness incarnate. It was only a matter of time now before my will wouldn't be strong enough to resist the temptation.

I needed the control desperately. I couldn't just slash and dash. Not everything required a death blow and I would feel better if that wasn't the only thing available to me. I knew it, but it didn't make the learning of it any easier. Stella offered me a hand up and demanded I continue.

I was finally dismissed after many failed attempts and only some half-failed ones. When I stumbled back into my root and collapsed on top of the mattress next to Luka, he didn't look up at me over his book. My head was pounding. It would be a steep learning curve, especially after so many years spent never accessing it.

Now that I was free from the collar, I found the burnt vanilla smell of his Magic delectable. The night before, I had been too drunk to notice it.

"I saved you dinner. You were gone all day."

The thought of food made me sit up. Luka handed me the plate of bread and deli-meat before going back to his book. I stuffed it down, barely stopping to breathe.

"Did you see Judas today?" I asked, attempting nonchalance.

He shook his head. I could almost see the pity in his eyes. I laid back down. My muscles were stiff from sitting on the floor all day.

"Did you find out when Loral leaves?"

"Micah said he was meant to go yesterday, but he was worried about you. I think he left this morning."

I grunted. Loral hadn't come to say goodbye.

"Where did you get your necklace?"

"My mother gave it to me."

He leant over me, inspecting it.

"May I?"

I shrugged. When his hand gently brushed my chest, goosebumps broke out against the skin. Luka picked up the heavy garnet stone, the intoxicating smell of his power was immediately cut off.

He dropped the pendant and looked at me in horror. "What is it?"

"A dampening charm."

His eyes widened. "It dampens your Magic? Take it off!"

"No." I looked at him in horror. "It gives me better control. I've worn it since I was a child."

His reaction was almost comical. He was worried about a dampening charm when he had denied me my Magic for nearly three months.

"Have you taken it off?"

"Never."

I suddenly realised how close Luka was. His platinum eyes bored into mine. "Why?"

How stupid. He wanted to know why I didn't want my evil Magic to rage out of control. I smirked, sitting with my back against the wall. "Have you ever wanted to be a Blood Mage?"

He genuinely pondered my question for a moment. "You have so much Magic."

"I wish I didn't."

His head cocked as he searched my face for the lie. When he didn't find it he went back to his book. I put the empty plate on the ground and closed my eyes. I would clean up later. He was so close that when I readjusted myself my hand brushed his elbow. A sense of calm filled me. My Magic flowed down my arm and pooled at my fingertips. It was effortless. I hadn't even had to think about it.

I sprung up, staring at him in bewilderment. Luka continued his book. I crossed my legs and smacked the book out of his hands. Before he could protest, I intertwined our fingers. It was like two magnets sliding into place. Ignoring his raised brow, I closed my eyes and steadied my breath. With each deep breath, my power grew smaller and smaller until it was easily contained in a small ball in the centre of my chest.

"Arina, what are you doing?"

I shushed him. I didn't want him to break my concentration. He sat steady, nothing if not patient. I placed my upturned hands in his and let the Magic flow down and pool in my palm.

"Knife."

I didn't want to go rummaging around the waistband of his pants. He handed it to me without a word of protest. I sliced my palm carefully. For once my power didn't rage out of control. It stayed in a tight ball. The black smoke travelled down my arm, the tingling feeling continuing as I pulled on it like a string. I was giddy as I wove the simple rune for light without having to move a muscle. I could see the shape in my mind, the lines as familiar as the back of my hand. It was like Stella had told me. A ball of light filled my palm and illuminated the entire room. Luka gasped, pulling his hands from mine. Immediately my power begun to shiver and revolt. I grunted as I tried to regain control of it. The rune flashed behind my eyes, the lines refusing to comply. The ball of light would only stay for a moment longer.

Shit, shit, shit.

I launched myself at Luka, pushing him down onto the bed. I shielded his body with mine before the power exploded out from me in a deadly wave. I managed to direct it away. It hit the wall. Our carefully-folded clothes scattered across the floor, and red dust was shaken loose.

I sucked in oxygen, my lungs were on fire. I had nearly killed him. When I mustered the courage, I push myself up off Luka's chest. When I opened my eyes I was only inches from his face. A tendril of awareness prodded at the edges of my psyche. I slammed down my mental shields and shoved myself off Luka and crumbled back into the mattress.

"That was amazing. Did Stella teach you that?"

I could barely lift my head to answer. The exhaustion was so complete, I wanted to sleep for a week.

Chapter Twelve

"Lilith! Come join us for lunch," Valerie yelled from the dining room. She was so bright and cheerful. It grated on my nerves.

Valerie had first shown us to the group. Originally I had thought her to be no older than sixteen. She was so innocent and pure. But she had corrected me when I asked her about schooling. She had said that she was actually twenty-one, only one year younger than me, yet it felt like I had lived a lifetime more. Her eyes were filled with trust and there was no regret keeping her awake into the early hours of the morning. Her sunny personality made me jealous for a life that I might have had. I found myself keeping my distance from her and her friends. They were hard to be around.

I walked to the table and joined the group with a stiff smile. I needed to eat between torture sessions with Stella.

Valerie sat with Nick and Maddie. The shifters liked to hang together. I wondered how they could stand to be in the confined spaces for so long. It was getting to me and I didn't have to shift into giant wolf every few weeks. They couldn't stay in human form forever. Loral had told me they had joined the rebellion once the Elect had destroyed their homes in Galway and left them no choice.

"You look so much better already," gushed Maddie. We had celebrated her eighteenth birthday last week. "What can I get you?"

"I'll get it." I rose from the table and begun to fill my plate with bread and baked vegetables. Valerie's father must have cooked. It was better than the peanut butter sandwich I usually had.

"Where's Noah?" Valerie asked me. She wasn't very good

at faking casualness. My eyes narrowed. It looked as if she was blushing.

"I'm not sure. I haven't seen him since before breakfast."

I had a good guess where he was. He had been spending more of his time in the gym, but I wasn't going to give her any ideas. Watching Luka shirtless, slick with sweat was enough to make even the purest have dirty thoughts. If Valerie got wind of his workouts, he would be performing for a crowd.

"How long have you two known each other?" Maddie added.

"A long time. We met through bounty hunting." I ate my food quickly, the personal questions made me uncomfortable. The more questions they asked the easier it was for someone to trip us up. I had to make sure Luka knew what I told them.

"He knows what you are and still stayed friends with you?" Nick sputtered, shocked. He was young, only fifteen, and didn't know how to bite his tongue yet. Valerie smacked him behind the ears.

The bread hovered in front of my mouth. I was taken aback by his question. It was easy to forget the stigma surrounding Blood Magic living in my bubble. Even though Stella had lived here for some time it was clear a majority of the group found her uncomfortable to be around. Hundreds of years of hate couldn't be undone quickly.

"My Magic is just like everyone else's, Nick."

"Everyone else doesn't steal power."

His sister looked at him, wide-eyed. I swallowed my temper. He was a child, a stupid ignorant child. Maddi grabbed Nick around the bicep and pulled him from the table.

"Have a good lunch." Maddi smiled in my direction and yanked Nick from the room. No doubt he would be getting an earful once they were alone. He didn't look happy at being shoved around by his older sister. Valerie cleared her throat.

"Noah said that when the two of you were on a bounty together, he saved your life from a goblin. Is that true?" She finished her meal and leant over the table on her elbows. Valerie's eyes sparkled with interest, her friend's earlier transgressions so quickly forgotten.

Is that what he had told her? That he had saved my life? I laughed. Of course he had twisted the story to make himself the hero.

"Hardly," I scoffed. "Have you ever seen a goblin?"

She shook her head, eyes wide. I put my fork down.

"They're the size of a horse and mean as a snake," I exaggerated. "If I hadn't used my Blood Magic, he would have been squished like an ant."

I brought my fist down onto the table for dramatics. She gasped.

"But he said he captured the most dangerous bounties."

"He was the best in the business."

I wasn't lying. Luka had tracked and found even me. He had hidden from my rune Magic and snuck up on me. I should ask him how he did it.

"Lilith? Are you and Noah…" She paused, clearly embarrassed.

I quirked an eyebrow.

"You know." She grabbed my plate and went to wash up. The deep blush on her face was evident as she rushed away from me.

"Bumping uglies?"

The plates clattered in the sink. I had to restrain a laugh. I had swallowed my first choice of words. She would have had a heart attack.

"No, ah yes. Together, I mean." Her voice was quiet.

I leant back on my chair.

What did I say? Had Luka laid plans that I wasn't privy too? Valerie seemed so young. I should spare her the heartbreak. This felt like a conversation I would have had, had I been to middle school. Loral thought we were together already. But what about Judas? Would he feel betrayed? Why did I care anyway? He hadn't spoken to me since the collar had been removed. No matter what I said, the group would know by dinner time. There wasn't much to do underground but gossip.

I pondered for a moment and settled on the truth. "No,

we're just friends."

She exhaled and turned to face me. "Are you sure?"

"Unless you know something I don't." Her face brightened. "But Valerie, Noah's life is dangerous." She frowned at me. "He's much older than you."

"I'm twenty-one," she reminded me.

"I know." I gave her a small smile.

"Lilith!" A tiny shrill voice screamed as small feet ran into the kitchen.

"Hello Rosie." I bent down to her level. There were only three children in the Compound and most of the parents kept them away from me. Rosie was different. Her mother couldn't keep her away for long. I suspected that she liked the feel of my Magic. She would seek me out whenever she could. She had bright brown eyes and black hair that hung just above her shoulders. I had no experience with children, but I did enjoy the fact that there was no fear behind her eyes.

"Hello, Valerie." She seemed to remember the other woman.

"Are you hungry?" I asked her, holding out a buttered piece of bread. Her little hands grabbed it from me and chowed down.

"You said you were going to teach me to fight like you."

"Later."

"You promise?"

"Yes, I promise."

She intertwined our hands, her chubby fingers looked tiny in my hand.

"Rosie!" Judas appeared in the threshold and shouted from across the kitchen. It startled me to finally hear his voice. He had been ignoring me so fervently. "Come away from her."

She looked perplexed for a moment. Judas strode over and snatched away the small child.

"She's dangerous," he muttered under his breath as he strode from the room.

Valerie stood awkwardly and shot me an apologetic glance. The words stung. I had thought Judas was a friend. Before I could do something stupid like cry I fled the kitchen and went to find the healer. By the time I found Davis in his office, my emotions were back under control. I stood in the threshold of his office, Davis had his head in a book. I cleared my throat. When he looked up, his warm face brightened.

"Lilith, how wonderful to see you looking so well."

"Hi, Davis."

"How can I help you?"

I looked over my shoulder and moved further into his office before closing the door softly behind me. "I was after a book."

He looked at me amused. I felt stupid to even ask the question, but I couldn't shake the strange feeling about how my Magic acted when I was around the Hunter.

"About a magical connection between Mages."

"Hmmm." He sat back in his chair. "I might have something. I have a number of banned books here."

He popped up from his chair with a speed that didn't match his age and rifled through his voluminous collection. "Any particular reason?"

"No, I just heard an old story from Noah that interested me." I tried to keep my voice light.

"Are you talking between family members?" He looked at me over his shoulder.

"No. The story was between strangers. They could channel their Magic easier in each other's presence."

He pulled a thin book from his shelf and turned to me. "I think this might be what you're looking for. I remember seeing a similar folk tale. It was a love story, Romeo and Juliet type thing."

He placed the book in my opens hands, the cover was worn with age. It felt so fragile. I tucked it under my heavy sweater. "Thank you Davis. Have you heard when Loral will be back?"

"Sorry, Lilith. No word yet."

Chapter Thirteen

I shuddered with fatigue, but still Stella wasn't satisfied.

"You're too slow," she huffed, bored. Stella wasn't the most patient Mage, but she was a good teacher.

"I know. It's *my* eyebrow that's gone." I gestured to my face which was now minus an eyebrow. I would have to glamour a fake one on for weeks until it grew back.

We were standing in the corner of the gym that was reserved for Magic sparring. No one wanted to throw Magic at me. Luka was the only volunteer. I guessed it was so he could spy on me and make sure I wasn't betraying the oath. He had been lazily lobbing fireballs at me all afternoon while Stella watched on. We were practicing using my new casting technique in combat simulations. So far I had been unsuccessful. I was either too slow at getting the shield up, or it was so weak that Luka's Magic burned right through it.

"I have shield runes tattooed on me. There is no point in casting like this."

"Fine. Try and use the rune tattoos this time." She faced the Hunter. "Turn up the power."

My hand hovered on my dagger and I readied myself to slash my palm. I centred my power and locked eyes with Luka. No doubt I looked ridiculous with only one eyebrow, but he had yet to openly mock me. I could see the glint of humour in his eyes. When I felt the telltale flare of Luka's power, I slashed my palm and slapped the blood under my collar bone. Before I could force enough power into the rune to activate it, I was forced to roll out of the way of Lukas attack. The massive ball of flames brushed past my shoulder and went out as it hit the padded wall. I returned to my feet. There was a sizeable hole burned into my sweater. It hung awkwardly off my shoulder and the skin underneath was red and peeling.

I turned my glare to Luka. "This was my favourite!"

He shrugged, not offering up any apologies.

"I think you need some more motivation." Stella strode over to Luka. She gripped his shoulders and manoeuvred him next to me. The spark of power that flowed between us still unsettled me.

"What are you doing?" I hissed and yanked my grip from Luka's hand.

Stella skipped to the other side of the room and grabbed one of my daggers. She balanced it awkwardly in her hand. It was clear she was inexperienced with weapons. Even though she had amazing control of her power, she would be a liability in close combat. She sliced her palm and the smell of her Magic was combined with Luka's. The combination made me light headed. Her long hair rose on its end and her eyes turned black. It was eerie to see the effect on someone else's face.

"He won't be half as nice to look at without eyebrows."

If Luka was phased by Stella's comments he didn't show it.

"Just throw it at me Stella. I'll do it this time."

"We've tried that already."

"It's not going to make a difference." I drew my blade and dragged it across my palm anyway. Luka gripped my bloody hand and intertwined our fingers, stopping me from using the shield tattoos.

"It's fine." He gave me an easy smile. "I'm sure Loral has some sort of potion for missing eyebrows."

When my eyes met his, the connection flared to life. Power exploded between us. It had to be a side-effect of the oath. Powerful Magic had side-effects that couldn't be predicted. I ignored it the best I could. Stella conjured a fireball and flung it across the space. Luka's eyes kept mine as it hurdled toward us. His faith in me was unnerving. The rune flashed behind my eyes and the shield exploded out from me not a moment too soon.

The powerful blast knocked Stella off her feet and she landed square on her ass, mouth agape. I ran over to her.

"Oh God, I'm so sorry Stella." I helped her to her feet. "Are you okay?"

"Let's go again." It was the most animated I had ever seen her.

She wiped her hands on her leggings and ushered me back toward the other side of the room. "I don't think I can do it again."

I could feel the beginnings of power backlash creeping behind my eyes. Apparently it didn't matter what I thought. Luka grabbed my hand. Stella's Magic stretched and expanded before she drew blood, and a ball of flames suddenly winked into existence. What Stella lacked in raw power, she made up for in finesse. When she hurled it toward me, the shield appeared almost without thought. My Magic bent to my will like never before. I could see the intricacies of it as it wove in beautiful glittering designs. Stella braced herself against the impact but still skidded back a few meters.

I expected a wave of exhaustion to overwhelm me, but I felt better than I had in a long time.

"That was amazing!" Luka had a wide smile across his face. His joy was infectious and I found myself smiling alongside him.

Stella joined in our celebration. "I've never seen such raw power before. If you just learn to channel it, no-one could stop you."

Luka dropped his arm, the joy seeming to extinguish. "Is that enough for today, Stella? I have a few things left to do."

"Sure. Thanks for your help," She gave him a radiant smile and waved him off.

As he left the room, a sick feeling entered my stomach. Would Luka try to collar me again? I didn't think I could take the loss; especially not after I had just started to become more comfortable with my power. It was stupid of me to practice my Magic in front of him. He was my enemy. You don't show your enemy your hand before the battle.

"I have to go. Thank you again for your help."

"We'll practice again tomorrow."

I gave her a small smile and rushed from the gym.

I was an idiot! I had just shown the Elect that I was a deadly, unstoppable weapon. I would never be free now. No way would they agree to letting me go once they knew the power I possessed. Luka was probably getting the paralysis potion ready for me. I had fallen for his facade, let down my guard, and now I would suffer the consequences. I had to find him.

I weaved through the corridors of the compound, back toward our bedroom.

"Hey." Valerie brushed past me. I grabbed her arm before she got too far away.

"Have you seen Noah?"

"Yea, I saw him walking that way." She directed behind her. "I think he was going to get ready for dinner. Are you coming? Sylvie's cooking."

"I'll see you there." I waved her off and stalked in the direction she pointed.

Our bedroom was empty. I moved on to the gym.

Empty.

Where was he?

I stalked through the compound. It was so large, only a fraction of the rooms were filled. There were so many parts of the underground bunker that had never been used. He could be anywhere. I needed to talk to him before he made any rash decisions. I came to the springs. The burnt vanilla aroma of his Magic filled the small space. I had been to the springs before, a lot of the compound swam there for fun. I waded further into the room. The black structures of rock holding up the walls were pock-marked and slick with condensation.

"Noah?" My voice was barely above a whisper, yet it echoed around the cavern. All the lamps suddenly went dark.

Out of nowhere I was tackled to the ground. My feet were swept from under me and I fell. A hand cradled my head and stopped me from hitting the ground. Luka's heavy body was crushing me, trapping my arms to my sides.

"Get off. I just want to talk."

I wiggled violently under him. Tepid water dripped onto

my face. It was impossible to see anything in the dark and I didn't want to cast any rune Magic in case I scared him further. I wiggled my arms free.

I shoved hard against his chest. He didn't let up. He adjusted his position, straddling my waist and trapping my hands. Genuine fear rose within me as I remembered the ferocity in his eyes when he dangled the paralysis potion in front of my face.

"We made an oath, remember? We're on the same side." My words came quickly.

No doubt he heard the thin thread of fear that wove through my words. It had been a while since I was afraid of Luka. He laughed and shifted his weight. In the next moment he was standing and he held a flame by his face. There was no malice in his eyes. His long hair was sopping wet and he wasn't wearing a shirt. The fear vanished as quickly as it came.

"Why are you wet?"

"I was swimming."

I rolled my eyes. "You left so quickly, I thought…"

"Why does Stella need to cut herself so deeply before she can use her Magic?" He cut me off.

"I think she needs more blood to use her power."

He hauled me to my feet. The rest of the lights returned. "I heard Sylvie's making dinner."

There was a strange joviality to his voice. It made me uncomfortable, the lightness didn't fit him. I eyed him with suspicion. "We better hurry before Tony and Levi eat it all."

The kitchen was busy. It always was when Sylvie was cooking. Most of the group were already sitting down with their meals, I grabbed my plate and piled on the rich-smelling food. I nestled on the edge of the bench beside Sylvie. Over the plates of buttery mash, gossip was traded like poker chips. In the compound, no one's secrets were safe for long. Upon seeing me sit down, Valerie got up and sat opposite me. It wasn't me she was waiting to speak too. Her hair was expertly curled around her face and her makeup applied with a heavy hand. I had done the same thing waiting for Judas a few weeks ago. Now he glared at me from the other end of the table. I could feel his eyes burning into the side of my head.

"You look nice, Val." I gave her a small smile.

Her tan skin blushed a deep red. Finally the target of her affections came into the dining room. As when I had first laid eyes on him, Luka entered the room confidence first. His body was lean and deadly and he tactfully ignored the number of eyes that locked on him. As it was, I averted mine, focusing instead on the half-eaten meal in front of me.

Luka took his quasi-assigned place next to me. He slid me a plate of bread.

"You need to eat more."

"You still look like a skeleton," Stella joined in.

"Thanks."

"Lilith, Stella said you've been doing really well with your Magic." Sylvie turned to face me.

"I couldn't do it without her help."

"And Noah's!" Stella said.

"He risked his eyebrows for me."

I was still missing mine. I hadn't had time to glamour myself a new one.

"Did you hear from Loral, Sylvie?" Valerie asked.

I tried to keep my calm façade. No one ever gave me any information. I believed Luka when he told me that he would relay anything of importance. He would never sugarcoat anything. It was one of his redeeming qualities.

"Everything is going according to plan, Valerie." She smiled. If I looked closely, I thought I could see a tightness in her eyes, but perhaps I was imagining things.

"I want to go on a mission," Valerie stated. She had made the same complaint too many nights to count.

"Don't be ridiculous. What if something happened? You can't defend yourself," Sylvie brushed off her daughter with a wave.

"Yes I can! Noah's been helping me learn how to fight. I'm getting better, right Noah?"

I shot Luka a glare. He hadn't told me he was training anyone outside our classes.

"Not quite good enough yet, Val, but you'll get there."

"But Loral goes on missions all the time and he can't fight." She crossed her arms over her chest.

"Loral is one of the most powerful Potion Mages alive and he can fight," I reminded her.

"Noah will protect me. I'll go on the next mission he does."

This was Luka's fight and I would leave him to it. Dinner didn't seem quite so inviting anymore. When I got to my room I flicked on our bedside lamp and retrieved the book I got from Davis. I had hidden it under the mattress. For some reason it made me uncomfortable to think what Luka would say if he found it.

I flipped open the worn cover and reread the same page I had found the night before.

Soul Bonds

A Soul Bond occurs when a pair of souls are deliberately and tightly bound to each other. It occurs in only extremely rare circumstances.

Each Mage has their own unique magical signature—it is how wards are erected. When a Mage enters a Soul Bond, their magical signatures are intertwined. Their mind and Magic become permanently connected. Senses and memories can be shared and, in some cases, the pair can transfer their Magic reserves. With all things Magic, the effect relies on the strength and circumstance of the Mages involved in the Bond.

Familiar Bonds

This bond is a connection of the minds only. Familiars are connected rather than bound. The animals work in tandem and stamina is increased between both parties.

Although bonded to the Mage they serve ...

I knew all about familiar bonds. They were common. I had never heard the term soul bond before. Closing my eyes, I stretched out my awareness and thought of Luka. *Nothing.* I couldn't sense anything. I was alone in my mind. I felt like an idiot. I slammed the book shut, and hid it back under the mattress. I had let my emotions get the better of me. A handsome man had laid on top of me half-naked and dripping wet, and the next thing I was doing was reading up on soul bonds. Loral would never let me live it down--if he ever came back. I spent the rest of the night reading the other books Davis had given me. Luka hadn't come back to our room before I fell asleep, so I stayed on the mattress. If he wanted to go to sleep at a ridiculous hour he could sleep on the floor.

***

My mother's emerald-green eyes pleaded with me through the crack in the door. I could save her if I left the pantry, but I couldn't move.

Dark blood seeped under the door, the thick liquid lapped at my bare feet.

I was frozen and could only watch as my mother's blood curled around my feet. My power finally laid dormant, silenced by my terror.

"Arina," a deep voice called in an urgent whisper.

They've found me.

Pure dread shot through my veins. I burst through the pantry door, not sparing my dying mother a second glance. I had to go.

"Wake up."

My eyes flashed open like I'd been doused with ice water. The room was pitch black and warm hands pinned me to the bed by my shoulders. *Trapped.* I began to struggle violently. The scent of burnt vanilla filled my nostrils, soothing my panic. *Luka.* It was just Luka.

"We need to talk."

Nothing good had ever come from those four words. I

nodded, a stupid thing to do in the dark, but I didn't trust my voice. He must have taken my silence for an assent because his warm hand closed around mine and he pulled me from the bed. At his touch, the last of the icy fear was chased away and the dream gone. We shuffled in silence across the room and into the bathroom. The light remained off and I could feel the heat from his body radiating in the tiny space. When had I gotten so comfortable with his company?

"Can you ward the room?" His voice was quiet and low.

"Okay." I tried and failed to disguise the tremor in my voice. He passed me a knife and I nicked my finger. I drew the rune for silence on the bathroom floor. It would be easy enough to clean up. I gave Luka a nod when the rune settled over us.

"We need to discover how they are funding the movement. They can't operate without money. It's the easiest way to dismantle them."

It shocked me to hear him speak about taking down the rebellion after so long without mentioning it. I could have almost forgotten about our oath.

"The Elect will kill you. You've agreed to this."

I knew what the Elect was capable of first-hand. They had given me recurrent nightmares as a parting gift the last time we had met. I wiped at my bare feet, half expecting to see them covered in blood once again. Luka was right, this was the oath. This was the price for my freedom and I had agreed to pay it.

Incarceration is a fate worse than death. My mother's phrase ran through my head like a mantra.

"I can speak to Loral, see if he'll tell me anything. He doesn't suspect me."

Because who expects their best friend to stab them in the back?

"Once we stop the money, we cut the snake's head off. They won't recover."

I recoiled in horror. My back hit the cold wall, "You mean Joshua?" I whispered, barely hiding my disgust.

"He's the leader, the only one who knows how and where each cell is operating. Valerie told me all the orders come directly from him. Only Judas and Loral know the actual location of this compound. Everyone else arrived blindfolded. It's the same for the other safe houses. No one knows where they are except for one or two in the cell. If we take him out, the rebellion would be too displaced to pose a threat to the Elect. They won't kill them. You'd be free, Rina."

I tried to convince myself that I was too moral for murder, that the price of my freedom was too high. But the truth was, I had done much worse for less. My time spent in Dunlap was testimony to that. Every moment in my life where I had to choose between myself or another, the choice was never close. I had never faltered in my decision to save my own life. This wouldn't be different. It was how I had survived.

I agreed to his plan quickly, before rushing from the now claustrophobic bathroom and dashing under the covers. My emotions had been stuffed down for too long. The brittle barrier had finally cracked and guilt had welled up between the fissures and flooded my conscious. My reality was all too clear. My life had been spent killing, lying and cheating; never had I spared more than a thought for another. Snippets of my life whirled behind my eyes making me gag.

I was revolting. I was worse than the Hunter. It didn't matter. I couldn't change now.

"Loral will understand."

That was the blackest of the guilt that had coated my insides. Tears wet my cheeks and I brushed them away before Luka could see. Loral wouldn't blame me. He wouldn't even be angry at me. Luka's weight shifted on the mattress as he sat down beside me. He let out an unsteady breath.

"When I was a child I *hated* Magic class. I use to sneak out and take a boat to this small lake behind the school. One morning I took a friend with me and we rowed out into the centre. We hadn't been there more than ten minutes when it started to sink. We had to swim to shore. I turned back up at school sopping wet and covered in mud. I couldn't think of an explanation fast enough and they suspended me for a week."

I could almost imagine a younger, more playful Luka covered in mud with a sour expression.

"My father was livid, the son of the Hunter skipping class to go daydream in a boat." I turned over and faced him in the dark. He had never spoken openly to me about his life.

"Your father was the Hunter before you?" My voice was rough.

"Yes, he was my toughest teacher."

"Was?"

"He died on the job." His voice was tinged with sadness. "I sort of inherited the role. When my father passed, the Elect each put forth someone to take the trials. As the Hunter's eldest son I was automatically put forth in his place. He had trained me for the position my whole life, honing my magical and physical ability. I passed the exams and destroyed my opponents. They were impressed with my savagery and immediately elected me, even though I wasn't old enough to hold office."

I had seen his viciousness first hand. He could be terrifying. Luka didn't seem terrifying now. In fact I could taste his regret in the air. It was sour on the back of my tongue. I needed to submerge myself in his secrets and forget about mine.

"What happened?"

He paused, deliberating. The air seemed to grow heavy around us. "The trials go for a month. The first week is all intellectual challenges, test after test. It's incredibly tedious. If you pass that round you move on to the next two challenges. The second week is to test your magical abilities. They push you to your limits, see how far you can stretch your power. I collapsed more times than I can count. I was certain I was behind in the rankings. The third and fourth week are against your fellow challengers. We have a target we need to hunt, the first to capture it wins. The challengers don't usually go after one another, but..." He paused again. I could sense his hesitation, I knew where this story was headed.

"But?" I prompted him.

"Two of us were closing in on the target. If I had stayed the course, I probably would have won. But I didn't want to take the chance. I laid a trap for him. He lost his leg, but I achieved my goal." Subtle notes of shame played through his words.

Had the man been a friend? He would have done anything to get what he wanted, no matter the cost. I could understand that. I didn't like it.

"Valerie asked me about us."

"Mmm?"

"She asked if we were bumping uglies."

"I can't imagine her asking that."

"Well, not in those words."

"What did you say?"

"I told her the truth."

"I hope not the whole truth."

I bit at my bottom lip. "No."

"Goodnight." I could feel his weight shift before he pressed his warm lips to my forehead. The small, unexpected gesture caused my Magic to escape its confines. The black smoke billowed out from me; suffocating the room. His sharp intake of breath gave me enough control so I could quickly reel it back in. I was worse than a teenage boy.

The necklace was getting less and less effective. Before I had met Luka, I had never had such issues with control. My power used to be dormant. It had been a tar that slid through my veins, it only drew attention when I concentrated on it. Now, unless I was actively constraining it, the power blew away from me.

"Your Magic." He was breathless.

"I lost control," I bumbled out, I could feel the blood pool in my cheeks. I was just glad that he couldn't see my face in the dark.

"It's beautiful."

What? I knew people could feel it when I lost control. It was like an oppressive wave crushing everything in its path. No one but me was able to see it, unless they were a Blood Mage. I didn't like the thought that Luka could see the black evil clouds emanating from me. I could only imagine how I looked when I was actively using Magic. Darkness billowing out from me, my bright red hair standing on its ends, and my eyes turned to black holes. It was a horrifying thought.

"What are you talking about?" I was almost angry. How could he say that? Ever since I had gotten the collar off, I had been more aware than ever, I knew what it looked like.

"Your Magic. It's amazing to see."

My voice was low, dangerous. "It's not amazing and it's certainly not beautiful."

"What?" He seemed genuinely confused. "It's all glittering gold. Even now I can see how tightly you hold control of it."

"It's an illusion. Every time I use it, I can feel the stain on my soul growing. You saw me perform yesterday. My eyes turn black, Luka. Don't be fooled by some pretty colours. It's death Magic."

He had no response for me, no further words of encouragement. I knew the truth and so did Judas. It was why he now avoided me as if I had the plague.

Chapter Fourteen

I was sitting in the dining room. The clock read 4:45am, too early for any sane person to be awake. My sleep had been restless and nightmare-filled. I would have the world to myself for at least an hour more. There was a shuffling behind me. I whirled around, half expecting Luka. In the doorway stood Judas, his blonde curly hair mused from sleep. Even with the freezing temperatures he was wearing only track pants. I moved my eyes back to my breakfast and waited for him to leave. Our last few encounters had been frosty to say the least. He sat down across from me, muscled arms nursing a dark coffee.

"You're up early. How did you sleep?"

I stared at him with my mouth agape. He hadn't so much as grunted at me in a month and now he was worried about my sleeping patterns. I peered up slowly, not bothering to hide my annoyance.

"You know who you're talking to, right? You're not sleepwalking are you?"

His full lips pulled down on one side. He was not impressed with my sarcasm. Even though neither of us had seen the sun in some time, his skin was still golden and tan.

"Yes, I know who I'm talking to." He snorted as if *I* were being unreasonable.

"You haven't so much as willingly glanced at me in weeks. Have you forgotten what I am?"

"I just wanted to say that we heard from Loral. He will be back later today with word from Joseph." His hand rubbed the back of his neck. *Was he uncomfortable with my presence? I hoped so.*

"Fantastic."

Tension rolled off my shoulders. I was glad Loral was

safe. Maybe I could get some information from him, volunteer Luka and me for the next mission. We slid back into awkward silence. I finished my eggs and we sat staring at each other.

I was the one to break first. "You've been ignoring me."

"That's not true."

"We've barely spoken since my collar was taken off. Every time I come into the room you glare at me and leave." I couldn't hide the hurt in my voice.

When I was collared, we had spent a majority of our time together. I hadn't even been back to the fields. "I thought we were friends."

I fiddled with the gold coin around my wrist, the one he had given me. It was meant to bring the wearer good luck. It didn't seem to be working.

"You're a Sorceress," he spat.

The air seemed to grow cold, and adrenaline made my lungs heavy. I had wished, in some part of my brain, that he was angry at me for lying to him. But that wasn't the case. It hurt to hear the words aloud. My oldest fear come to life, Judas had seen the real me and turned away.

"That's not who I am, Judas. I'm still me. I'm still Lilith."

I needed Judas's friendship. He was a bright ray of sun in the compound. His eyes narrowed as he stared at me. I could see the calculation behind his pallid eyes. What was he weighting up? He glanced around the room. "I know who you really are." He leant over the table toward me. His voice was quiet. "I know what you did. You're a murderer."

When I was younger, my father would push me on the swings. I would jump off and see how high I could fly. One day I let go too late and landed flat on my back. That was how I felt now, all the wind had been knocked from my lungs. I tried to inhale, to exhale, to do anything but let the word bounce around inside my head.

Murderer. Murderer.

He knew. He knew.

"There's a two-million credit bounty on your head. You're a wanted criminal." His words were rushed and intense, as if he wanted me to deny it.

The bounty has gone up.

"You're a murderer! That's why you were collared." He shot at me accusingly. The words were like a wasp flying around my brain, stinging every time they hit the side of my skull.

"I..I didn't."

"You didn't kill that vampire?"

"I had no choice! He was killing an innocent woman."

His face hardened and he looked disgusted. Judas's once-friendly face had curled into something unrecognisable. I had confirmed everything he thought of me.

"What did you expect me to do, let her die?" I stood up over the table, leaning toward him. My voice reverberated through the kitchen.

The bitter taste of rage filled my mouth. *I had saved that woman.* The vampire would have sucked her dry before help arrived.

"You didn't have to murder him!" He matched my outrage. "I guess I shouldn't have expected more from a *vile Sorceress. Did it feel good to steal his Magic?*" Judas spat at me from across the table.

I *hated* that word.

His words snapped something inside of me. I couldn't see through the red haze that clouded my vision. There was a sharp pain on the inside of my cheek as my molars ground down. The coppery taste of blood flooded my mouth. My power came roaring to the surface. It yearned for violence. I yearned for violence.

I ripped the gold bracelet from my wrist and slammed it down on the table between us. "You're right. I am a vile Sorceress! I killed that vampire without even needing to take a step."

My Magic fuelled my temper, forcing it to burn out of control. Magic blanketed the room, replacing all the air. I would show him what a vile Sorceress I really was. I watched, uninterested, as the gifted golden pendant melted and burned under my attention.

"My only regret was that I didn't savour it more." I moved around the table. He needed to pay for his insolence.

"You're a monster." His eyes widened in horror.

In their glassy reflection I could see my black irises mirrored. He stumbled back, falling over his chair. I sauntered toward my prey, letting out a dark chuckle. His demise would be slow and painful.

"Arina!" An urgent voice interrupted. Luka stood in front of me, his warm hands encircling my biceps. Instantly my Magic retreated. The effect was dizzying and some of the rage dissipated. It still simmered just under the surface.

Luka was standing in front of me, stony-eyes serious. As I stared up at him, icy regret wormed its way through my body. Judas was cowered behind the table, eyes wide. Hastily I sheathed the dagger I hadn't remembered palming. Would I have killed him? Probably. My features schooled into ones of indifference. I couldn't show any more weakness. I shoved the anger down deep.

"I'm not your enemy, Judas." I pushed past Luka and strode from the room. I struggled to keep my Magic and mood stable as I stalked to my bedroom.

Instead of pacing the length of the room, I tensed up my muscles and sat on the mattress. I snatched a book from beside the bed and yanked it open. The page could have been blank for all it mattered. My fingers were strained white against the pages and I had to stop myself from tearing the thing in two. Anger pulsed under my skin. Luka hovered on the edge of my awareness. I could feel his energy pulsing in a silent threat.

"What the hell just happened?" he finally growled.

When I glanced up, the dim light from the bedroom shadowed his sharp features.

"Nothing," I snapped. "Just a disagreement"

His disapproval bristled on my raw nerves.

"He knows who you are," he said, his large frame loomed over me.

"He knows my name and that there's a bounty on my head." I kept my eyes glaring at the book.

Apparently he couldn't tell that my temper was barely contained, or he simply didn't care.

"What did you do to make him so angry in the first place?"

I clenched my jaw, my molars grinding against each other. I took in deep, calming breaths and tried to once again focus on the book.

"Arina." He snatched the book from my hands and demanded my full attention.

In the next moment I had Luka pressed against the wall by the neck. I pushed the full length of my body against his. "He hates me because I'm a *vile* Sorceress." The words tasted foul on my tongue.

The memory of the unbridled hatred that radiated from Judas caused my Magic to spark. I pressed myself harder against him, my body straining under the rage.

"Clam down." He chastised me.

His eyes held no fear in them. Maybe he had forgotten how close I had come to killing him the second time we'd met. I wanted to roar at him, remind him how terrifying I was. He grabbed my wrist where it was pressed against his neck. He threw me across the room. Luka hurled me as if I weighed nothing. By the time I got to my feet again I was buzzing with anger. He planted himself in front of me.

"You want a fight?" He shouted.

I shook my head and crossed my arms over my chest. My teeth ground as I struggled to keep my temper in check.

"Come on. Pick on someone who can fight back." He shoved my chest hard and I stumbled backward onto the mattress.

"Did Judas say something mean to you? Did you get your feelings hurt?" he taunted and settled into his fighting stance, beckoning me forward.

How dare he belittle me! I launched myself at him with a shrill screech. We traded blows. Luka caught me with a stinging shot across my cheek. I spat blood onto the floor and grinned up at him. I launched myself toward Luka, pummeling his face and chest. He grabbed me roughly and threw me off him once again. I hit the wall hard, winding myself. It took me a moment to get to my feet and then I lunged forward.

He didn't check one of my high kicks and my heel caught him flush on the temple. The Hunter wobbled for a moment before turning his sharp glare on me.

"Did that hurt?" I fake-pouted.

He barked laughter in my face. In retaliation, I hit him in the stomach. The Hunter bowed over and I pushed my advantage. I shot in aiming to kick his knee but he grabbed my shoulder and pulled me down with him. We managed to fall half on the mattress. I scrambled to gain a better position but he tied my legs up with his and straddled my hips. When I lashed out, he grabbed my hands and pinned them beside my ears. I kicked and bucked to no avail.

The anger began to simmer and was replaced with shame. My arm was definitely broken and Luka's face was covered in blood. He wore a mask of calm when he looked down at me. There was no condemnation in his eyes.

"You're lucky I woke up when I did. I've never felt your Magic so…" He searched for the right words, the anger sliding off him. "So uncontrolled. I thought you were in trouble."

I took a deep breath, letting the sweet smell of his Magic fill my lungs. I had lost my temper so easily.

"Don't do that again. I could have killed you."

He rolled his eyes. "You wouldn't have."

He was always so confident in my control. I wasn't. If I had used my power he would have been dead. I had tried to leave my monstrous side back in Dunlap, but it seemed I could never be free of it. He let me up and I retreated to the bathroom. The rage had left, and in its place was an icy sadness. I splashed my face with water to clean the worst of the blood. I had hoped Luka would have left the bedroom but he was still sitting on the mattress. I couldn't ignore him forever.

His face was badly bruised and blood had dried on his cheek.

"You shouldn't have taunted me."

"I didn't want you doing something you would regret later."

"Let me heal you." I took his hand in mine and he handed

me his dagger. I sliced it across my thigh.

I dipped my finger in the blood and drew the rune on the back of Luka's hand. With barely a second thought, the shape flashed to life and the bruises disappeared from his face. He seemed to sit straighter and breathe easier. I repeated the process on myself before crawling back into bed.

Luka left me to my misery.

I couldn't leave the room the rest of the day, the thought that the others secretly felt the same as Judas left me with a rolling nausea. I counted the cracks on the ceiling and daydreamed about a life I could have lived if I'd not been born an abomination. At some point Luka had brought me food, but it remained untouched on the floor.

Judas had been so terrified of me and he was right to be. I was a murderer.

"Arina?" Loral's familiar voice came from the entryway.

He had returned. The thought brought me from my stupor momentarily and a ghost of a smile crossed my lips.

"Are you ill?" There was concern dripping from his words and the sound of his shuffling feet as he moved closer. I shook my head.

"Noah told me what happened with Judas." It took me a moment to realise he was talking of Luka. "What an ass. He's lucky you didn't punch him in the throat."

I had done much worse than punch him. Did Loral know how close I had been to turning into a monster? Luka wouldn't have told him.

"You'll come with me on my next mission. Some fresh air will do you good. Plus I could use the extra protection."

"Can Noah come with us?"

"He's the one who came up with the idea."

Of course he had.

"Thank you, Loral, I can't wait." My voice sounded hollow and I turned my face so he couldn't see my eyes.

"Would you like to join me for dinner?"

"Noah already bought me food. Thank you."

Silent accusing stares were something I couldn't face today. Loral hovered by my mattress. We had never been the type of friends to comfort each other. He placed an unsure hand on my shoulder before leaving.

I wasn't certain how many hours had passed until Luka came and sat beside me, his large frame jostled the bed. "We're going with Loral on the next mission. He needs protection."

I murmured my consent. At least I could look forward to the fresh air.

"Come with me."

I shook my head. The thought of leaving the bed made my bones ache.

"It's late. No one is awake now."

When I sat up to face him, our light was no longer on and we sat in complete darkness.

"Where are we going?"

"I want to show you something." His tone left no room for argument and I reluctantly took his outstretched hand.

Our bare feet were silent as we hurried through the corridors. It made me nostalgic for my bounty hunting days. I missed the adrenaline of the hunt and the simplicity of a target. I had felt fleeting happiness for the last two years. I wished I had savored it more. We wove deeper through the caves. I didn't dare ask where we were going. The further we travelled, the lighter my mood seemed to get. I could almost imagine I was back on the hunt. Luka and I would have been a formidable team.

The silence was suddenly broken by a soft bubbling of the underground springs. Luka summoned a ball of flames that illuminated the cave in warm light. I was careful not to fall into any of the running streams. There was a reason I had not joined in on the swimming. Luka led me to the deepest section of the caves, and to a dead end.

To my complete surprise he begun undressing.

I spluttered. "What are you doing?"

The ball of flames was quickly extinguished as it neared the fabric of his shirt. His control was astonishing to watch. He seemed perfectly at ease with his Magic, the same Magic that was now illuminating his expectant grin. I turned away.

"When I was exploring last time, my clothes were

destroyed. I only have three sets left. I can't risk another."

When I turned back around he was down to his briefs. I tried, and failed, to look at anything other than his distracting body.

"Are you going to stand staring all night?" He grinned at me and I motioned for him to turn around.

He turned, extinguishing the light. I looked at my favourite sweat pants. I weighted the choice of ruining my pants or Luka seeing me in my underwear. I stripped down quickly.

"Where to next?" I grumbled. The caves were freezing. Luka didn't turn and stare like I had.

Instead he motioned to a high up ledge that I hadn't seen earlier. "Up there."

The entrance looked barely large enough for him to fit through and it was at least a meter above his head. There was no way I was getting up there alone. He motioned me forward and rested his elbows on his knees, creating a platform with his hands. I stood on him and was quickly propelled to the lip of the stone. The sharp rocks cut into my fingers as I hung there for a second.

"Too much time off?" he taunted as I wiggled up and over the edge.

"Come on then, Hunter," I scoffed over the ledge.

I waited for him, arms crossed over my chest as I scooted back so that he could join me. He scaled the ledge much easier than I had and somehow managed to keep the flame alight. I didn't give him the satisfaction of a grin, instead I motioned for him to lead the way. The cave floor slid steadily downward and I struggled to not slip on the wet stone. The thought of the teasing I would have endured if I had fallen on my ass was enough for me to keep my balance. I would have killed for a pair of boots. We made our way lower and lower, I couldn't see where we were going. Eventually we came to a tight crevice. Luka shoved himself through the tiny space. If he was wearing pants they would have been ruined. I followed, the rocks scraping at my skin.

I hope he knows where we are going.

I squeezed my way through to the other side. The sound of

the springs became louder and louder. The further we travelled, the lighter the passageway became. *How had they gotten lighting in here?* Luka dropped his firelight. A large pool was bathed in cool light. I looked around to see where the lamp was. Luka didn't wait for me, he dived headfirst into the navy water. He popped back up a second later, his hair looked black in the cool light all traces of the red hidden. Luka waded in the seemingly bottomless water. Anxiety shivered up my spine.

"What are you waiting for?" Luka shouted back at me.

I hesitated, my weight shifting. "I can't swim."

The revelation was met with silence. At least it wasn't laughter. Luka swam toward the edge and motioned me forward. I wasn't about to get into freezing water.

"What I want to show you is just up ahead. But we need to swim there."

I sat on the edge, my legs dangling in the tepid water. It was surprisingly warm, like a giant bath.

"Hold on to me. You'll be fine."

His confidence was infectious. I had never shied away from a challenge and I wasn't about to start now. Sliding into the water, I kept a death grip on the ledge. Luka managed to pry my hands and wrap them around his neck. I could feel the fire under his skin where we touched.

My kicking wasn't in sync with his. I had never been in open water before. The feeling made me uncomfortable. Luka dragged me along until we reached the other side. I was huffing from exhaustion by the time we reached the ledge.

I crawled out and laid flat on my back, struggling to catch my breath. Luka sat beside me. He breathed easy despite carrying me across the lake.

"I wouldn't think a Fire Mage could be so comfortable in water," I groaned. The sound of Luka's deep laugh filled the cavern.

"There's not long to go now. It's just up here." He reached a hand out for me and I took it. Immediately I was yanked to my feet. The light was stronger here. I could make out his face.

"What are you showing me?"

He simply rewarded me with a smile. After walking for a while longer we reached a circle enclave. There was a flat rock sitting in the centre which Luka perched on. I sat beside him, his body warming mine.

Why did he bring me here?

"Look up." He leaned back and lay against the rock. I did the same.

My breath hitched.

There was a large opening in the top of the cavern, through which I could see the pitch black curtain that had draped over the sky. The stars were milky speckles spattered in random patterns. A smile tugged at my lips. Nothing in life could touch me here. I studied the silver glow of the moon. The night had always brought me peace. It hid my flaws, my imperfections. Sweet-smelling rain started to fall through the hole and I relished the feel of cool air blowing on my face for the first time in months. It was cleansing.

A laugh begun to bubble from within me and I couldn't hold it in. I wanted to dance in the rain. Luka's knuckles brushed against my own, his fingers grabbing gently for mine. I sat up, my laughter vanished.

"What are you doing?"

He looked confused. "I'd never heard you laugh before. I…"

"Don't touch me." I scrambled from the stone bench. What was *I* doing? This was my enemy. We had touched before plenty. This felt different. The gentleness of the contact had sent goosebumps along my flesh and my stomach squeezed in protest. My body knew this was my enemy, even as my mind forgot.

"I'm sorry, Rina. I wo--" He sat up, blustering with his words.

"—You don't call me that, Hunter," I sniped.

"That's not my name." He stood, his face returning to the sneer I hated.

"But it is who you are." My words were cruel, I knew it, but I could not stop them.

"If I am to be reduced to my worst parts then so shall you,

Sorceress."

My fists clenched and unclenched in rapid succession. My eyes burned from unshed tears. "I hate you."

He was too close to me now, his hot breath tickled my cheek. "I don't think you do."

I scrambled backwards, my back hitting the cool stone. He stared at me a moment longer, his eyes drinking me in. I must have looked pathetic, pressed against the wall. He left the clearing without another word.

I sunk to the ground and wrapped my arms around my chest. When he left it had felt like the warmth had been sucked from the space. Tears squeezed from the corners of my eyes and fell onto my knees.

I sat in the dark for hours, Luka did not come back.

Eventually, the small cavern was filled with the yellow light of morning. I raised my hand and let the sun rays filter through my fingers and onto my face. The yellow gold light kissed every crevice in the cave. It wouldn't be long until someone came searching for me.

I unfolded my stiff muscles and made my way past the entrance.

It was a walk of shame and I hadn't even gotten laid.

The pool of black water stretched out forever in front of me. It was much larger than I remembered. To my relief, a rope had been secured from one end to the other. My chest felt tight.

"Stupid rope," I muttered. It seemed solid enough.

I slid into the tepid water and clung to it for all my miserable life was worth. Fist over fist I eventually made it to the other side. The rest of the way was easy enough to get through. I shoved myself back through the tiny crevasses and climbed back uphill to the ledge where we had first entered. There was another rope strung from the top. I ignored it and hung from my fingertips. The drop to the ground below jolted my bones but nothing broke.

My clothes were still dry when I redressed. I set off to find Loral, to pick another fight.

Chapter Fifteen

"How does it feel to be out in the real world?" Loral grinned at me from the front seat. I couldn't keep the smile from my face, the fresh air was like a drug. I never wanted to go back to the cramped space of the compound.

"So what are we doing on this mission?"

It looked like we were on our way to Ka or maybe Nexus. Loral had still not told us what exactly the plan was, just that we were required for protection. It seemed silence was the way of the rebellion just as it was the Elect. There were a number of large duffel bags sharing the back seat with me. Loral had warned me not to open them. Apparently the contents were volatile.

"We need money to survive," Loral eventually mumbled.

I shared a pointed look at Luka from the back seat that he dutifully ignored. "So we're working?"

"The hard works done. We're just going to deliver this package and collect the cash." Loral tightened his fingers on the wheel.

I wondered, not for the first time, why he needed protection. Loral didn't know about my old reputation, but he did know I could fight. I was just hoping we weren't doing any deals in Dunlap.

"What's in the bags?" Luka asked nonchalantly.

"Potions." Loral shrugged and flashed a worried look between us in the back seat. We had been frosty to one another since leaving.

"No doubt they were created by the best." I raised an eyebrow in his direction. Loral just laughed me off and turned up the music.

He was leading us right to the rebellion's source of

income. All Luka and I needed to do was to find a way to cut them off from the money. It sounded deceptively easy. The rest of the journey went too quickly. I focused on the passing houses and dimming light. We had yet to even pass a single Enforcer. The road was unsealed and not well travelled, but Loral seemed to know where we were heading.

Loral must have been nervous, I couldn't remember the last time he had stayed silent for so long. With Luka and I not on speaking terms, the road trip went very slowly. When the sun was on its way back down again, Loral decided it was time to stop. He had eventually told us that we would reach Dunlap tomorrow. My teeth gnawed at my cheek. Loral unlocked a small shed off the road. We all trundled into the small room. There were two twin beds. I was in half a mind to force Luka and Loral to share. Loral stuffed the duffel bags under a bed and Luka put our bags on the other.

"Keep watch. I'm going to go hide the car. The bags are heavily warded, so don't even try, Rina."

He didn't bother with my fake name when it was just me and Luka. Pfft, like a little warding, had ever stopped me before. I stood awkwardly in the room waiting for him to leave. He gave me one last warning glare before making his escape. As soon as Loral left I ignored his warnings and pulled a bag from under the bed. Luka hovered above my shoulder. The bags looked unassuming enough. No one would spare them a second glance. I kneeled over it.

"Can you break the wards?"

After the incident with Judas I was terrified to use my Blood Magic again. It was clear I had been using it too often with Stella. I had nearly lost control and killed him.

"Yes, but it might take a while."

"I'll keep a look out."

He gave me an encouraging nod, at least he was speaking to me now. Retrieving my dagger from its sheath on my thigh, I leaned the tip of the blade against the ward. It was stronger than his usual work. If I hadn't been so experienced with Loral's Magic they would have been impossible to break. I forced my will into the dome of power, searching for a weakness. It would have been easier had I spilled blood, but it seemed unwise to tempt fate. Loral was a skilled wardcrafter, but no one was perfect. I knew where the tiny imperfections in his signature lay. I found a tiny opening. Anyone else would have missed it. I pressed my knife against it until the ward fell. Salty sweat fell into my eyes and trickled down my back. Luka wasted no time in ripping open the bag.

I was lost for words. A gasp escaped Luka's usually stoic expression.

Inside the bag lay hundreds of vials containing a bright red powder.

Traxxy.

The drug had flooded the streets of Nexus and Dunlap for many years, had destroyed people's lives and families. It was insanely addictive and destroyed a Mage's power to the point where they lost their minds. The wolf packs were the main traffickers. They fought over territory constantly. My time as a mercenary had often placed me in the middle of the drug wars, killing for whatever pack payed the most. A shiver ran down my spine. It wasn't a time in my life I wanted to relive. I moved to the tiny bathroom.

Loral is making traxxy.

Even though I had made it my life's work to break the Elect's rules, there was something distasteful about dealing in traxxy. A sick feeling entered my stomach. *How many lives had been destroyed at the rebellions hands?* The line between good and bad was not as clear as I had thought. Luka didn't seem shocked at the turn of events, how much was he keeping from me? I plastered a pleasant expression on my face and perched on the other bed. I locked up my feelings of mistrust. I would study them when I had a moment to myself. Loral came with our pre-packed bags of Elect approved rations from the car.

I was starving and stuffed my face with the bland squares of food. Luka looked at me with disgust, his lip curling. I gave him a stuffed sneer.

"I'm not sharing a bed," Luka stated after dinner. The *with her* was implied.

"Fine. I'll share with Loral." I crossed my arms.

"Fine."

"Fine," I parroted.

Loral pinched his brow in frustration and muttered something about children. The night went slowly and we awoke the next day before the sun rose.

We entered Dunlap by nightfall. Run down houses begun sprinkling the streets and my stomach twisted in knots. We stopped at a motel on the outskirts of the city. It looked like the rebellion had some contacts, the motel hadn't even taken money from us. There was even a safe in the room. Loral locked the bags in the vault and turned to face us.

"I need to meet up with one of my contacts tonight."

"Okay," said Luka. "Where are we going?"

"The Pick Pocket," Loral replied.

I smiled and got dressed without alerting either of them to my discomfort. I didn't particularly feel like sharing my colourful past in the city's most infamous bar.

As expected, The Pick Pocket was crowded and overheated. It had been a mistake to wear leather. Species of all kind were drinking together like one big, volatile family.

The three of us wove our way through the rowdy crowd. People shuffled aside to let us through. Luka cut a particularly intimidating figure. One mangy-looking man didn't get the message. He stopped in front of me. He licked his thin blistered lips, his pupils were dilated. The wolf's eyes flittered around the room. He thought that I was an easy mugging victim. He probably didn't even see the mountain of a man standing beside me.

Luka moved from behind me and gave him a hard shove. He growled in the shifter's face. As he loomed over the skinny shifter, his grey eyes hardened. The wolf's yellow eyes widened in terror. He scrambled to the side not wanting to mess with my new bodyguard. I wouldn't have wanted to mess with him either, he was terrifying. Luka seemed to know as well as I did that you couldn't be seen as weak in a place like this. You would be swallowed by its underbelly, never to be seen or heard from again. There were no Elect members patrolling the streets and no one would come if you screamed. It was violent and deadly, but I found myself missing the unpredictable nature of the city, especially when considering the monotonous routine of the compound. The excitement was easy to miss.

After much whining by Loral, the bartender decided to serve us. Three lukewarm beers were placed on the counter. Luka had completely shed his stiff Hunter persona. He was bursting with arrogance. Lounging on the bar, he looked mean.

"That's the person I need to see," Loral leant over and whispered in my ear.

I peered through the crowd, looking for the person he was pointing out. No one looked particularly menacing, just a bunch of gangly teenagers laughing boisterously and spilling their beers over the run down table.

"Stay here. I don't want *you two* to scare them off," he ordered me and Luka.

"Fine, stay close. Yell if you need help."

The bar dug up memories that I thought I had escaped. Before I had left Dunlap, I had been infamous. Hopefully by now my face would have left recent memory. The first time Wesley had made sure I disappeared without a trace. Rumours would have circulated for a few months about what had happened to me. Maybe I had finally met a target I couldn't kill, or maybe the packs had thought me too dangerous and finally taken me out themselves. No one would have searched for me and my name would have slipped from their lips and minds. Hopefully Wesley had stayed quiet about my resurrection.

"Well, well, well." A nasally voice interrupted my thoughts. I whipped around, my gaze landing on a vaguely familiar man. "Look what the wolf dragged in."

Panicked, I flipped through my memories to try and place him.

"Wesley was telling everyone that you had blown back into town, but I didn't believe him," he sneered at me.

I risked a glance over at Luka and saw his poker face still firmly in place. "I don't know what you're talking about."

"It's hard not to notice when you walk into the room little love. The wolves have a long memory."

Wesley! The damn snitch. I would rip his arms off and feed them to him.

The man looked like a werewolf enforcer, I had long-forgotten his name and who he belonged to. The man was built like a tree trunk and his only memorable quality was his baldness. It was very unusual for a werewolf. Enforcers were all brawn and no brain. They executed their orders by using intimidation and beat downs, something I had been on the receiving end of more than once. It left me with a grudge and a healthy respect for their fists.

"Run along back to your owner," I spat and turned my back on him. Luka raised a questioning eyebrow. I shook my head. It wouldn't be wise for him to fight this battle for me. I nodded in Loral's direction. He needed protection more than me if things turned south. The wolf's heavy footsteps stopped close behind me.

"I reckon Alpha Lucian will wanna speak to ya."

I fought the urge to turn around and punch him in the face. I forced the ire down and tried to imitate Luka's calm facade. The bitter beer slid down my throat, making me feel nauseous. "That's too bad. I don't want to speak to him."

His meaty hand fell on my thin shoulder.

Big mistake.

When he spun me his hands turned to claws. His wrinkled, pock-marked face was so close. I could smell his rancid meat breath. I jumped off the stool and swiped his legs out from under him. His massive form crumbled to the ground. Before he had time to take another breath, my daggers were unsheathed and I was on top of him. The polished edge of the blade was pressed against the thin skin of his neck. I could see his artery pulsing frantically.

"Did you forget *who* I was?"

His eyes widened and I twisted my blade so that it broke the skin. My power bubbled to the surface. It would be so easy to allow my Magic to burn through his veins and take his power. I shook with restraint.

"Cool it love, I was just playing." His voice was shaky and he gave me a weak smile. It was satisfying to see my reputation still held. It took all of my self-control to force myself from the enforcer and allow him to scuttle away. No one in the crowd looked up from their drink, it was all standard in Dunlap. I sauntered back to my stool and Luka passed me another drink. I was grateful for once that he kept his silence. My mood turned more black. Wesley had tattled on me, letting everyone know I had returned from the dead. It had taken so much planning and effort to disappear the first time. Out of the corner of my eye a familiar figure sashayed toward me. This one was much friendlier. I felt the fragile skin on my face stretch into a smile.

"Go check on Loral," I whispered to Luka. He didn't argue.

I skulled the drink and ordered another one. The icy blonde woman slid onto the stool beside me. Her deep brown eyes stayed forward, neither of us acknowledged the other.

"Imelda." Her musical voice was just as I remembered it. I had been expecting her to change in some way, but of course that was absurd.

"Lucia," I responded.

How much had I changed? She had known me since I was a child, what did she think of me now? She had captivated the poor bartender completely. He was leant over the bar in front of her like a doting puppy. Lucia tapped the counter with her sharp nails and he began pouring her drink enthusiastically. The sweet smell of cinnamon invaded my nose, her drink order hadn't changed.

"What name are you going by now?" She asked.

"Arina."

"I thought you'd gone legit," Lucia murmured into the glass, just loud enough for me to hear.

"Mmm, so did I."

To those standing around us, it wouldn't immediately be clear we were talking. Lucia always liked it that way. She had few friends and didn't like to make her acquaintances known. I was glad she had made the choice to come see me, word travelled fast in Dunlap.

"Shame." She almost sounded bored. I suppose after living for hundreds of years nothing was surprising anymore.

"Anything exciting happen while I was gone?"

A tinkling laugh escaped her pale pink lips, her sharp fangs peeking out. Lucia finally turned fully toward me and I was caught in her aura, just as the bartender had been. For a moment, I couldn't look away. I shook my head to dispel her hold. It was easy to do. She wasn't truly trying to spell me. Lucia gave me a warm, teasing smile.

"There may be new players, but the game always stays the same my dear."

"I've missed you, friend." *And I had.*

"You know where to find me. Where ever I am, you are welcome." She flashed her fangs and in the next moment was gone.

I stared at the chair that she had just vacated with a strange longing. My life with Lucia had been full of tough love, yet I missed her. When I looked over at Loral and Luka, they were laughing in the corner with beers in hands. It was as if they were old buddies, catching up on the weekends events. It made me wonder if I had ever really seen the true Hunter. As I made my way over to the pair, slimy regret slid under my skin. Why had I even left Dunlap? I was an idiot to think that I could have a life out of the shadows. If the packs didn't know of my return already, they would tonight.

There would be no escape for me.

"Are you done?" My voice was husky. I was impatient to get back to the hotel room and out of this godforsaken bar. Loral's cheeks were flushed and his words were more jumbled than usual.

"Nearly," he brushed me off. "Have a drink. Relax."

I faced Luka. "Take care of him. I need to clear my head."

His slate eyes assessed me, obviously deciding how much to trust me. Luka gave me a curt nod. I wouldn't have stayed, even if he had tied me to the tables. The crowd parted for me as I stormed through. I reached the streets. They were blessedly empty. The wind whipped the short hair around my face. The night air was crisp and I breathed it in, relishing in the temporary freedom.

I could go to Lucia. She would take me in. Her barracks weren't far from here.

The Elect left the covens alone because they were powerful and old; the vampires had existed before the Elect had formed and would exist after they perished. The closer I got toward the barracks, the darker the streets became. The shadows seemed to have eyes. Could I become a pit fighter again? Or even a mercenary?

My heart beat faster the further I got from the bar. Adrenaline made me feel alive. My clunky boots beat the cobble stones as I stretched my legs into a run.

Free. It felt so good to be free.

The city was familiar. I turned down a small lane, taking the long way toward the manor. In my distracted state I hadn't noticed the distinctive scent of Luka's power until he stood directly in front of me. I skidded to a halt, nearly smacking into him in the process. The cool air seared my lungs. I hadn't run like that in a long time.

How did he find me? My freedom had lasted all of forty minutes.

"Where's Loral?" Maybe I could knock him out and make a run for it.

"I took him back to the room and then I came looking for you." He crossed his arms, power radiating from him in waves. "Where are you going?"

"I was going for a run."

He eyed me. "Arina, no one can escape the Elect."

In the darkness I couldn't read his emotions. He waited for me to understand. When I didn't he cursed under his breath.

"I don't want to go back." The desperation in my voice was discerning.

"Loral's in the motel alone with two bags full of traxxy. It's not safe. We have to go back for him."

Guilt rose up and unplanted my feet. I couldn't leave Loral

undefended.

I trailed after Luka as he led me through the winding alleys, away from the manor and toward the centre of the city. I couldn't help but think I was willingly walking back to my prison. It didn't matter how alluring my jailer was.

Dunlap wasn't a beautiful city, it was all harsh lines and secrets whispered behind closed doors. People stayed hidden in the shadows and the occasional flair of power burst from the forts that were disguised as houses. Maybe it was my home.

Back at the motel, Loral was sprawled on the bed fully-clothed. His gentle snores filled the room. We shuffled past his sleeping form and into the second bedroom. Luka shut the door softly, his back to me. He took a deep lingering breath, the moonlight illuminating his tense form. Through his shirt I could see the tension in his back.

I stood with folded arms. *I shouldn't have come back here. Screw the oath.*

"I'm sorry for how I spoke to you Arina." Luka's words were barely above a whisper.

My arms fell to my side. I had never expected to hear an apology from the Hunter's mouth. "It's okay."

"It's not. I have been cruel to you."

"We have been cruel to each other," I said.

"Then we are even." He turned to face me, some of the tension had leaked from his shoulders.

"How did you find me?"

"I don't know." His hand curled into a tight ball. "I can track your Magic somehow."

"Using a spell?" I asked.

Please let it be using a spell.

"No, I don't think so. I think it's the oath." His voice was quiet, cautious.

"Oh," My voice was breathy. I couldn't muster up a full sentence. The bland cream walls of the small room seemed to close in on me. There was so much unsaid between us. I slunk back onto the hard mattress, my arms wrapped around my scratchy pants. I rested my chin on my knees. Despair had settled deep in my bones. Freedom had never felt so far away.

"I wasn't sure until tonight."

I should have shouted at him, forced him into a fight, but I couldn't find it in me to get angry again. There was no sound other than Luka's measured breathing. After a moment he pushed himself off the wall and strode toward me, lowering his weight onto the bed.

"Rina, if you run, I'll hunt you." His tone was as grave as I had ever heard it.

He fiddled with his fake ID band. It was a nervous motion, one that didn't suit him. "Or you could pretend to." My voice was small, but the words I had whispered loomed large between us.

"You don't understand."

He stood to walk away and I grabbed at his sleeve. Luka flinched. The movement hurt more than I cared to admit.

"Then help me understand." He rarely showed vulnerability. I only ever saw glimpses of his true self. "Please."

He sighed, the sound heavy.

"I wouldn't want too, but I would be forced. They control me as much as they do you. I have only the illusion of freewill."

His words crushed the air in my lungs. I desperately wanted to scrub the sadness from his face. His controlled facade had slipped and I didn't know if it would ever fool me again. "We can leave together. We'll go now. They won't find us." I was almost manic in my musings.

"I can't, Rina."

"The covens will hide us. I have plenty of favours to call in. We can disappear. I've done it before." *I'll visit Wesley tonight, get new identities. We would have to be at Lucia's before the sun rose. She would know a safe house we could go to temporarily until the heat died down. By morning it would be like we had never existed.*

"If I leave they'll kill my sister."

What?

His words crashed into my train of thought. I hadn't thought Luka would allow himself a vulnerability so large. *The poor girl was probably imprisoned and being tortured just to keep him in line. Why hadn't he freed her?*

"Her names Ingrid, she's only sixteen. She lives a cushy life in Ka, but if I take a step out of line…" He paused, unable to finish the sentence, "I have to see this through."

I wrapped an unsteady arm around his broad shoulders. The rational voice inside my brain told me feeling sympathy for the Elect's Hunter was dangerous. The voice was easy to ignore. He shrugged off my arm. Before the silence could drown us he changed the subject.

"A few years back I tracked a bounty down to Nexus. He begged me to take him in, said he would rather face the wrath of the Elect than let the baby-faced killer find him." He aimed for levity but failed.

"I hate that name. For a while some people got it into their heads it was *baby killer* or just *baby*. I don't know which was worse."

"Will you tell me how you got the name?" He flopped back onto the bed..

I crawled toward him and sat cross legged at his head. His hair was inky-black in the limited light. It was much longer than when we first met. I wanted to run my fingers through the lengths. I weighed up telling him. Maybe it would make him see me for who I really was.

"Do you know about the fighting pits?" He made a non-committal sound, his poker face firmly in place once again. "After my parents were killed I ran, and I found myself in Nexus alone. I was so young…."

I stared at the slither of night peeking from between the curtains. How naive I had been. *Never again would I be helpless like that.* Luka grabbed my hand and stretched my fingers flat. My sharp nails had formed little crescents on my palm. They had finally grown back. I realised he was waiting for me to continue.

"After Nexus, I left to Dunlap and found a vampire woman who trained fighters for the pit. She let me stay and train as long as I cleaned and took care of the barracks. I had nothing else. Fighting was my life. I was sixteen when I first stepped into the pit. I'd always had a small frame. No one thought I was older than twelve."

A sad laugh left my mouth before I could stop it. I would never forget the look on the crowd's face as I marched in. Lucia had said that it was the first time she had seen me smile in eight years. "I fought for a year and made enough money to leave. My reputation from the pit preceded me and I fell into mercenary work. I was called many things in the pits but baby-faced killer was the one that stuck. No one knew my real name so they whispered about me in the shadows. I worked for whoever paid the most. My only loyalty was to myself and I wasn't picky with my targets."

He was still gently tracing shapes on my open palm. I spat the next words. "I told myself I would do one or two jobs and leave this god forsaken city, but I didn't leave."

I waited for his repulsion. It never came. I ripped my eyes from the night sky and met his equally dark gaze. There was a deep well of sadness behind the marble of his eyes, one I couldn't understand. I had expected disgust, even hatred, but not this soft emotion.

"The fighting pits are no place for a child."

Tears welled in my eyes. I beat them back. Had he not heard what I said?

"I chose to stay. I liked the killing. It was the only thing that made me feel alive." My words were a blade I wielded against my target. I wanted him to hate me as much as I hated myself.

Luka didn't flinch as the words found their mark. Instead he leant close to me. "I know what it's like to be numb to anything but the adrenaline."

I shrunk back as I recognised the emotion shining in his eyes—*compassion.* I could almost believe he understood the addiction, the ultimate power trip. He was so close. His scent of burnt vanilla invaded my senses and his power caressed me. It was almost a physical touch.

"Maybe we should find a more productive hobby." My voice stammered. Before I could flee, his hand closed around mine.

"Stay."

I hesitated, frozen in place for a moment too long.

"Forgive me. I forget myself." He dropped my hand like it had burned him.

The formality in his voice stung. I left the room, careful not to look back. The door took my weight as I closed it behind me.

My bag was sitting beside Loral's snoring body. I quickly changed out of my boots and jeans and tried not to think about the feel of Luka's calloused hand in mine.

Loral had spread out on the bed, the covers pulled tight under his body. I perched on a corner of the bed Loral had not taken up. It wasn't like I hadn't shared a bed with Luka before. There had been many nights in the compound when I had collapsed into the bed next to him.

This felt different. Both of us had shared things not easily spoken of it. It was too intimate. I tried to crawl up next to Loral, but he hadn't left me any space. The air conditioning was freezing and my muscles cramped in protest. At least that's what I told myself as I hopped off the bed and opened the door to the bedroom. Luka was still laying in the middle of the bed and he remained motionless as I shuffled over to the side. If I ignored the laser-like attention of his power, I could almost pretend he was sleeping. The sheets were scratchy as I quickly slipped beneath them.

I lay on my back, eyes fixed to the ceiling. Luka's body radiated a familiar heat. It was oddly comforting. His hand slithered out and touched mine. He entwined our fingers, and the burden of my odious past suddenly didn't feel so heavy.

Chapter Sixteen

We'd been set up.

It was *meant* to be a simple transaction. We had the potions, they had the money. But now I was staring down the barrel of a gun. The werewolf holding it had a mean snarl on his face. He didn't seem to know who he was pointing the weapon at.

We had arrived at the meeting in good faith and they had pulled weapons. They wanted the goods, but weren't willing to part with their cash. Luka looked surprisingly comfortable with the gun aimed at his chest. It made me wonder how many times he'd had it happen.

Poor Loral didn't look at ease, he clutched the duffel bag like a shield across his stomach.

"Gentlemen, this is no way to treat a lady," Luka drawled. He had shuffled so his shoulder was slightly in front of mine, blocking half my body.

Sniggers rose from the pack.

"You're no lady." The cool metal from the butt of the gun poked me in the chest, the smell of the enforcer's breath hit me with full force. It smelt like rotting meat. Some of the members without weapons had partially shifted, sharp claws sprouted from their hands.

"We had a deal," I spat. The brute snarled in response.

His yellowing teeth came way too close to my face. "Give us the bag."

"No." Luka's voice was deadly calm. There would be no negotiating.

Beside me Loral was shaking like a leaf. I would have to take out the man holding him hostage first. *I really didn't feel like getting shot.*

Before the wolves could get shooty, a wall of fire rose between us and the pack—courtesy of Luka. I unsheathed my daggers and crouched into a fighting stance. I didn't trust my magic after the incident with Judas. It would be just as likely that I would kill Loral and Luka in my rage. I tightened my fingers around the cool hilt of the blades. Knives it was.

Luka's control was extraordinary to watch. He held the wall and hurled spheres of blue flame through it. I had never seen anything like it. The smell of burnt fur filled the air and some of the wolves squealed.

"Go!" I yelled at Loral. He abided my instructions and scurried toward the truck.

They continued to stalk forward, some had fully shifted. They were waiting for Luka to exhaust his Magic. The three wolfs holding guns seemed to remember they were armed and begun firing toward us. I dove for cover behind a pile of crates. Luka did the same. *Stupid human weapons.* His wall of flame fell and he pulled out a gun from a hidden holster. I had never seen him wield one before, but he did so comfortably. Where did he even get the weapon from?

I didn't know how any of them held them for as long as they did. Just the memory of firing one sent a shiver up my spine.

"We need to get rid of their weapons!" he shouted over the top of his fire. "Use your power."

I shook my head aggressively. "I'll lose control."

I would expose myself . He ducked out from behind the crates and began shooting. One of the enforcers dropped his gun and shifted into his wolf form, snarling and leaping toward us. I popped up from behind the box and hurled my dagger. It landed in between his eyes. The wolf froze and crumbled mid-step.

I retrieved my spare throwing knives from my satchel. I spent a second weighting them in my hand before jumping up and pitching them at two separate shifters. One of my daggers hit its mark, the other I had thrown with my left hand. It had gone wide, hitting his shoulder.

A curse escaped my mouth. *Rusty*.

It had the desired outcome anyway, all of the wolves were now disarmed and they had all been forced to shift. When I poked my head above the crates I counted nine left. We were badly outnumbered and under-armed. Neither of us had been expecting a fight.

Luka holstered his now empty weapon. Our eyes met for a moment before we exploded from our hiding place and into the fray.

The first wolf crouched before me. There was no time for assessment.

My dagger slashed out at him before he had a chance to pounce. His roar of pain was deafening. There was no time for prisoners.

He fell dead but two more stalked me. They met the same fate and I was left with a deep gash across my ribs for my efforts. The wound was messy and burned with the telltale signs of poison.

Luka grunted in pain as two circled him, one already lay in a burnt husk on the ground. Blood covered Luka's arm and his Magic saturated the air. My nose twitched and my eyes fixated on the blood pulsing from the wound in time with his heart.

A wolf threw itself at me and broke the hypnosis. Claws dug into my shoulders and his hefty weight threw me to the floor. My head rung like a bell against the concrete. It took all my strength to keep the wolf's teeth from clamping down on my neck and my power at bay. Blood seeped from the wound in my side in time with my racing heart. The jaws of the animal snapped at my face, its spittle hitting my cheek. My blade had been knocked from my hand in the fall. I reached towards it with one outstretched arm while the other pushed at the creatures gross, wet snout.

My arm begun to shake under the strain.

The wolf's head landed next to my face. My eyes squeezed shut as a torrent of arterial spray rained down on me. The weight of the wolf disappeared. I took a deep breath and my throat became clogged with sour blood. I frantically wiped at my face, desperate to clear my eyes. Before I could lash out, a warm hand grabbed my own and pulled me to my feet.

"Are you alright?" Luka murmured.

The tip of his sword rested on the ground and he looked as horrid as I felt. I nodded. We were both still alive, for the moment. We stood together to face the two remaining threats. The scent of Luka's magic had disappeared from the air and was replaced by only the reek of wolf blood. I pushed a bloody tendril of my hair behind my ear and knelt down to yank my blade from the closest wolf's chest. I threw it at the animal as it thundered toward me. The dagger landed flush in the creature's chest, but it did not fall. It kept running at me, its black eyes filled with a hunger that I understood only too well. I would be eviscerated before I could stop it.

"Rina!" Luka lobbed his sword at me. I caught it and chopped down. The creature dodged my strike and skittered back aside.

Luka let loose more spurts of fire but I could taste his weariness in the air. The wolf swiped at my thigh in a movement too quick for me to track. My balance faltered and I fell to one knee. He lunged toward me to deal the killing blow.

My sword met his middle. He faltered for a moment but kept snarling. I pushed the sword in deeper into its fur with a scream. The wolf died and I felt a cavern of relief open within me.

Dead.

My satisfaction was cut short by Luka's anguished yell. His Magic had faltered and the wolf was on top him, his sharp teeth ravaging his neck.

No!

My Magic exploded out from me, my eyes bled black and my hair stood on its ends. My power drilled into the veins of the animal, turning his blood to smoke. I brimmed with stolen power. It sung in my veins and sparked at my fingertips. The monster crumbled, as if its skin was suddenly empty. Warmth flooded my cheeks and made me giddy. I wanted to do this forever.

Luka lay motionless on the ground in a puddle of his dark blood. Everything wild within me was suddenly quiet.

I sprinted towards him and crashed to my knees. The pain

barely registered. My hands closed over the gaping wound on his neck. Blood squirted between my fingers. I ripped his shirt and painted a large healing rune on his chest.

"Is he okay?" Loral shouted. I drowned his frantic yelling and focused on draining my Magic into the rune.

I heaved Luka's limp bloody form onto my lap, my eyes blurry with tears. There was nothing of the fire under his skin. His body was ice cold.

I couldn't sense his Magic. The thought rolled over and over in my mind. It was the only thing I could think of.

"Luka!" I begged, the rune was working too slowly. Healing Magic couldn't bring people back from the dead.

I felt my own breath leave me.

I slashed my palm with a bloody knife and grasped at the golden thread of my power. I looped it round and round to weave the complex character needed for healing. A hoarse scream wrangled itself from my throat as I forced all my available power into the rune and threw it toward Luka.

He was dead. I would be left alone in my misery. His sister would die and all his sacrifice would be for nothing. I cried as if my skin was being shredded from the inside. Grief poured from my every pore, the weight of my emotions fueled my Magic. It wasn't enough. The gem from around my neck began to spark and burn. Without a second thought, I yanked the thin chain and threw it to the ground, shattering it in the process. My Magic flared.

I forced everything I had into his limp form begging him to just take a breath.

He couldn't be dead.

I had nothing left to give, my power went eerily silent for only the second time in my life.

"You can't die," I babbled.

I cradled his body close to me. The scent of burnt vanilla tickled my senses. He begun to breathe, taking deep slow inhales. His body turned hotter until the touch from his skin almost burned me. I couldn't let go. The blood covering his body had cooled and turned sticky. It wet my hair as I buried my face in the crook of his neck.

"Rina?" His voice was gravelly, as if his throat had been damaged. I pulled back and watched his eyes flutter open. Exhaustion crashed over me. I had given too much.

"You're alive."

"It would seem so."

His response pulled a dry laugh from me. I buried my face in his chest. He stiffened for a moment before softening and wrapping an arm around me. I inhaled the sweet smell of his Magic. Before he could see, I swiped at my eyes to wipe the tears from my cheeks.

"You're bleeding."

"I'm fine." I had expended all my power. There was no Magic left for another healing rune. I cradled my ribs protectively, holding the pieces of my singlet together.

"We should go," Loral whispered. He had collected the bag of money and held it to his chest.

"Leave the traxxy," Luka ordered.

Loral followed his direction and dropped the duffel bags in the middle of the scattered bodies. He looked bashful. He had never told us what was in the bags. The healing rune had worked perfectly. Luka seemed to be back at full strength. He slipped off his destroyed t-shirt to reveal four thin lines across his chest and neck. The blood coating his body was dried and I could almost convince myself that it didn't belong to him. He looked at his body in wonderment.

"I feel perfect."

He balled his shirt and pressed it to my side. My vision had begun to grey from blood loss. It had taken all my power to yank him from deaths icy grip and now I was paying for it. I wouldn't examine the feeling his lifeless form had exposed. His strong arms slipped under my knees and he cradled me to his bare chest. Loral drove us back to the motel, oddly silent the whole drive.

Luka insisted on carrying me into the motel room when my eyes struggled to stay open. Pain was radiating from my entire body and I ground my teeth together to keep silent. Despite my effort, a groan escaped my lips as Luka placed me gingerly down on the bed.

"Do you have enough Magic to perform another rune?"

I could only shake my head, my Magic was still deathly silent. It made me wonder if it would ever come back.

"Poison." It was the only word I could spit out.

"Loral, I have medical supplies in my bag. Will you grab them please?"

Silently, Loral rushed over to Luka's bag and retrieved the supplies. After he deposited them off to Luka, he went to the bathroom and came back with a bowl of hot water. Loral sat in brooding silence. If the pain wasn't blindingly distracting I would have demanded to know why he was behaving so strangely.

Luka cut down the front of my shirt exposing the wound. My skin was ashen and clammy, and my hands shook slightly.

Loral handed me a silvery potion. "For the pain."

I took it greedily. The effects were almost immediate. My senses were covered in a heavy wool blanket. Everything was muted, even the feel of the warm cloth as Luka gently washed my wounds. It must have been human medicine.

"Sleep, Rina." Surprising panic rose within me.

"I'll be here when you wake up," he said and rested a hand on my cheek. With his platinum eyes gazing at me, my eyes slipped close and I fell into a deep sleep.

***

In my hazed state, I could just make out fervent arguing. The world was covered in clouds.

"She called you *Luka*?" a voice whispered.

"Calm down. You'll wake her." A deeper, bored sound came from closer by.

"Who are you?" The first voice sounded frantic.

My breath caught as I rolled onto my side. The pain was excruciating. A grating moan came from me in response. My body was on fire. A cool cloth was dabbed on my forehead and comforting words were murmured in my ear. My lips were wet with a sour tasting liquid and I fell back into a restless sleep.

***

There was a war raging within me. My body was drenched in sweat yet still I shivered violently.

"The poison is burning her up faster than her Magic can heal her." Luka's horrified moan came from beside me. The metallic-tasting potion was brought to my lips and I drunk the liquid like it was the sweetest water. The relief was instant. I drifted blessedly away.

"She'll be okay." Loral's voice sounded far away, like I was floating above my body. "She always is."

The sound warmed me for some reason. It was a pleasant feeling and one I clung on to in the sea of pain.

***

Gentle snores filled the room. I hurt from the roots of my hair to the tips of my toes, but the pain was bearable. I opened my eyes to darkness. Beside me I saw Luka's muscled form propped up by a stack of pillows. His face was lined with stress.

I gasped as I rolled over. Luka's eyes snapped open. His features were laced with concern and he begun fussing over me, dabbing the cool washcloth over the wound on my chest. My body felt as if it had been dragged through a blender, but I didn't feel like I was actively dying anymore. Luka brought another potion to my lips, but I pushed him away. I'd slept for too long already.

We needed to retaliate on those that had betrayed us. I pushed myself up, ignoring the pain in my ribs. My Magic had finally returned, but it only slid quietly through my veins. It would be enough for now.

"I think I can perform a healing rune," I croaked, trying not to wake Loral, who was snoring on an arm chair. He hadn't left my side. I didn't deserve him.

Luka didn't question me, he just handed me my blade. I slashed my palm and with my free hand, I intertwined my fingers with Luka's. I had done it subconsciously but immediately, my power centred. The golden thread of Magic slid down my arm and I let it pool in my hand with the spilled blood. It wove into the rune for healing, the power spluttering and shivering in protest. By the time I had completed the rune I was shaking. Sweat dripped from the end of my nose. Luka didn't ask if I was okay, his faith was comforting. I pushed every last iota of power into the rune and finally felt the click of it taking hold.

Immediately a calming cool washed through my body taking with it the pain. I let out an audible sigh of relief.

"Better?" Luka whispered and pushed a sweat and blood-soaked lock of my hair from my face. I murmured and stretched out my joints, feeling them click and pop back into place. Pulling the blankets away, I tugged at the edges of the carefully-laid bandages that decorated my chest and ribs. Underneath, the skin was smooth and unmarred except for a thin angry pink line. I pulled the remainder of the bandages from my side and thigh. Luka had cleaned most of the blood off, yet I could still feel sweat and grime caking my body. I needed a shower. I needed to wash the memory of Luka's bloodied body from the forefront of my mind.

"Help me up," he obliged and lifted me from under my arms. Once I was standing I brushed his hands away and stumbled toward the bathroom. My body was now unmarked, but I was completely drained of power. Luka trailed behind me like I was a baby deer taking its first step. My knees wobbled every step I took. It felt like I had been collared for the last six months.

I let the door frame take my weight.

"I'm going to shower."

"I'll be here." He turned from the door, facing away from the bathroom as I flicked on the light.

I didn't argue. I didn't have the energy to. Quickly I stripped off and moved under the hot stream of water, sitting in the bottom of the shower. The loofa rubbed my skin until it was red and raw. I scrubbed my hair viciously trying to get the sweat, blood and debris from my strands. It had grown past my shoulders now.

"Are you alright?" Luka whispered over his shoulder.

I grunted my assent and let the water rush over my finally-clean body. Once the water ran clear, I gingerly lifted myself from the floor and wrapped my body in a thin towel.

Luka held my bag out, his eyes still averted. I rifled through my belongings and slipped into a clean tracksuit. My hair was wrapped into a towel and I plodded back into the room. Loral was still snoring in the arm chair. Luka shook him softly. Loral startled awake and searched for me with frantic eyes.

"I'm fine," I quickly placated him. "I healed myself. You can go to bed now."

I could see Loral's sharp eyes assessing me and I flicked on the lamp beside the bed before lifting my sweater to reveal my now-smooth skin.

Loral picked up his blanket and wound me in a tight hug. "I'm glad you're okay."

"Me too."

Loral shuffled to the second room, fatigue evident in his every step. When he left, I collapsed onto the bed. Luka took the chair.

"Thank you for saving my life." His voice was full of sincerity. "It's not a debt which I can ever repay."

I waved him off with a flick of my fingers and rolled over. "There's no debt between friends."

Were we friends now? I didn't know. The uncomfortable knowledge that I had almost traded my life for his, settled behind all the other things I didn't want to think of. I yawned as Luka shifted his weight in the chair. My wet hair had made me uncomfortably cold. Sitting up, I threw my feet over the side of the mattress. Using all my remaining strength, I grabbed his large hand in both of mine and dragged him into the mattress.

The bed was filled with the warmth of his magic and I could finally breathe. He kept away from me, only allowing his fingertips to trail up and down my forearm. The pleasant feeling finally lulled me into a peaceful sleep.

Chapter Seventeen

When the morning came I was feeling much better. My muscles ached but my mind was clear, and the worst of the pain was gone. Luka's arm was flung over my waist and his nose was pressed into the crook of my neck. His breathing was even and he looked peaceful for once. The cruel set to his brows had disappeared in sleep. I reached up to rake my fingers through his black hair. It was softer than I expected. It fell easily through my fingertips. His grip around my waist tightened. I froze and raised my arm so as not to wake him.

When he pressed his face closer into my neck and threw a heavy knee over my body, I tentatively wrapped my arm around his shoulders and let my fingers fiddle with the hem of his sleeve. The gentle contact was so foreign. Not since I was a child had someone held me without expectation of repayment.

The hand around his shoulders begun to shake and my heart thudded unevenly. I could hear it pounding in my ears. Luka's eyes flicked open and he came awake all at once. He looked at me with brows raised before jumping from the bed. He pushed his hair back behind his ears, his dark eyes darted around the room.

My mouth stayed glued shut.

"I'm going to shower," he muttered, adjusting his pants. I struggled to keep my eyes on his face. The crease between his brows was back.

I didn't like it.

He came out with a towel wrapped low on his waist. With a shake of my head I disappeared into the bathroom and shut the door behind me. I sat in the cold shower until Luka had banged on the door threatening to come in. I dressed quickly after that, avoiding my reflection in the toothpaste-stained mirror

Now that the threat to my life had passed, it seemed Loral was giving me the silent treatment. I wondered how long I could pretend I didn't notice. I had convinced him that we needed to go shake some trees until we found out who had betrayed us. It was partially an excuse to find out who the rebellion was supplying to so that we could cut it off at the source. Luka had insisted that Loral needed to stay at the motel. There was no way we could protect him and do what we needed to do.

Luka and I had come better prepared this time around, both carrying long swords and a number of Loral's most potent potions. We sat in the car in fresh clothes.

"So what's the plan?" I cracked my knuckles in front of my body. I needed to say anything to fill the heavy silence that was between us.

"Loral gave me the name of his contact - Eurice. Apparently he's a member of the Crescent Eye Pack."

"Alpha Giovanni," I sneered. "If my memory still serves me correctly."

"No doubt he will be looking for us too."

"I have someone who owes me. They can set up a meeting."

He cocked his brow, but I paid him no attention. I had promised Wesley I would give him another visit. It wasn't good to not follow through on your threats. I was a better woman than that, if I made you a promise I was keeping it. I gave Luka the directions to his house. The lights were off. He was probably still asleep even though it was nearly midday. It was a good thing. I wasn't sure I could hold a shield rune for long. His house was much the same as it had been when I had last shown up. How stupid I was to think it would be my last time in Dunlap. I wasn't at full strength, but at least I was still strong enough to break Wesley's shitty wards.

No potion bombs flew in our direction as we strolled in. Maybe he wasn't home. My fist rapped on the door and I called out in a sing song voice, "Wesley darling!"

From inside his messy apartment I heard him scrambling

before he flung open the door. I tried to hide the fact that I was out of breath. He was too strung out to see that Luka was holding up most of my weight.

Luka shoved his way through. Wesley was in dirty pyjamas and his greasy hair hung over his eyes. He looked like he had been on a two week bender. I shoved him against the wall and held my dagger to his neck. I wouldn't be surprised if he had nightmares about me. I liked the thought that I occupied so much of his mind.

"I heard you had opened your big mouth Wesley. I believe I made you a little promise the last time I visited."

"I'm sorry! Please don't kill me, A. I'll do anything you want. Anything!" Pure terror flashed from behind his eyes and he tried to wiggle free of my grip. It took more effort than usual to contain him. It was lucky Luka stood behind me.

"Looks like it's your lucky day. I need an audience with Alpha Giovanni." I leant more weight against the knife. Wesley shook his head and screwed up his face.

"You owe me." My voice was low and dangerous.

"Okay, okay. I can request a meeting."

"You will get us the meeting. If he doesn't show, your life is forfeit."

"Okay! Anything, A. Anything you want."

"We will meet him at Fluffy's at 8pm tonight"

I knew the owner well enough. He could be paid off.

"If he brings more than two *friends,* we walk, and you're dead," Luka demanded from behind me.

I sliced my finger on the edge of my dagger and called to my Magic. I probed at him, letting him feel my power.

"I'll make sure he's there," he shouted, eager to please. I shoved Wesley away from me, unable to be near his rancid breath any longer.

"That wasn't so hard, and Wesley—remember you're only alive because you were useful." I flipped my daggers and re-sheathed them. I didn't know if I could actually kill Wesley, let alone torture him. But he believed I could.

I had to hope that Wesley wasn't going to lob a potion bomb our way as we left. I had no power left to defend them.

He scurried back inside his house and slammed the door behind us. We walked undisturbed back to our car. Luka hopped into the driver's seat and when we were far enough away from his house I slumped in my chair. *I was so tired.*

"Are you alright?"

"I'm fine."

"I need to rest before tonight. I'm still not at full strength yet." His Magic saturated the air. It didn't seem likely that he needed to recoup. I eyed him suspiciously. He looked honest enough. If I didn't feel his power, I might have believed him. Instead of arguing, I simply nodded and let him drive me back to the motel.

***

My power was nearly back at full strength as I walked into Fluffy's with Luka at my back. Never did I think I would feel safe with the Hunter standing behind me. I strolled up to the bar like I owned the place. When I lived in the barracks with Lucia I used to spend all my free time and money at the place. My mask was back on, black kohl lined my eyes, and my lips were painted red. I felt like myself again for the first time in many months.

"Can I speak to Fluffy?" I sized up the green-looking bar hand. He blanched.

Except he wasn't looking at me, he was looking behind me. I narrowed my eyes and swung around to see Luka looking particularly mean. He was an asshole, stealing all my scary thunder.

Fluffy came to the bar looking cranky. He was almost the size of a bear and just as hairy. I had always guessed he was some sort of shifter, but I hadn't dared enough to ask. When he spotted me, his face softened. Even though I brought more than my fair share of trouble into his bar I had always been a generous tipper. I had won a lot of fights and spent most of my winnings on his whisky.

"I didn't believe the rumours—"

I tilted my head.

"—That you were dead." He spoke like it was obvious and eyed Luka. "Who's your new boy toy?"

I tried to keep my face stoic.

"He's a friend." I didn't know why I felt the need to clear up our relationship to Fluffy of all people.

"He looks like your type if I remember correctly. You never had any issue getting—"

"—Fluffy! We need to use your back room." I interrupted him before he could embarrass me further. He knew what he was doing too. There was amusement dancing behind his eyes.

"Can you pay?"

"Always."

It was a bluff. I hadn't brought enough cash with me. I would have to come back. He led Luka and me back behind the bar and opened the door tucked aside. The ruckus of the bar immediately quietened. Fluffy moved around in the dark and switched on the light, illuminating the private area. The walls were covered in warm timber slats and the smell in the room burnt my nose. Alcohol had soaked the floor on more than one occasion.

"Alpha Giovanni and two of his goons will be meeting us soon. Can you let them in?"

Luka pulled out a pouch of illegal money and handed it over. Where had he got that? I resisted the urge to shoot him a look. Fluffy weighted the bag in his hand, apparently satisfied he shot me a smile before motioning us to sit. I sat at the round table. It was a second before Luka dragged the chair out beside me and sat his considerable size down. Fluffy dropped two glasses in front of us along with an unmarked bottle of whisky.

"Loser cleans."

"I remember the rules." I waved him out and dragged the bottle toward me.

I had never met Alpha Giovanni but he would know who I was and my reputation hopefully still held enough sway. If it didn't work we would need to find a way to stop Loral making the traxxy. Luka had guessed there were labs in the compound in places we had yet to explore, maybe in secret caverns like the one he found in the pools. Luka and I sat in silence. I didn't know what to say. The last few days had changed something between us. We had both done bad things to survive. Both of us were victims of the Elect and also perpetrators of violence. I tipped the glass of good whisky back and relished in the familiar burn.

Before I could pour a second glass, the door slammed open and noise from the bar floated in. Shadowed against the light stood a skinny man whose black hair was like wet seaweed. There were two massive mountains of men beside him. His main enforcer, Everly, wasn't beside him. I narrowed my eyes. She was probably lying in wait in case the shit hit the fan. He strolled into the private bar area with a confidence that rivalled Luka's.

I leaned back in the chair and kicked my boots up on the table with an arrogance I didn't feel. You couldn't show weakness in front of an Alpha. They sniffed it out and went for the throat. He stared at me, his beady eyes not wavering. Our silent standoff went on for a few seconds until finally Luka broke the tension.

"Thank you for accepting our request to meet."

With the tension broken, the waif-like man floated into the room. His two gargantuan wolves quickly pulled out his chair and took their posts behind him. He managed to look down his hooked nose at me, even though he was no taller than I. As unassuming as the Alpha looked, I knew he was a ruthless leader with no mercy. It would not do us well to provoke him.

"Where's Everly?" I demanded, inspecting my dirty nails. They were hardly interesting enough to draw my attention.

"Ah. So the rumours are true. I don't believe we've formally met."

He had never wanted to meet me, I had always dealt with one of his lackeys. If he had hired me for the job, it had meant it was a dirty one. Werewolfs had no aversion to killing, but even Alphas had protocols and rules to follow. I was never one to tackle things gently, might as well dive right in.

"Your dealings with the rebellion have come to an end."

"Says who?"

I could tell Luka was bristling beside me. He wasn't a man used to taking disrespect. Well… from anyone but me.

"Says me." I lifted an eyebrow, daring him to challenge me.

"You're no one. You don't dictate who I do business with girl."

Luka growled beside me. I quickly rested my hand on his thigh. Time to pull out the big guns.

"You know Giovanni," he snarled at my disrespect. "Before my hiatus, I remember leaving pieces of your Beta strewn on your front lawn."

The colour left his face and he dismissed his bodyguards with a wave of his hand. Silence fell over the room. I gave him a self-satisfied smirk. We had the upper hand. He eyed Luka.

"Dismiss your guard," he growled.

I shook my head. A tinkering laugh filling the tense silence. I felt giddy with a different kind of power. It wasn't often that you one-upped an Alpha. Perhaps I had a death wish.

"He's not my guard." I took a sip of the liquor. "I, along with everyone else, was led to believe that Alpha Lucian ordered the hit on your man. Imagine my surprise when I discovered that you were behind the request." I poured myself another finger of whisky. "I imagine ordering your second-in-command's torture and murder is frowned upon in polite werewolf society."

I was goading him. He knew as well as I that if word ever got out it was him that had ordered a pack mate killed he would be dethroned and exiled. All the money at his disposal wouldn't be enough to save him. The shifters were loyal above everything else.

"I don't know what you're talking about."

"Don't play dumb, Alpha. It doesn't become you. I'm promising my silence."

He rose from his chair, his woody Magic swirling around his body. "You threaten me. You threaten the whole pack," he whispered.

Giovanni swung around, his black eyes bored into Luka's. When he didn't flinch, his steely gaze switched to me. I could see in his gaze he had broken many a person stronger than me. Before I could kneel and beg for forgiveness, Luka closed his hand around mine. My posture straightened and the power flowing through my veins bolstered me.

The Alpha's hands morphed into terrifying claws, his bones shifted under the leathery skin.

"I should kill you both now."

The words didn't sound right, like he was having trouble keeping his jaw in shape. I drew my dagger and flipped it, slicing my palm. With the power already coursing through my veins, as soon as my blood hit the air, my eyes flicked back and my hair stood on its ends. I felt juiced, like someone had given me a shot of adrenaline. My Magic was back and I loved it. The Alpha stumbled back.

"You're welcome to try," Luka added.

"Sorceress,' he hissed.

I let my Magic flow out of me, my eyes draining back to their normal colour. Luka lunged over the table and in the next second he was standing behind the Alpha with a dagger to his throat.

"Apologise," he demanded quietly.

I was going to tell Luka that it was fine, but the look he gave made me swallow my words. The fiery Magic contained in him was shining through his eyes. I could see the depth of his power and it took my breath away.

"She's a monster."

The dagger nicked the thin skin at his neck and bright red blood beaded before falling in a thin line. Before the drop could stain his white collar, the door was thrown open and his two bodyguards appeared along with five others. Everly was among them. They growled as they took in our stance.

Everly looked puzzled for a moment before glaring at me from across the room. We used to have some sort of truce but it seemed that had ended. Luka pocketed the dagger and leaned casually against the table, like he hadn't been holding a knife to the Alpha's neck mere moments ago.

"Do we have a deal, Alpha?" I smiled sweetly, tucking away the monster for now.

He gave us a curt nod and stormed from the room, the rest of his pack following. As soon as the door shut I sagged against the chair. I had just painted a giant target on my back. I would add it to all the others.

"You didn't have to do that," I snapped.

I didn't need anyone to defend me.

"He disrespected you."

"What he said was the truth. There's no need to get your knickers in a knot."

"You're not a monster Rina." He was fervent.

I didn't care enough to argue. "Okay."

"You don't believe me."

"He can call me anything he wants."

He poured himself a glass of whisky and took the seat opposite me. "Better than mopping blood off the floor."

I peeked over at him. His cheeks flushed and a small grin threatening to break into a full-fledged smile. I wanted to see him smile, his genuine smile was so rare. I slammed down another glass of whisky, enjoying the buzz.

"Fluffy hasn't made me clean yet."

He looked at me, perfect eyebrow arched. "So you've never lost? Explains a lot," he mumbled.

"I found that after I beat a few of the bigger ones up they tended to leave me alone." I poured another large shot for me and one for Luka. He downed his immediately. "It's embarrassing losing to someone that doesn't look far out of puberty."

He shot me a look that said he disagreed.

"You think you can beat me?" I let out a giggle—out of character. "I'm not weak like I was before."

"I'm aware."

I stood, leaning over the table. "Are you?"

He didn't squirm under my full attention. Instead, he met my stare, daring me to look away first. Luka wasn't scared of me, but there was another emotion shining through the cracks in his stony eyes. I threw the whisky back and enjoyed the warmth that settled in my belly. I walked around the table and hopped up on the table, my legs swung up and I sat my boots on either side of his chair. The alcohol was making me reckless and foolish. He was looking at me as if I was a tall glass of water and he hadn't had a drink for months. Before I could do something stupid like straddle his waist, Fluffy slammed open the door.

I met Fluffy's self-satisfied grin. So what if I had a type? Luka didn't even bother to turn around.

"Get out of my bar," he said. The spell was broken and I hoped off the table, the anxiety returning in a rush.

Luka went to hand over more money, but Fluffy waved him away.

"I won't take money from the dead," he laughed, but as we left his look was something closer to pity.

"I've already come back from the dead once, it wasn't so hard." I snatched another bottle of liquor off his shelf.

We rushed back to the hotel, moving quickly between the shadows.

"We need to leave Dunlap." My voice was surprisingly calm, despite the ever-increasing panic rising under my sternum. I might have just declared war on the pack. They would strike back soon. When we returned to the hotel and slammed open the door, Loral sat on the bed staring up at us wide-eyed.

"We need to go," Luka said. He moved around the hotel room like a hurricane, throwing our belongings into bags. He didn't seem too fussed about whose stuff went where. Loral said nothing to me, but his lips twisted down in displeasure and the silence between us was heavy with accusation.

"You need to warn the other members of the rebellion that deal with the packs. They will come for them now."

"What did you do?" he demanded.

"*I* did nothing. They were the ones to betray us!" I shouted more loudly than the conversation needed.

"It wasn't an open declaration of war." His voice rose louder still, the terse silence from before now forgotten.

"Did you forget the part where they nearly tore me in two? Or is selling traxxy more important to you?"

As the words had left my mouth, I regretted them. They were cruel, selfish words, and ones I had no right to say.

"Sometimes sacrifices need to be made for the greater good. Not that *you* would know anything about sacrifice." He spat the words with venom. My vision misted red.

Before I could retort with more words I would regret, Luka grabbed my arm. The words died on my lips.

"Come, help me pack." His calming voice soothed some of the ragged anger in my chest. I spun on my heel, and begun to tear through the bathroom to shove our toiletries into a bag. When Luka and I had our stuff packed away, Loral finally grabbed the keys and stormed out the door behind us.

I wasn't going to be the first to break. So we sat in silence until Loral handed us back the blindfolds to put on before coming to the compound. We sat in darkness for nearly an hour, much longer than any time previously. I let the twists and turns lull me to sleep.

"Rina, we're here," a male voice murmured. His warm hand cupped my forearm. I jerked awake, scurrying back until the seat belt choked me. "It's me," Luka said. I had never thought those words would ever be comforting, but still my breathing steadied. He threaded his fingers through mine as we were led back down into the compound.

Chapter Eighteen

The roof of the compound seemed lower than I remembered. Our bedroom was more suffocating despite being larger than the motels we had stayed at. Luka's boots wore shallow tracks in the floor as he paced the room. I snatched one of the rock-hard pillows from the bed and hurled it toward his head. He plucked it from the air and glared at me, like *I* was the annoying one. Something was bothering him but I didn't want to know what it was. I wanted to live in my ignorant bliss a little longer.

"Stop pacing," I growled.

"What are we going to tell Loral?" He threw the pillow back at me and restarted his pattern.

"What about?" I picked up my book of runes and began to flick through the pages.

"I know why he's not talking to you. It's because he heard you call me Luka."

I stopped. "What are you talking about?"

"When I fell, you said my name."

Blood flushed my cheeks. The desperation in my voice had been too telling.

"I'll tell him it's your real name, that I knew you from when I grew up in Dunlap." I waved him away, his nervous energy had swallowed the room. I had never seen him so riled up. Unease settle in my gut. I hadn't thought Loral could ever betray me. He held friendship as something sacred. But his words from before echoed in my mind.

"The oath will kill us both. My sister, Rina. They'll kill my sister." He grabbed me by my shoulders, eyes frantic.

I was suddenly filled with overwhelming panic. I yanked away from him and it disappeared.

"Calm down." He didn't acknowledge me, instead he

continued to pace. "Luka, I'll fix it."

I hopped off the bed and turned to leave the room.

"Do you want me to come with you?"

"No. Go... be normal. Hit the bag or something."

When I turned, he was standing too close. I grabbed him around his biceps, the feeling of panic returned. I beat back at it.

"Luka."

Our eyes met, I could almost hear the thoughts racing in his mind. No wonder the Elect had so much control over him. When his sister was involved he became totally irrational It was so out of character. He was usually in such tight control of himself, but now he was spiraling in a panic. He stared at me and I watched as his face smoothed back into the mask I was so familiar with. When his nervous energy finally settled, he nodded. I left the room and made my way toward Loral's bedroom. One more lie. Just one more lie.

True to form, Loral was hunched over the cauldron on his small desk, muttering to himself. When he looked up at me, the hurt in his eyes was palpable. It stopped me dead in my tracks. I stood planted in the door frame. He didn't avert his gaze, instead his green eyes locked with mine. All my words were suddenly stuck in my throat. This was the same man that had collected me, bloody and bruised, whenever I had called, the friend that had singlehandedly turned me human again. After years of fighting pits and mercenary work, I was cold and barely human. He had warmed my heart and helped me see I was more than just a killing machine. I owed my life to him and now he looked at me as if I had yanked his beating heart from his chest and held it in front of him.

I'd come prepared to weave a story of how Luka and I met. Maybe it could have been true if our lives weren't so fundamentally different. We would have met in one of the dingy bars in the centre of the city, where all the transactions were done under the yellow light of night. We would have commiserated over the difficulties of living in a city such as Dunlap. Anything to throw him off the scent of who he really was. The lie died on my lips.

All the air was sucked from the room.

"I'm sorry." It was all I could bring myself to say. It wasn't enough.

Realisation hit me like a brick to the face. I was still imprisoned. The Elect had imprisoned me as soon as Luka had found me. The Elect may not have locked me in a cell, but I was stuck all the same. There was only one way to free myself. "I'm so sorry," I choked. "I've lied to you. Nothing I have ever said has been the truth." He didn't look surprised, but the sadness in his eyes deepened. "I'm not who you think I am." I took a steadying breath. "I was wanted by the Elect."

He turned back to his work. "I know that."

"They found me—"

—A heavy hand clamped down on my shoulder. I spun on my heel and away from the looming figure.

Judas stood in the doorway.

"I've been looking everywhere for you! I'm so glad you're back." I shared a puzzled look with Loral.

"We were just in the middle of something, Judas," Loral hinted, but he stayed put.

The glint of hatred in Judas's eyes was now buried so deep that I couldn't see it. His smile was as I had remembered it before he had discovered what I really was. It was easy and reached his eyes. There was no hint of mistrust in his features. Loral looked as shocked as I did.

"Can I steal her from you, Loral? I promise I'll give her back." He wrapped his fingers around my bicep. Loral looked resigned.

"Sure. I'll speak to you tomorrow...Lilith." There was a sour taste in his mouth as he spat out my pseudonym.

Judas pulled me from the room and into the tiny corridor. We moved into an unused nook. When he faced me he wore a smile. "You're back." He sounded relieved.

Did I trust him?

"Yes."

I didn't move to leave. I should have. If he started spewing hate again, I didn't know if I could control myself.

"I'm sorry. I shouldn't have said what I did to you. It

wasn't fair." If he wasn't still holding my arm, I would have fallen back in surprise. "I want to make it up to you."

"You don't have to. I was out of line as well." I wiggled my way from his grip. His large body was blocking my exit. I couldn't pass unless I pushed him.

"I'm so sorry. Please let me make it up to you." The sincerity in his clear eyes melted some of the ice in my chest, I gave him an uncertain nod. He wrapped me in a tight hug. "I missed you."

My body tensed in response to his sudden change in demeanour. What had changed?

"I spoke with Stella," he said softly and rested his chin on the top of my head. "I didn't understand before. I was a real asshole."

"We were both assholes." I laughed nervously, but relaxed into the hug nonetheless. Maybe Stella had finally made him see the light. I didn't want to ask any questions, it felt nice to have a friend back at least for a few nights.

He finally released me and gave me one more wide smile. "I'll see you later."

He gave me a wink and disappeared into the maze of halls. When I returned to my room, Luka had continued to wear tracks into the floor. When I stopped in the threshold he paused and looked up. His brows were knitted together. I couldn't tell him now.

"It's done." When the words left my lips he released a breath.

"Are you hungry?" he asked.

I shrugged but he led me to the dining hall anyway. It was busier than usual. The bustle of the group was soothing. When we entered, Sylvia turned around from her place at the stove. She smiled and wiped her hands on the front of her apron.

"You're back. We missed you."

I forced a laugh past my lips as Rosie rushed over to wrap her arms around me in a hug. "You missed Noah's cooking."

"That as well." She laughed, and the sound warmed the room.

Luka plastered a smile on his own face and took an apron

from Sylvia. Rosie led me to the end of the dining table. She was too big to be picked up now. She presented a little chatterbox to me. It was coloured and numbered. Some of the corners had worn down like she had been demanding people pick a colour all day.

The others in the hall were murmuring and laughing amongst themselves. I looked up for a moment and just watched. I wanted to remember this, Luka and Sylvia cooking, the smell of fragrant vegetables heavy in the air. Sylvia even wrapped an arm across Luka's wide back and gave him a squeeze. Others were talking or laughing. Even Levi and Anthony sat across from each other whispering conspiratorially. I was surprised they hadn't begged Luka to train with them as soon as he walked in.

Rosie shoved her paper creation toward my face, breaking the trance

"Pick a colour," she demanded.

"Pink." I pointed to the panel. I wanted to remember her too. Her pin-straight black hair was wild, it was barely controlled by the bright scrunchie at the nape of her neck.

She moved her fingers, spelling out the word. Rosie opened the chatterbox, the inside was filled with numbers.

"Pick a number."

"Seven."

She grinned up at me like I've picked the wrong one. Still, she moved the chatterbox again before pushing it back in my face.

"Pick again."

"Three."

"Not that one."

I hovered my finger over another number and she shook her head over each one until I reach the nine.

"Nine," I said.

She flattened the paper and pulled open the carefully folded tab. Her smile was pure mischief when she looks up at me. "Who do you love?"

I pretended to think for a moment, putting my finger to the corner of my lips. "Hmm I love you."

"Who else?" she prompted.

I realised I hadn't ever said the words in my adult life. Rosie had asked them so casually. No doubt Sylvia spoke them to her every night. I hadn't raised the courage needed to ask what had happened to her father, but I could imagine well enough. There were only a few scenarios which might have led a single mother into the arms of a doomed rebellion.

"I love your mum and Loral and Davis."

"No." She huffed like I was being purposefully daft. Rosie covered her mouth with her hands, trying to hide her giggle.

Before she could push me further, Sylvia came and placed a plate of vegetables and white meat in front of her. The chatterbox was forgotten and she dug into her lunch. Luka placed a plate in front of me. It seemed he was still trying to fatten me up. The others lined up to get food. I hadn't expected Luka to be a good cook, but he was. He was almost as good as Sylvia. He sat across from me with an easy smile that I couldn't match.

"It's good to see you both back in one piece."

"We were lucky the trip was uneventful." The lie slid from my lips.

The meal was lively and I found myself smiling and laughing along with the group. After lunch, I returned to our room. Luka collected a towel to escape to the gym. I fidgeted, wringing my fingers and trying to read the book Davis gave me. I tried to think of things to say to Luka, how to explain to him that he needed to take me back to Ka. When he finally returned all the nervous energy had disappeared. I jumped up as he entered the room, but he paid me no attention and retrieved a book from his large pile.

My careful speech was forgotten and the words tumbled from my lips.

"You need to take me back to Ka."

He froze. "No."

"You have to or I will tell everyone who you are and void the oath."

His eyes narrowed as he turned toward me. "What are you talking about?"

"I don't want to lie anymore."

"It's a little while longer and then you'll be free."

"I won't betray the rebellion. You have to take me to the Elect." The treacherous words tumbled from my lips.

"They'll throw you in one of the Blood Mage camps." I shrugged. I had quickly made peace with the idea of spending the rest of my life in a cage, if only to never see the look of betrayal on Loral's face again. "You'll be collared."

Once again I lifted my shoulders. It was all I could do to not burst into tears. Luka grew frantic. He knelt in front of me and took my hands. His eyes searched mine.

"We can escape. There's a few people that owe me. We can disappear back to Dunlap where the Elect won't find us."

"I won't ask you to trade your sister's life for mine."

"I have been planning to get her out for years. There's a few more things to put in place." He looked calculating for a moment. "It will take six months to a year max."

I grabbed his hands. "They will all be dead in six months." I didn't need to tell him who I was talking about.

"You don't understand. Please. There's a reason they don't even talk about the camps in Dunlap. They are worse than you can imagine." I would take a bet that it was the closest to begging Luka had ever come.

I moved my clammy hand to rest on his cheek. As I focused on it, the cut about his brow knitted together. The first time I had met him, the Magic in his blood had almost driven me mad with desire. I wanted to drain every last drop of his power and bathe in it. Now it was easy to ignore.

"I want to try and do something right for once in my life."

He examined my eyes for any signs that I was wavering. "When?"

"Tomorrow?"

"Okay."

"Thank you." I resisted the urge to lean forward and brush my lips against his. It would have been so easy.

"I'm sorry, Rina."

"Me too."

We sat in silence after that.

***

I laid in the dark, listening to Luka's soft snoring. At the start of the night we had been on opposite ends of the bed, now he was intertwined around me as I lay on my back. His leg was flung over mine and his arms wrapped the whole way around my body. I didn't think I could move if I had wanted to. With tentative fingers, I traced shapes across his shoulders. He tightened his arms. The movement caused his fingertips to slip beneath the hem of my singlet. The press of his warm skin on my hip sent a scattering of goosebumps down my arms.

"Are you scared?" he murmured into my shoulder.

"No." I stopped my tracing. To my surprise, Luka didn't pull away. He just adjusted his hand so that it was resting on the outside of my clothing.

"What's bothering you?"

I hesitated for a moment before speaking. "My parents would be ashamed of me." I felt his weight shift but tensed my arms to keep him in place.

"There is nothing for them to be ashamed of."

"I'm a bad person." My words were so small and pathetic that I wanted to snatch them back into my mouth. They soured the air.

"I thought Stella helped you understand. Your Magic isn't —"

"—It's not my Magic. It's my actions. It's me."

He drew calming circles over my hip. "Few of us are granted the luxury of peace. You did what you needed to in order to survive."

I had no reply. Instead I wrapped my arms around him and buried my face into his hair. The scent of his power was soothing and I drew it deep into my lungs. His hand was wrapped around my forearm and he squeezed it twice.

"My father taught me this."

"What does it mean?"

He squeezed my arm again. "Squeeze." And pressed. "And tap. It's used in tactical communication because it can't be mistaken for something accidental. It means I'm here, I'm with you."

He did it again. Squeeze…tap. I'm here, I'm with you.

The blaring sound of an alarm rang through the compound.

Someone had breached the perimeter.

The siren wailed along the corridors, ricocheting off the walls and into our room. Overhead, the lights begun to flash red in warning. I jumped out of bed. The Elect had found us. Luka had moved faster than me and began throwing me clothes.

"We have to get everyone out!" I yelled over the screaming alarm. When I was dressed, we sprinted down the corridor until we reached the main intersection of the compound.

"Send everyone to the gym." His voice was surprisingly calm. I didn't hesitate and sprinted to the first bedroom.

"Get out! Get to the gym!" I screamed, running into the room. Sabrina and Max were half-dressed and moving too slow. With the urgency of my words, they fled. There had been no word from Joshua to stay vigilant, nothing to say that the Elect were closing in on the Compounds location. No one was prepared. I dashed from room to room herding everyone out and down. When the rooms were empty, I sprinted toward the meeting point. The group had gathered. There was almost thirty people all crammed into the small space. Luka ushered me out of earshot.

"Is Loral okay?"

His nod came too slowly. I almost shook him. "Judas isn't here."

My eyes widened. "The front entrance will be compromised first. Take everyone out through the springs. I'll go find Judas."

"No, it's too dangerous. I'll go."

I grabbed him by the arm. "If it's the Elect, you can't fight back. They'll know who you are. I have to go. I'll meet you at the springs as soon as I find him."

Luka pulled me close and pressed the hilt of his blade into my hand. The weight felt unfamiliar in my palm. It was engraved with a complicated crest I had yet to ask him about.

"Don't hesitate."

I met his intense gaze and gave him a curt nod before sprinting back toward the kitchen, keeping close to the walls. I wondered how long it would be until they found the entrance. How had they found us? The alarm light went out, plunging the area into darkness.

It hadn't even occurred to me that Luka might have been the reason. The thought made me stumble, but I kept running toward Judas's room. The line of thinking caused hot shame to well within me. He had earned my trust. The alarm went silent. The walls seemed to warp and move in the sudden quiet.

"Judas?" I hissed. It would be my luck that he had found his way back to the group when I was searching for him.

Judas was helpless. He had blanched at the very idea of sparring. If he came up against someone he wouldn't stand a chance. I needed to find him before anyone else did. I snuck down corridors, dragging my fingertips along the edges. My ears still rang from the alarm. I flattened myself against the wall and used Luka's knife to slice my palm. There was a flash of a shadow coming from further up. My power buzzed with anticipation, ready to strike out.

It had to be Judas. The door to the compound was so heavily barricaded, there was no way it could be breached without me hearing it. Luka's warning reverberated in my head. I couldn't take the risk. Before I could attack, Judas's worried voice came from the dark. "Lilith?"

I straightened, the tension leaving my body. "It's me." I rounded the corner toward his voice and sprung a small flame in my palm. "We have to leave."

"Rosie's in the kitchen. We have to go get her." When he came into view, his eyes were wide and frantic.

"Did you see anyone else?"

He shook his head. It was good enough for me. "Stay behind me." I kept my voice low and crept along the passageway.

I extinguished the flame.

I hissed at Judas. "Where is she?"

"She was right in there." He was so close that I could feel

his breath on the back of my neck. Before I could round the corner into the kitchen, my blood turned to ice in my veins. Something wasn't right. Goosebumps rose on my arms and I sliced my hand to ready my power. The uneasy feeling grew until eventually I spun around to check if Judas was still behind me. I was tackled. The back of my head smashed the floor and a heavy figure sat astride my chest. I saw stars. Before I could strike out, something cold and familiar clamped around my neck. My power went silent and I howled. The shock brought me back to my senses and immediately I bucked the man from my waist, reversing the position, I held the dagger to his throat.

In the flickering candlelight, I stared down at Judas.

"Take it off," I spat into his ear. His struggles were futile, even collared he was no match for me.

A cruel laugh left his lips. "And let you kill me?"

My mind raced. I didn't want to believe it was Judas. The betrayal was heavier than the weight of the collar. Judas took my lapse in concentration to try and wiggle free. It was fruitless. Although muscled from working in the fields, he had no mind for combat.

"I'll kill you anyway." I pressed the blade into his neck to let him know just how serious I was.

"I don't think you will."

Before I could smash the handle of the dagger into his temple, I froze in place. I had been so certain we were alone, certain that I would have heard anyone breaking in the door. I hadn't even thought that perhaps the enemy had been welcomed in by one of our own. In the struggle we had fallen into the kitchen which was lit by a number of candles. I hadn't noticed the figures in trademark red standing around the outskirts of the room. Elect enforcers, armed to the teeth, slowly circled us. I had been so focused on Judas I hadn't seen them. *What has he done?*

I pressed the dagger to his neck and felt his warm blood drip through my fingers. If I was captured, he would go down with me. Before I could slice the dagger across his artery, a small figure was pulled to the forefront of the crowd.

Rosie.

Her eyes were filled with tears and her small frame vibrated. The sight turned my blood cold.

"I wouldn't do that if I were you."

"Let her go." My voice was deadly calm.

"Once you release Judas, she's free to leave."

I reluctantly opened my stiff fingers and the knife clattered to the ground. Judas scuttled away from me like the cockroach he was. I spat toward him.

"You've got your mutt, now hand her over."

One of the enforcers shoved Rosie toward me. She stumbled and I wrapped my arms around her. Heaving sobs racked her frail body and I smoothed her hair in an effort to keep her calm. I knelt in front of her and took her cold hands in mine. Tears wet her face and there was a bruise starting under her right eye. I leant close to her face.

"Listen to me, Rosie. You have to run as fast as you can to the meeting spot. Do you remember it? You need to find Noah and tell him what happened." I wiped a fresh tear from her cheek. "Can you do that for me?"

Her nod was jerky and unsure. It would have to do. I stood and faced the enforcers. Rosie and I were in the centre of the large space, we were too exposed. I tucked her behind my body.

"I'll come peacefully if you let her leave."

"She's free to go." The man closest to me spoke.

I turned to Rosie once more and tried to keep the fear from my eyes. "It's going to be okay." With a shove, she stumbled toward the entrance of the kitchen. She would find Luka. He would make sure she got back to Sylvia no matter what. The small girl seemed to stumble, her body moving too fast for her feet. As she entered the threshold I heard the unmistakable twang of an arrow. I leapt toward her. The crazy wisps of her hair caught in the dim light. I wanted to brush them back into her braid. Her shoulders bunched as the arrow buried itself in her back. Her bitten-down nails scrunched into fists that did not break her fall.

"Rosie!" The scream ripped from my mouth.

My legs gave way under me and I scrambled toward her. She looked so small crumbled face-down on the floor. I snapped the shaft of the arrow and gently rolled her onto my lap. Her dark eyes searched mine frantically. I bit my tongue and let blood fill my mouth. I hauled my power to the surface and desperately tried to push it past the constraints of the collar. My Magic buzzed like a swarm of wasps under my skin, but I could not access it.

I tucked the stray strands of hair back behind her ear with shaking fingers. She gasped, her arms lolling uselessly at her side. "It's okay Rosie. You'll be okay."

"Lili," she managed to gasp. "I'm scared." Her mouth opened and closed as if she was trying to suck in oxygen through torn lungs. I pressed hard on the wound, but it made no difference. The blood coating my hand was so warm.

"I'm here. I'm not leaving, Rosie."

The child clutched my shirt in her small fist and screamed. She gasped and moaned, and I could do nothing to help her as more and more of the too warm liquid spilt over my hand and onto the floor. Then she was quiet and it was worse. I rolled her onto her side and stood.

Tears wet my face, blurring my vision, but it didn't matter. I knew my enemy well enough. Deep, cloying rage buoyed from within me. It didn't need power to fuel it. "What have you done?" My voice was as sharp as a knife's edge.

Judas stood shoulder to shoulder with the other enforcers. He hadn't even glanced down at Rosie but flicked his slimy eyes toward me. His mouth lifted in a grin.

"You can imagine my surprise when I saw the Elect's Hunter waltz into the compound towing you behind him."

"What have you done?" I repeated, my voice hoarse with rage. It was the only coherent thought I could manage. He shrugged. I *hated* men that shrugged.

Rosie is dead. I am not.

In a swift movement I collected the dagger from the floor and flung it at the nearest enforcer. The hilt stuck out of his chest. He looked confused for a moment before tumbling to the floor. The remainder of the enforcers stormed me. Two of them lunged at once, one had a short sword. I kicked his wrist. He dropped the blade and I scrambled for it on the ground. They would all die. With a scream, I thrust out wildly. They needed to pay. I had killed two before a long sword slashed across my rib cage. Three more went down in a tear of rage and teeth.

"Don't kill her!" someone screamed. I didn't care. I couldn't feel any pain.

Someone struck out at my lead hand and the sword clattered to the ground. My fingers wouldn't respond. It didn't matter. None of them had weapons anymore as they circled me. I was tackled and my face smashed into the dirt. I struggled frantically under the weight of the enforcer and screamed obscenities into the dirt. Eventually I wiggled out from under him, but two more were standing in front of me. I struck out again. If I died here I would take as many with me as I could. I used instinct alone as my flesh hit theirs. Pained moans came from one of the enforcers and he was crouched on all fours after I had delivered a particularly nasty blow between his legs. I managed to grab onto a knife and slice wildly, their screams a balm to my soul.

In the flurry, a second group of enforcers had come up behind me. A potion smashed into my back and my body was on fire. I collapsed into the ground as electricity raced through me, the burning pain indescribable. I couldn't scream, only a low groan came from my lips. Judas crouched beside me, his white pants had blood stains on the knees. He stroked my hair. I wanted to yank it out at the roots so he could never touch it again.

"At first I had thought you were an innocent, a tool used by the Hunter to get an in with the rebellion. I even grew to like you. But when the collar was removed, I saw you for what you truly are." My body wouldn't cooperate, my mouth wouldn't form any coherent words. "A monster."

"Lu..ka." I managed to spit out.

Judas began laughing, the hollow sound echoing through the room. I rolled over, my body still a dead weight. The rest of the enforcers joined in on the joke. One of them stood over me, placing his boot on my bleeding gut. He pressed down. Every nerve in my body was on fire. I searched for Rosie, keeping my eyes on her now slack face and empty eyes.

"The Hunter won't come for you. He's the Elect's most loyal subject. He was using you."

The heavy boot from the enforcer slammed down on the side of my temple and everything went black.

Chapter Nineteen

Instead of Luka's soft, rhythmic snoring, I awoke to a haunting silence, the type that only occurs within an empty space. My moans of pain were muffled by a foul-smelling mattress. My senses were assaulted with the rancid smell that permeated my pores. My body felt like it had been hit by a train. The memories of what had happened the night before flashed in my mind and my hands flew to my neck. The metal was freezing cold under my fingers.

Collared.

Terror threatened to overwhelm me before a second more horrible thought came to my mind.

Rosie.

Her tiny body crumbling as the arrow struck her in the back. Rosie's pallid face and lifeless eyes stared back at me, accusingly. I had failed her. A wave of torrential grief washed over me. The tiny innocent girl had been struck down where she stood, her life snuffed out before it even had a chance to begin. Did the Elect take her body or did they leave her in the dirt? Her mother would never know what happened to her. The compound had been breached. No one would ever return. It would be too dangerous. I couldn't think of her laying there alone on the dirty kitchen floor.

Everyone that had a hand in taking her life would die.

I opened my eyes and took in my new surroundings. The cell was tiny and dark. There was no window. The only light came from beyond the thick bars, a place where I could not see.

There was a bucket in the corner, and the thin, slimy mattress that I had been deposited on but nothing else. The bricks were decayed and covered in moss, water dripped from the roof. The freezing air bit at my exposed limbs. I climbed to my feet and shuffled over to the bars that now held me prisoner. I shook them, violently. The thick, rusted metal shrieked in protest but they did not budge. I tried to look outside the bars but they were too close together to get my head through.

The hall to my right seemed to go on forever, a yellow flame lit the sloping corridor every few meters. A steep staircase sat on the other side. Perhaps it led to the outside world, I couldn't see in the dim light, no matter how hard I strained my eyes. I threw myself at the bars, crying out in frustration. I needed to tell Sylvia what happened to Rosie, to beg her forgiveness. The movement caused a sharp pain to burn across my chest. I fell to my knees and swallowed a scream. Crawling back to my tiny mattress, I inspected the painful cut just below my breasts, it ran from one side of my chest to the other. Lowering my thin singlet, I collapsed and cradled my head in my hands. The darkness enveloped me in its cold embrace. Everything and nothing folded into me, constricting my lungs until I was gasping for oxygen and fighting off the urge to vomit. There was no way out. No one would know where Rosie had died. Hysteria and guilt began to beat at the inside of my skull and I clawed at my face trying to distract myself from the overwhelming emotions.

I had to get a grip. Revenge needed me to be cold and calculated, not hysterical. I drew in deep, shuddering breaths until the urge to vomit had passed. No doubt the confinement would compound the effects of the collar and I had to stay sane long enough to extract my punishment.

When would the torture begin?

It seemed as if Judas didn't know that I had struck a deal with the Elect, and they would never admit to actively working with a Blood Mage. At least it explained his odd behaviour. I took solace in the fact that the rebellion would continue its mission without me. I would no longer pose a risk to their operation. This was what I had wanted, to surrender myself, to save my friends, and protect Luka's sister. *Hadn't I?* Judas had just beat me to it.

My choice had been taken from me and Rosie had been murdered. Seething anger burned through me, chasing away the panic. No longer would I be an unwilling passenger in my life. My next decision would be mine alone. For Rosie, for me.

The Elect would not break me.

I needed focus. How long had I been unconscious for? There was no daylight and I couldn't even roughly gauge the time. I might have been unconscious for minutes or for days. The spell I had been hit with was strong. I still felt the groggy after-effects. I hobbled along and inspected every square inch of my tiny cell. In the back corner was a soft spot in one of the bricks about the size of my palm. But there were no other weaknesses. Sitting back on the mattress, my mind was filled with images that I had long since forgotten. It seemed my nightmares were coming back to haunt me.

Eventually I heard a door open. I rushed to press my face to the bars. Two heavily-armed enforcers strode down the hall toward my cell. I shifted my features into a menacing snarl. The woman was holding a small roll of bread and a soft satchel of water. My mouth was dry and I had never been more hungry. My stomach growled in protest. Without a word, one of the guards tossed the bread and water into my cell and turned on their heels to leave.

I was tempted to yell after them, but I wouldn't show any weakness. When the door had closed I scrambled to retrieve the bread and water. In the rational portion of my brain I knew that I needed to save the rations. I didn't know when I would be getting my next meal, but my stomach didn't care when my next meal was, it was only concerned with the present. The hard, dry bread was gone much too quickly.

I took a sip of the water and hid the half-full container under my pillow. It took all my willpower not to guzzle it. Judging by how thirsty I was, it was likely I had been unconscious for quite some time. I retrieved a small stone from the dirty floor and scratched a mark into one of the bricks before crawling back onto the hard mattress. If I couldn't keep track of the days, my mind would turn to mush. I laid down and closed my eyes.

Would they move me to one of the Blood Mage camps that Luka was so terrified of? Or would they leave me in the cells? The thoughts swirled around my mind until sleep took me again.

Luka grinned at me, his platinum eyes lighting up. His smile was infectious. I smiled back like a love sick puppy.

"Is that the best you've got?" His stance was wide and his body slick with sweat. His shirt had been abandoned some time ago and the view of his hard muscles was distracting. We were in the sparring gym I frequented in Ka. Erin's tinkling laugh rang through the space, it soothed my soul. She and Jax leant against padded walls, taking in our stand-off.

I rolled my eyes at Luka, ignoring the burning pain in my lungs that demanded I stop. His fingers stretched. It was all the warning I needed. I rolled to the side, narrowly avoided a kick to the head. Luka threw it lazily and tried to jump into guard on top of me. He was too slow and I was on my feet before him. We traded blows, evenly matched, especially when I couldn't use my Magic and Luka pulled his strikes. Eventually Luka managed to take me down and straddle my stomach. His legs locked around mine and I was trapped.

He leant his mouth to my ear. "You need to wake up."

"What are you talking about?"

"Wake up, Rina."

Frantically, I swung around looking for Erin and Jax, but they were no longer there.

I was alone. Luka was gone.

A terrible, keening sound filled the space.

My hands clawed at the metal around my neck. The loss of my power was a physical pain, an insatiable gnawing hunger. My eyes flashed open and I was once again surrounded by three brick walls and a set of bars. I slammed my mouth shut, stopping the gurgling noise.

They will not break me.

I repeated my prayer, my lips stumbling around the silent

words. A moldy loaf of bread lay at my feet along with a canister of water. The bread was hard but filled some of the emptiness in my gut. It was the first time they had delivered food since I had awoken. I marked the occasion on the bar, next to the other lines. After stuffing the food down, I began my monotonous routine. It was getting harder to ignore the burning pain that nearly brought me to my knees every time I breathed in. The circumference of the cell was exactly sixteen steps, I paced the dirt floor until I was covered in a light sweat and my bare feet hurt. My joints popped and protested as I stretched for as long as I was able. I then sat back on my mattress and attempted to meditate until I was delivered food for a second time. Then I would allow myself to sleep and begin the whole process the next day. The routine kept me from being swallowed into a pit of despair.

My only goals were to stay sane long enough to send word to Sylvia and to take my vengeance. I would take it in any form. In the silence between meals, I heard the heavy wood door creak open. My dream had put me on edge and I was waiting to hear the now-familiar gait of the enforcers. I wondered who it would be; the fat one with the thick moustache who would aim the food at my head, or maybe the muscled woman with a thin braid who would set the food gently on the floor by my feet. There didn't seem to be a set schedule, none that I could predict with any accuracy at least.

Instead of the usual two sets of footsteps, I heard *more*. Three people? The change of routine after four long weeks made my ears prick.

The distinctive smell of power flooded my cell, Magic I would recognise anywhere.

It couldn't be.

I raced to the bars and pressed my face to peer down the hall. Immediately I recognised his confident aura and easy swagger. "Luka?" I yelled, my voice hoarse from the prolonged silence.

He didn't acknowledge me. Perhaps he didn't recognise me. I was covered in filth and mud, and my Magic was being hidden by the collar. "Luka!" My words turned to a desperate scream. I reached through the bars toward him. If I could just touch him, maybe he would recognise me. I needed to know if Rosie had been found, if they had told Sylvia.

He came for me!

I was wrong. Judas was wrong. He hadn't betrayed me.

Luka stood with two guards. He was dressed in a perfectly pressed black uniform. His mahogany hair, which had grown long in our time at the compound, was now shaved close to his head. It stuck straight out. Luka's eyes were hard, and all emotion was locked away behind their steel casing.

He was so different, harder, more disciplined. I barely recognised him. If it wasn't for his distinctive Magic, I might not have recognised him at all. He was the Hunter once again. What I had thought of as the real Luka was hidden away. My outstretched arm dropped. If I could just touch him, I knew the spell would break and he would grin at me. His smokey eyes met mine in the firelight. Even different as he was, the contact was like a salve to my soul. I wanted to ask him about Rosie, ask if everyone had gotten to safety, but I stayed silent.

"She'll be dead soon." His voice was dismissive, his lip had curled and the disgust was plain on his face. "You better question her soon or all you'll get is the ramblings of a mad woman."

Shock smashed into my chest like a blow and I stumbled back from the bars. *What was he doing?* "The collar will burn through her. How long has she been in here?"

The information suddenly seemed like a lifeline. It was real, something solid to hang onto. The gruff looking man with salt and pepper stubble seems to think for a moment before answering.

"Six weeks, give or take."

I had thought I had been in here only a month.

"It wouldn't surprise me if she's hallucinating already."

Was I hallucinating now? I reached up to touch the collar. It was solid under my fingers. Tumultuous thoughts swirled in my head. I spun to face the back wall, my hands running through my knotted hair. This was real, wasn't it? I was in this cell. If I turned around now would Luka still be there? Or would he disappear like he had this morning?

What would be worse, if the Hunter was standing in front of me, arms crossed and eyes cruel, or if I was alone once again? I wanted to remember Luka as he had been in my dreams, long hair flopping over his eyes and an easy smile showcasing his perfectly-pointed teeth. My teeth bit through my bottom lip, the pain centering me. I kept my eyes closed as I spun around to face the bars once again. The unmistakable clicking of a heavy lock forced my eyes open. The Hunter was standing in the threshold, boredom plain on his features.

This was real.

He had betrayed me. Every word, every touch had been a lie.

Backing up into the corner of my cell, I prepared to fend off the guards. I could most likely take the two of them, but a fight with Luka was one I wouldn't win. It didn't mean I wouldn't try.

"Careful, she's dangerous," he warned as the guards closed in around me. One of them had the audacity to scoff before I smashed my head into his nose. Blood poured from his face and he bowed over in pain.

"Bitch," he groaned.

My right fist connected with the other guard's jaw in an upper cut. My power was pathetic and the guard barely flinched. Instead, he grinned, showing me a row of his stained and misshapen teeth. Salt and pepper beard seemed to get over his broken nose and grabbed me around the waist before slamming me onto the floor. The air was forced from my lungs and I could smell my blood. I guessed it was from the back of my head, but the adrenaline was masking any significant pain. Without letting him get on top of me, I scrambled to get back to my feet. The other forgettable looking guard seemed to regain his senses and dove for my knees as I fought to get up.

Luka had the audacity to laugh. I shot him an evil glare. For a moment I thought I saw the ice melt in his eyes, but I realised that it was simply a trick of the light. They smothered me using their size advantage and wound up one astride my chest and the other over my thighs. Handcuffs trapped my wrists and ankles. Instead of standing up with them, my body went limp. They would have to drag me out.

"Get up," salt and pepper shouted at me.

I stuck my tongue out at him, childish as it was. My action was met with a swift slap across the face. The hot metallic taste of blood filled my mouth and I spat the mixture onto the floor.

"Carry her," Luka demanded. They both looked wary. Finally, the one with the plain face leant down to scoop me up. As soon as he was close enough I bit into his shoulder; *hard*. He reared back in pain.

"Stupid cow!" he screamed.

His blood filled my mouth and I let it dribble down my chin as I eyed salt and pepper. I was ready to headbutt him again if he got too close. He didn't seem to want his nose smashed again because he stayed back.

"Oh seven hells." Luka strode over to me, his granite eyes met mine. In a flash, he unsheathed a dagger and held it to my neck.

"If you bite me, you'll regret it." His voice was low and dangerous. The knife should have stung against the skin on my neck but my body was numb to anything but the pain of his betrayal. I searched his grey eyes for any signs of familiarity but found none.

I pressed toward the sharpened edge of the blade and let it bite deeper into my skin. My blood ran warm against my neck as it trickled down my front. His gaze was steady and he didn't flinch at the wound. His once-beautiful eyes now seemed too angular and sharp. There was nothing but burning hatred within them. Trembling, I tipped my chin further into the sharpened edge, tempting him to end my suffering, half hoping he would.

He seemed to take delight in my pain.

I kept my mouth closed as he scooped me up roughly under the arms. Luka begun to drag me from the cell. I knew

I didn't want to go wherever they were taking me. My legs kicked violently and I began screaming as loud as my damaged voice would go. The two guards seemed to follow his lead and grabbed my feet. Luka completely ignored my struggles. He looked as serene as if he were walking a dog. They took me deeper into the confines of the underground prison. The ground eventually started to slope and I had the impression that the cells down here were much worse than mine.

We stopped in front of a large steel door. Luka swiped a pass on an electronic scanner and the door unlocked. They carried me into a dark room, the air seemed to turn colder. Goose bumps raised on my skin. The guards dropped my feet and flicked on the fluorescence light. The room was larger than my cell, but not by much. A reclined chair sat in the middle of the room. It came straight from my nightmares. The walls were adorned with various devices of torture, I tried not to look at any of them too closely.

Luka released my arms and I fell to the ground, he wiped his hands as he moved back toward the door.

"I'll get Louis."

"You don't want to stay and watch?" I taunted him, licking my lips.

He didn't spare me a glance. Instead he shut the door without turning around.

The two guards had wrestled me onto the chair and now secured my hands and feet. Both of the guards were considerably more bruised and bloodied than when they first entered the room. It wasn't as satisfying as I would have liked. We waited in silence for whoever Luka had gone to get. I doubted very much I would like the next person who walked through the door. I kept my face blank. No need to let them see how terrified I was.

Finally the door clicked open.

The figure that walked in could have been a man or a woman. They were tall and lithe, and their features were distinctively androgynous. When they turned their head, a thin dark pony tail was secured at the back of their head. They stared at me, bored, as if seeing a person strapped to the chair was nothing to phone home about.

"Hello, Arina." The voice was bland and monotonous. It made me question whether or not they had a soul. I guessed it had been destroyed by the Elect long ago. "I'm here to ask you a few questions."

The original two guards seemed to shrink away from the person, as soon as they walked over to me, the guards fled to stand by the door. I schooled my features into ones of serenity. They would *not* break me. If nothing came from my mouth, there would be nothing that could betray my friends. No doubt Luka and Judas had told them everything, I wouldn't be corroborating their information.

My breathing slowed, as I focused as Stella had taught me. I imagined my non-existent power forming a contained golden orb, I could almost feel the glorious burn as it chased away the icy terror in my veins. My eyes closed and my brain filled with memories of power rushing through my body. I longed for my Magic.

"Where has the rebellion moved too?"

Maybe Luka hadn't told them everything. My lips stayed sealed and I tried to remember the faces of my friends back in the compound. Davis, with his kind eyes and his single minded pursuit to breaking the enchantment on my collar.

A dark cloth was stuffed into my mouth and placed over my face. I tilted backwards.

I thought of Stella, with her intense eyes who I had once thought of as crazed. She had spent hours selflessly teaching me not to fear my Magic. She had made me a stronger, better version of myself. Frigid water flowed, in my mouth, my nose and all over my face. I held my breath as long as I could, but eventually I was forced to breathe. I was drowning. Sheer panic overtook me. The stiff leather of the restraints bit into my skin as I thrashed.

I struggled to bring up memories of Loral in his messy potion room. His zest for life which entered the room before he did.

Water dripped unrestrained into my lungs. *I couldn't breathe!* The freezing cold I had initially felt was now completely gone. A wave of heat filled me and my heart begun to beat in frantic panic. The urgency for air was overwhelming. The water stopped.

I lurched forward and threw up in my lap. Water and bile mixed with my already putrid smell.

Louis asked me another question, but I couldn't hear it over my hacking coughs. The rest of the water was splashed over my chest and body. I began violently shivering, my muscles ached and cramped. Surely, I had never been so cold.

"Where are the other Blood Mages living?" The woman demanded. "You can't be alone. Where are the others?"

I didn't dare open my eyes, less tears begin to escape. The chair was tilted backwards again and the cloth stuffed back into my mouth.

I thought of Loral bringing me unapproved food when he knew I was miserable. He had picked me up bounty after bounty without a complaint. My lungs filled with water—they burned. It wasn't the sweet feeling of my Magic, but one that would break me if it went on for too long. I imagined Lucia, her never changing appearance through the years and the tough love she had shown me through my childhood. It was the affection of an immortal. If I had stayed with her none of this would have happened.

Surely, I had never been as close to death. Every inch of my body screamed for oxygen. Finally, after what felt like hours, the water stopped and the cloth was removed. I ripped air into my lungs. My throat stung with sweet relief. Violent retches tore through me and more water expelled from my body. If I started talking now, I wouldn't stop. I would tell her everything I thought she wanted to know and more. Even if I didn't know the answers. I was never meant to be a martyr, I was a *mercenary*. Not long ago I would have said anything to have the pain stop, but there were people who were more important to me than myself. Those people needed me. The thought steeled me.

I opened my eyes. Louis had a sadistic smile plastered to

her face as she weighted a hefty hammer in her hand.

I needed to protect those people. That was my choice and it *would not* be taken away from me.

"The Hunter said we can't touch your pretty face or break your skin because you're too fragile." She fake pouted, "But there are other ways to get information."

Luka had said she wasn't allowed to cut me? A small spark of hope started in my chest. I stomped on it. Maybe he was scared the collar couldn't hold my power. He was an Elect member through and through. I had forgotten what a chameleon he was, and believed I had seen the real man underneath. How wrong I was, I had believed a facade.

"You'll get nothing from me bitch," I spat.

I knew the blow was coming and I tensed in preparation, the knowing didn't soften the pain.

The hammer slammed down onto my hand. The thin bones of my fingers splintered into untold fragments. Everything was pain. A violent scream tore through me and my mind took me far away, to some primitive place that knew how to deal with the kind of agony I was feeling. My vision was overtaken with violent colours that merged and moved without pattern or reason. I was unstrapped from the chair. My hands were secured in front of me tightly, and she pushed me onto the floor. The beating continued and no further questions were presented. My silence had angered her. The blows caused the wound on my chest to burst open. After her heavy boot connected with my face, my mouth filled with blood. It seemed the Hunter's rules didn't matter anymore. Time ceased to exist. There was nothing before the pain and nothing after.

"This is what you deserve." She wasn't wrong.

When the beatings stopped, my body was slick with blood, bile and salty tears. The guards tugged at my cuffed hands and sharp pain lanced through my head and colourful spots flashed in front of my eyes. Black mists swirled at the edges of my mind, calling me to oblivion. Before I was allowed to embrace unconsciousness, icy water was splashed over me once again. I didn't think I could muster the energy to walk back to my cell.

The two guards dragged me from the room, seemingly more comfortable around me now. My body was broken, but my mind was intact. They dropped me roughly onto the hard mattress. I half-heartedly lunged toward the salt and pepper haired guard. He scrambled back and landed on his ass. I let out a deep hacking laugh that ended with me doubled over spitting blood. The pain was worth it. They left me quickly after that, shutting me back in my tiny cell. I wasn't sure how long I had been gone for. It could have been hours or days.

Gingerly, I placed my battered body down on the mattress, cradling my broken hand to my chest. I cried until my tears dried up.

"Rina."

Gentle hands pushed back my stiff hair from my face and cradled my cheek.

They had come back for me.

Adrenaline forced my eyes open and I scrambled back, ignoring the pain that flared throughout my body. My back hit the wall and air was forced from my lungs. I couldn't see anything in the dark. A hand was placed over my mouth.

"Shhhhh, it's me."

Luka? His familiar power caressed me, welcoming me into its embrace like an old lover. My clothes were still soaking wet and my muscles ached from the tremors. In the silence, I could hear the chattering of my teeth. A lamp in the corner of the room suddenly lit. Luka's Fire Magic caused my skin to tingle. I latched onto the pleasant feeling. I was no longer in my cell, but instead in a large cave. When I saw past his shoulder, there was a large pool of water. Memories of freezing liquid pouring into my lungs flooded my brain. I sucked in big gulps of air and my heart began to flutter in my chest. A keening sound escaped my lips.

I wouldn't drown again.

Luka caught me around the waist and I struggled against his grip. Silent tears marked my cheeks. I could take torture from strangers, but not at the hands of Luka. It would break me.

"Rina please, I'm not going to hurt you." His voice was warm and he wrapped his arm around my thighs to stop me from kicking out. His fingers gripped around my bicep. Squeeze…Tap. *I'm here…I'm with you.* My vision took on a strange haze and a comforting warmth filled me. *Of course!* I was hallucinating. The effects of the collar mixed with torture and starvation had taken their toll and my mind had checked out. I didn't mind the reprieve.

He wasn't the Hunter anymore, he was back to being my Luka. It was easy to pretend he was separate from the Elect, that the man who had held a knife to my throat was someone different. The metal of his eyes had softened, and the angles of his face were alluring once again. I reached up with my good hand and cradled his cheek.

"I'm not going to hurt you," he whispered. My breathing begun to return to normal. Nothing could hurt me here. It was just me and my Luka.

"Rosie," I rasped out. The despair in my voice was heavy.

"I know. I'm so sorry, Rina. We gave her back to Sylvia."

I nodded. It was good that they had found her and returned her body to her mother. His eyes filled with tears that glittered in the firelight. My mind felt foggy, like I hadn't slept in a month. I half-expected Luka's hair to be long again but it was still shaved close to his head.

"I like your hair longer," I muttered. He gave me a sad smile that didn't reach his eyes.

"We need to clean your wounds before they get infected."

I giggled. *How absurd.* He clapped a hand over my mouth and shushed me. Luka seemed so real. I studied his features. His eyes were no longer hard but filled with concern. A stiff uniform no longer adorned his body. Instead he wore a simple black t-shirt and track pants. His strong arms lifted me easily and I cuddled into his chest as he walked toward the pool of water. I was placed on the edge, legs tucked under me. Anxiety rose up within me at the sight of the depths. I stuffed it down to keep company with my other nightmares. I wouldn't drown here. Gingerly, Luka lifted my arms. The pain transcended even my hallucinations. My muscles felt as if they had been filled with concrete and my bones ground against each other. He pulled the damp singlet off me, the fabric had stuck to the wounds across my ribs and I gritted my teeth to avoid screaming out.

Luka inhaled sharply at the sight of me.

"I'm so sorry." His voice was strangled.

When I looked down at my body, I saw that it was painted in purple and green. The bruises looked particularly grotesque against my ghostly pale skin. I wondered how much damage had been done to my internal organs. After removing the rest of my clothes, Luka held me and slid into the steaming bath. Luka shucked his shirt. I had seen his near naked body before and my imagination did not disappoint. His skin was olive in the warm light and his chest and stomach held a litany of scars. There were four thin lines that I had healed, but the closer I looked, the more I saw. They spoke of a hard life. My body was finally weightless in the hot water. Tears of relief escaped my eyes. I didn't mind crying in front of dream-Luka. If I ever returned to reality, I would be back freezing and covered in blood. For now, I would take any respite offered.

Luka gently washed the dried blood from my arms and face. I couldn't bring myself to dunk my head under the water. His touch was exquisitely careful. He lifted my broken hand from the water and inspected it. Luka tried to harden his eyes, but I saw the flash of horror.

When I got the courage to look at it closely, I could see my fingers were mangled. It was swollen to three times its normal size and had turned an odd shade of blue. Would it heal? It seemed unlikely. There were some things even magic couldn't fix. Luka cupped some water in his hands and ran it over my hair, trying to dislodge the build-up of dirt and blood. I rested my head on his shoulder.

"Forgive me." His voice was thick with emotion.

"It hurts," I choked. He pulled himself out of the pool and fished a small silver vial from his pants.

I popped the cap and drunk the sour tasting potion greedily. The effect was immediate, the pain slid off me like water from a duck's back. It must have been human medicine. My eyes struggled to stay open and Luka pulled me onto his chest once again. The water was nice. I didn't want the dream to end. *Squeeze...Tap.* I am here, I am with you. Exhaustion had anchored itself to me and I was pulled down further and further into the deep abyss of unconsciousness. Finally I gave in.

Chapter Twenty

Luka

The hollow sound of Luka's footsteps echoed off the damp walls. His hands were clasped behind his back to stop him from ringing his fingers. The hallway seemed to narrow the closer he got to the two silver doors that signified the end of his walk.

Taking a steadying breath, he pushed open the doors and strode into the chambers. He schooled his features into the bored expression that was his mask. The rest of the Elect had summoned him to appear before them. Did they guess how deep his betrayal ran?

The room was how he remembered it, white and sterile. There were nine seats on a podium, positioned in a large semi-circle. It was designed to intimidate subjects, but one of those seats was his, and he would not be subject to their mind games.

"Master Highland, welcome back to Verinski."

The head of the Elect sat in the room, his salt and pepper hair was cut short and his blue eyes surveyed Luka intensely. His face was deeply-lined and pale from too many years spent indoors.

"Hayden."

He sneered at the subtle insult.

"I trust you have requested my presence for an important reason."

"The sorceress has been *silent*."

He bristled at the insult. "I delivered her to Louis days ago. Has she lost her touch?"

Arina had stayed quiet. He hadn't expected anything else. Hayden seemed personally offended at the suggestion.

"Of course not. But the sorceress refuses to bend."

"Maybe you over-estimated what she knows," he offered.

"Don't be ridiculous. You know her kind are never alone. They congregate in packs. She is a danger to our very way of life." Hayden chastised him. "You told me so yourself."

"Apparently she cries out your name in her sleep," Gianna added, her face screwed into an accusatory glare.

Of course she did. He had betrayed her. Ignoring the twinge of emotion in his chest, Luka's face stayed neutral.

"Your insistence that Louis cannot use more conventional methods is hindering us."

"Her wounds do not heal like those of a normal Mage. If she loses too much blood she will die without giving up any of the information we seek."

"Well, perhaps you can assist," the dark-haired woman sitting next to Hayden offered. It wasn't a question.

He scoffed. "I am not a torturer, Indiana."

"We must know what she knows, Hunter." Indiana spat, her temper barely held in check. "Her parents were integral in the birth of the rebellion. She's more involved than we realised."

He hid his surprise. He hadn't known that. He had convinced them that Arina had known where scores of Blood Mages were living to save her from the horror of the Blood Mage camps. He didn't think she would actually know anything not already given up by himself and Judas.

"I'm not your torturer." It was all he could say in response. He couldn't torture Rina, not even to keep her alive.

"But you are well-versed in brutality." Hayden provided with a smug smile. They all knew cruelty was what got him the job in the first place.

"Blood Mages are a danger to us all. Perhaps we should destroy her." Julien leaned back on his throne, his face plump and ruddy. Luka wouldn't give in to his games. The man was smarter than he looked.

"Perhaps." He shrugged. If he gave any indication that he

was sympathetic toward Arina, they wouldn't hesitate to slaughter her.

The Elect glared down at him from their thrones. Luka felt so far removed from them. How long had it been since he had sat upon one of those chairs and looked down at whoever stood by his feet?

Not long enough.

"So it's settled then. The Hunter will get the information we need from the Blood Mage or we will execute her." Hayden clasped his withered hands. "You're dismissed." He bowed and struggled not to flee from the room.

The once-familiar walls of his home now closed in around him as he moved to his bedroom. He slammed the steel door with too much force and began to pace the large space.

He noticed how bare the bedroom was, how devoid of personality. The walls were empty and the bed sheets were a pale grey. There was no pile of unwashed clothes on the floor, or empty plates sitting on the bedside table. It was sterile. His closet was filled with identical black uniforms and boots. The only thing which indicated that anyone lived in the space was the two long swords hanging on the wall.

He shuffled toward the window. The view was breathtaking. The entirety of Ka lay before him, the city streets lined up in perfect grids. It was cathartic to stare out at the perfect order and watch the people go by unaware. From up here he couldn't see the fear in their eyes as they glanced sideways at the enforcers keeping them in check. He couldn't hold off the Elect's plans for long. They would demand answers soon.

He needed to show his face at the next meal. Elect members loved to gossip. If he missed dinner again there would be speculation. After checking his uniform was spotless, he made his way through the brightly-lit corridors and toward hell.

If a person hadn't been to the prisons underneath, they wouldn't believe they existed. Everything above ground level was lit with white light. Verinski had no shadows to hide in. Luka's face was expressionless as he strode into the busy dining hall. It was a mask he had worn since childhood. The silence was so foreign after his time in the compound. Meal times had become boisterous and loud. The room had always been filled with easy conversation and laughter.

Verinski had only terse silence or carefully chosen words. People here made chess moves, not conversation. He used to thrive playing the game, but now he found himself despising it.

"Hunter, how nice of you to finally join us." The icy Gretchen flashed her white teeth. The woman was a viper.

"Thank you, Gretchen. It is good to be back amongst friends."

The dining hall was set out with a thirteen-seat table on a podium at the front of the room for the Elect and whoever had earned their favour that day. The rest of the room was set for advisors and other dignitaries. It seemed Gretchen had gained the favour of Julien because she sat nestled between them. Judas sat on the other side of Luka, next to Hayden. Silence fell over the room as the servers wheeled carts filled with plates of food into the hall.

Hayden was served first, the waiter shaking with fear as he placed the plate in front of him. The rest of the podium were given meals and only after the Elect and the ticks that had attached themselves to them begun to eat, were the rest of the meals served. The steaming plate of steak and vegetables in front of him turned his stomach. The crowd waited for Hayden to pick up his knife and fork before beginning. He liked to wait a few extra seconds to remind everyone who was in control.

"You must share with us how you survived living with those savages for so long," Julien said between mouthfuls of food.

Luka felt the mask slip back on more slowly than usual, the smile felt forced and unnatural. But the act was one he couldn't give up. If they guessed how far he had slipped, they wouldn't hesitate to punish both his sister and Arina.

His protests had been too fervent upon arrival and Hayden

decided to test his subject's loyalty. Luka should have stayed and watched, but even hearing her screams from down the hall had been too much. Giving her the human medicine was too risky. He shouldn't have done it. If he had been caught, they both would have been executed and her sacrifice would be for nothing.

"It was tough to hide my true feelings, but we do what we must in order to safeguard the Elect's reign."

Judas leant over Julien. They made eye contact and his gaze narrowed. He was still suspicious. He had seen Luka's betrayal first hand. If he had known Judas was a part of the Elect, he would have killed him. Who was he to question Luka? He was a no one. He was in the good graces of Hayden now, but the head of the Elect was a fickle man and Judas would be forgotten soon, relegated to sit back with the plebs.

For now, he was dangerous. He gave Luka a sly smile, a snake ready to strike out.

"It didn't seem too difficult for you to fit in with the sorceress, Hunter. You shared a room, didn't you?"

"I insisted on it. Before her face was ruined by Louis, she had a certain charm." Luka returned his smug smile. "I'm sure you remember. It's a shame you never got to experience it for yourself."

Bile rose in his throat. The Hunter's reputation as a womaniser was well-known. No one would have batted an eyelid that he had taken a shine to Arina.

Judas sneered.

"It's a shame we don't know where the remainder of the rebellion is. Is she still not giving up any answers?" Julien ignored the conflict.

"No, but she was close with the man above me."

Loral. Luka hadn't given up that particular bit of information, how much had Rina told him?

"He was her old roommate, he was the closest to the leader. He would have told her what to do in case the compound was ever breached."

"And he never told you?" Luka accused.

"No, he never liked me."

Loral was smarter than Luka had given him credit for.

After getting everyone out through the springs, Luka had told Loral that he had to go back and get Rina. When he had gotten to the kitchen, he had seen Rosie's tiny crumpled body in the mud. There had been no sight of Judas or Arina. The only evidence that Rina had been there at all was the number of dead enforcers littering the floor. At that point he hadn't known Judas had betrayed her. Luka had thought them both captured. He had cleaned up Rosie and carefully carried her. The memory of her slight weight in his arms still horrified him.

Loral had insisted he come with Luka to find Rina. It was only after he had come clean about who he was that Loral had relented. Arina was right, he hadn't even been mad at her. He had just wanted her safe. Luka was so close to getting her out. He had called in a number of favours and the plan to hide his sister would be complete within the week. Once she was safe, he was free to act how he wanted.

Luka wasn't sure if she would last that long.

Chapter Twenty-One

My routine had changed. My days were no longer filled with walking and stretching. My body was too broken for that. After my first meal, Luka would take me to see Louis. The first few days I had resisted and screamed. It was no use, I ended up there all the same and I needed my energy to survive the torture. Now I lay limp as he carried me out.

My mind quickly slipped into the sanctuary of more pleasant memories.

Lucia's immortal face was in front of me in all its beauty. She held my small head in her cold hands.

"Why are you crying?"

"Because it hurts." My voice was so small, so innocent.

"Have you never felt pain before?"

I had been too slow and one of the fighters had kicked me in my ribs. Lucia had found me sobbing on the edge of the training pit. At the time, I was no older than thirteen and still weak with grief.

"Do you want to be strong, little one? Or do you want to cower forever?"

She had never spoken to me with such gentleness. It was a salve to my ragged soul.

"I want to be strong." My voice was breathy from the pain.

"Then you must continue. There is no other option."

I got back on my feet and did as she asked. It was a lesson she had taught me time after time. There is no other option, but to continue. To do anything else would betray the memory of my parents. I was not weak.

This would be the same. I had faced the pain already.

My only option was to endure, and endure I did.

Day after day, Louis inflicted her worse. Some days she

used flames to burn my skin and other days she ripped out my fingernails one by one. I thought I knew what it meant to bleed, but I was wrong. Occasionally she grew frustrated with my silence and preferred to hear my screams and watch my blood pool on the ground underneath me. She never used a knife to cut my skin and it seemed the Hunter was content with that. Perhaps they didn't want me to bleed out too soon.

The books Davis had given me on Blood Mages had theorised that they had a higher tolerance for pain than other Mages. It said Blood Magic came from the pain of the self-inflicted wound, rather than the blood itself. Blood Mages were used to wielding their Magic and holding onto their sanity when all others would break under the mix of power and pain. Perhaps it was true. Despite the all-consuming agony, I still clung to a small corner in my mind. *They would not break me.*

After she had her way with me, I was deposited back into my room and left to tend to my injuries. My clothes were reduced to rags. Parts of my body wouldn't respond to my commands, the only respite was that those were the parts I couldn't feel. When I tried to shift on my mattress my body screamed in protest, and pins and needles shot down my spine. My dreams were rarely pleasant. Sometimes I screamed out for Luka and begged him to kill me. Instead I was met with the mocking grey stare of the Hunter. Some nights I was a child again, trying to silence my Magic by smashing into a wooden totem until my knuckles bled. Or I betrayed my friends over and over, Loral, Erin, Jax and even Wesley made an appearance. My subconscious was relentless in its assault. It was almost as bad as the physical pain. The last few nights I stood over my targets and watched as the life drained from their eyes and their magic rushed my limbs.

Those were the worst nightmares, the ones where I was reminded of what a monster I was. A small voice told me that perhaps I deserved what was coming.

After a while I couldn't decide what was real and what was not. The place I controlled in my mind grew smaller and smaller until eventually it was all I could do to keep silent.

Those were the nights I prayed for the sweet release of death. In the darkness I ran my blistered fingers over the sharp edges of the stone. A strained smile burned my cracked lips. The piece of slate had fallen from the wall in a session with Louis and I had stashed it in my underwear when her back was turned. It had taken me days of carefully grinding the edge against the bars to get it sharp enough.

A murky plan had formed in between episodes of psychosis. I needed to stay sane just a few hours longer.

My Luka had visited me last night. He had soothed my aching body and pulled together the ragged edges of my psyche just enough. Squeeze…Tap. Over and over, the wordless communication had kept me together. Upon waking, I cradled a vial that I had found under my pillow. It was solid in my hand, it was real. *Wasn't it?*

The plan. I needed to focus on the plan.

I was counting on the fact someone would come when I screamed. No sound had escaped my lips for weeks. It was one of the rules I had created. On some days those rules were the only thing that mattered. No one but *she* would bear witness to me breaking. Someone would come to investigate. They would have too. It wouldn't be hard to convince them I had finally succumbed to the collar, that I no longer had any information to give. When they stormed my cell I would kill as many as I could.

When I opened my mouth to scream, despair begun to worm its way into my head. *I was too weak.* The emptiness yawned open. It commanded the space my power had left behind. The black hole continued to expand, destroying every part of me that was left. I scrambled to keep a corner for myself. The collar was too powerful. I had overestimated my strength. There had been a reason for my silence.

Now the despair would destroy me.

Like a crystal vase that had fallen onto the floor, the last pieces of my sanity shattered. I couldn't reach down and put it back together, it was too hard. The pieces had been broken beyond recognition, too damaged to consider saving.

My chest ached as heaving sobs racked through my frail

body. The pain brought me back to myself for a split second. They *would not* break me. I slashed the sharpened stone down my forearm, from my palm to the crook of my elbow. My skin gave way easily and the sticky blood poured onto the floor, pulsing in rhythm to my weak heartbeats. Loud footsteps pounded the pavement. That had once meant something to me, but I couldn't think of what. I'd once had a plan. Large bodies stood behind metal bars. I watched them through my nearly swollen shut eyelids.

The static became louder, muffling everything. At least there would be no more pain.

"Quickly get the Hunter!"

The Hunter. A set of grey eyes appeared in my mind. Desperately I clung to the image. It was something I wanted to stay for. *Luka*. Time had ceased to exist. There was nothing but the emptiness and the set of dark eyes. It stretched out in my mind, devouring all conscious thoughts. People left and returned, the set of familiar eyes appeared in front of me. I wanted to look into them forever.

"Get her out!" Someone screamed.

Something was brought to my lips, but I refused to drink. I wanted to go. This world held nothing for me. The screaming stopped. I was weightless. There was nothing, just the horrible static as it grew louder and louder. It was all I could hear, the waves of sound crashed into my skull. Before it could pull me under, the gnawing emptiness was consumed by ravenous power. A gurgled scream tore through the static. My body had betrayed me in the worst way. I was still alive.

"Rina, the collar's off. You're safe."

Safe. The word seemed so foreign. *He brought the Elect into the compound. He killed Rosie.*

The betrayal stung deeper than any wound inflicted by my captors. *He needed to pay.* My Magic demanded retribution. It filled my chest, powered by my still spilling blood. I bathed in it. Thick black smoke rose from my skin, laced with gold. Power chased away the cobwebs of death still clinging to my mind.

If I couldn't have death, I would have revenge.

I exploded. Gone was my careful control. My feet left the ground, pure power causing me to rise. The traitor fell to his knees. His skin turned ashy.

"Why didn't you let me die!" My rough voice barely above a whisper. The memory of his apathy was a knife to my chest. His cold eyes had fuelled my nightmares for weeks. But when it had mattered, he had stepped in to prolong my torment.

"Rina!" He stumbled toward me, weak under the weight of my power. The balls of my feet landed back on the wooden floor. I forced myself closer to him. The Hunter was bare-chested, shirt in his hand. He hastily grabbed at my forearm and tried to cover the bleeding wound.

I yanked away from his touch, but the warmth of his hands stirred something inside of me. The Magic dissipated as quickly as it had appeared, and the pain came roaring back in its place. My legs collapsed beneath me.

"I'm sorry. I'm so sorry," the Hunter moaned.

Where was I?

From my position on the floor I looked around the room. I wasn't in a cell, but it was close enough. I sobered enough to really see the man crouched in front of me. The Hunter's eyes were ringed with black circles and his skin was too pale. My mind was filled with mud, my thoughts moved too slowly. Was this real, or was I imaging the power singing through me?

Surely death would have been more pleasant.

"I'll run you a bath."

The blast of power had finally knit together the skin on my forearm. I looked at the long angry line. Soon there wouldn't even be a scar. My body was still littered with injuries. Even my power wasn't infallible. The Hunter helped me to my feet, avoiding the most severe of my wounds. I desperately wanted to scrub the bruises from my skin. The bathroom was large and undecorated, just like the bedroom. It wasn't how I had previously imagined the Hunter's bedroom to be. In my imagination it was dark and homely, not this sterile environment. I sat on the cold tiles and the Hunter made his way over to the large bath. He hunched over the tub, steam rising from the water.

My emotions had been burned away with the power. I was numb. There was nothing left of me to take. My power had made me feel alive for a moment, but now it was gone again like everything else. I peeled off my stiff clothes layer by layer. They were ruined from blood, sweat and urine. Where was my burn bag? *I couldn't wear these again.* Standing awkwardly in the centre of the room, I hobbled over to the door looking for the familiar bag hanging from the handle.

This wasn't my bathroom. Where was I?

The Hunter pried the clothes from my hand and herded me toward the bath.

He hadn't put the plug in. Instead I sat next to the running tap. I took the washcloth from him. I scrubbed the blood from my body. It wasn't coming off. It was tattooed to my skin. I kept scrubbing with my good hand, desperate to rid myself of the pain that echoed in my brain. The water ran red until I grew dizzy. Handprints were painted in bruises over my body. I wanted them gone.

The Hunter left for a moment and returned with a number of vials.

"Drink please," he said. "Why isn't the bleeding stopping?" He asked more to himself than me.

I looked at my body. It was covered in a litany of cuts. Each one a reminder of Louis's torture. My Magic wasn't closing the wounds fast enough. I didn't care if the Hunter had brought me a vile of poison to drink, I didn't want to be in pain anymore. I plucked the first vile from him and let the sweet tasting liquid rest on my tongue for a moment before swallowing. He handed me the next one, and the next, until my wounds were crusted over and the bleeding was finally stemmed. They would scar. I hadn't used Blood Magic to heal the wounds. My body would always bear testimony to the Elect's brutality. It was lucky I had enough Magic left for the healing potions to even work. At least the worst of the pain had disappeared.

The Hunter snatched the cloth from me when my body was red raw and finally put the plug in the bath. I wrapped my arms around my knees and tried to reach for the amber stone that hung around my neck. My chest was empty. I had yanked it off months ago.

It was the only thing that remained of my parents and now it was gone. Like me, I was gone.

"This isn't real," I concluded.

"We're in the Elect's Headquarters. This is real, Rina."

"I'm not in my cell." I would humour him for now. When I awoke to find myself behind bars, the sadness could very well kill me.

"I told you I would come for you."

"I want to leave."

"We will, I swear it. You need to heal first. You're safe for a few more days."

That would have to do for now, a vague promise of freedom. The bath began to fill. In the dim light it was easier to inspect my body. The bruises had faded enough that I barely saw them. Still, my bones protruded from my elbows and wrists. All my strength was drained. My hand was the worst damaged. I couldn't move it out of the claw position, and all my fingernails were missing. Strangely, when I looked at my mangled hand, I felt only indifference, like it didn't belong to me.

The Hunter left me alone and came back some time later with a fluffy towel and clean clothes. The soft towel was scratchy on my sensitive skin. I avoided my reflection in the mirror and got dressed quickly. The clothes hung off me. They must have been the Hunter's. The short walk to the bed left me out of breath and I crawled onto the mattress. It was too soft. My brain demanded rest and, without a beat, I fell asleep.

I was yanked violently from my sleep. My throat was hoarse from screaming and my muscles spasmed and cramped. I was pinned to the bed. I thrashed violently, snarling in the Hunter's face. He hovered over me. "It's okay."

I nodded.

After that, the day had gone slowly. The Hunter had waited on me hand and foot. He brought me food and water every half an hour and hadn't let me leave the bed. The food tasted bland in my mouth and on more than one occasion I had thrown it up. My Magic was partially back, but it felt sluggish in my veins. My mind wandered and replayed the moment I brought the stone down across my forearm again and again. I wept like a child.

The Hunter dutifully brought me pain potions every few hours. His betrayal was clearer than ever. He had forsaken me the same as everyone else. It didn't matter the reasons. Only one thing mattered now. Pillows propped me up and he was laying at the foot of the bed in a sleeping bag. I was in a fresh pair of clothes and my hair was still wet from my fourth bath. The Hunter had eventually hidden the wash cloth from me when I reopened my scabs for the second time.

I doubt I had ever been cleaner, yet still my body felt dirty. My skin crawled with the thought that I was so close to the people who had tormented me my whole life, the people that had sanctioned the murder of my parents and hunted me like a deer. Judas was in this building. The horrors of my captivity were barely held at bay. The only thing that beat back at the torrent of cold despair was the thought of revenge. Revenge for my parents, for Rosie, for me.

The rebellion would have been temporarily disbanded, but they would rise again.

True rebellion never dies.

They would never trust me again. I couldn't return to the cause. But I could make a dent in the Elect. Their goons would die at my hands. I would feel the Magic bleed from their bodies. My legacy would be one of death. The Queen of carnage.

"Luka?" I called, my voice small in the dark, it had to be early morning by now.

"Mmmm."

"I'm too scared to sleep." I pulled the blanket up under my chin. "Do you have any sleeping potions?" The vulnerability in my voice startled me, I wasn't used to hearing it. Maybe I was not as strong as I thought. Maybe the Elect had broken me. There was a rustling and he appeared beside the bed, flicking on the lamp.

I looked up at him, eyes wide. My arms wound around my knees and I let some of the torment leak into my expression. His gaze softened. He strode from the room, closing the door softly behind him.

Did he truly care for me? *It doesn't matter. He led the Elect to you. He dragged you to the torture chamber day after day.*

I took stock of my power. It was erratic and sputtered occasionally, my rune work was going to be sloppy at best. It would have to do, I needed to act now before I ended up back in the cell. When he returned, I was sitting cross-legged in the middle of the bed. He held a tiny silver vial in his hand and passed it to me. I palmed the cold metal. He turned off the light and moved to leave. I crawled to my hands and knees and grabbed his arm. My power sparked when we touched.

"Please stay with me."

He watched me a moment in the dark before letting out a resigned sigh, Luka sunk next to me. The warmth of his bare skin was glorious, I had forgotten how good it felt to be close to him. I rested my head on his bare chest and his arm wound around me protectively. My hand was trembling as I traced unsteady runes on his bare stomach.

"Are you okay?"

I couldn't answer. Instead I pushed off him and sat up facing the edge of the bed. I wouldn't win in a fight. I needed to play dirty. Revenge was just outside the door.

I let out a breath. This was my only chance. I popped the cap from the vial of potion with my thumb, silently. There were only two drops of liquid. It would work. I swiped the potion across my lips quickly and made a show of placing the vial back down on the bedside table, cap in place. His concern was palpable, even in the dark.

"You're not going to drink it?"

My heart raced and my palms began to sweat.

Before I could lose my cool I climbed on top of him and straddled his waist. Leaning forward, I ran a finger down his cheek.

"I can think of a better distraction." I didn't sound sexy, I sounded scared. Still, he didn't push me off. I could see the guilt warring on his features. Perhaps it was evil to take advantage of it. I found I didn't care.

"Rina…" He hesitated, his warm breath tickled my cheek, his hands gentle on my hips.

"Please, Luka. I want to feel something other than pain." My voice broke on the last word and I watched something change in his eyes.

My eyelids felt heavy, the potion was taking effect too quickly. I needed to act. I leaned forward and lowered my mouth to his.

Our lips met, briefly. I had only planned to brush my mouth across his one time. But Luka's fingers dug into my hips and he dragged me closer, pulling my lips back down onto his. The pain disappeared for a brief, glorious instant. I inhaled sharply. My body was pressed against his muscled chest and I could feel the thunderous beating of his heart.

His lips softened as he deepened the kiss. All I could feel was him. His warmth, his touch, his Magic was caressing my back. He begun nuzzling my neck with delicate kisses, so faint, they were whispers. I urged myself to push away but I couldn't.

"Arina." He whispered each syllable as if to savour them.

My name had never been something extraordinary until it came from his lips. His hands trailed gently under my shirt, the delicate touch demanding. My sweatshirt was pulled over my head and forgotten on the floor. He captured my lips again. I drew my tongue over his mouth and swallowed his moan of pleasure. His hair had grown out some and I relished in finally burying my hands in the soft lengths. My teeth nicked his lip, and the coppery taste of his blood filled my mouth. My power roared to life and mingled with his.

I whimpered in pleasure.

His life force was so clear to me. I could see it in his chest, the flame bright and white, fueling his beautiful Magic. Strangling the last of my concentration, I crafted a healing rune. I had no idea if the effects of the potion would be negated, but tried, nonetheless. It had been a long time since I had used someone else's blood to power my runes, and never someone as powerful as Luka. It would be so easy to lose myself in the moment. I wanted to. I needed to be overwhelmed by his power. It was pure agony knowing that this would be the first and only time. My chest squeezed for something that might have been if we had been born two normal Mages. But we weren't. He was the Hunter and I was a sorceress.

Luka rolled so his weight was barely resting on top of me. The wonderful feel of his body left me barely enough concentration to activate the rune. He drew back, his mouth leaving mine. I lamented the loss of contact. Resting on his elbow, he swiped under my eyes collecting the moisture that had pooled there.

"Did you want me to stop?"

I almost wanted to laugh. I had never wanted anyone as badly in my entire life. He stifled a yawn. The potion was working. Frantically I shook my head and pulled him back toward me, smashing his lips to mine. My hands roamed his body desperately, clawing at his bare skin. I needed more of him. There was no time left for words. There was no time left. The exhaustion that had weighted me down only minutes ago had lifted, the healing rune worked. I felt better than I had in a long time.

With renewed strength, I rolled to sit on top of him. I kissed down his neck and to his muscled chest. Goosebumps rose on his perfect skin. Luka grabbed my arm, stopping me. The spell was broken. I covered my breasts, suddenly awkward. He gently tugged at my hands, his strength gone.

"I'm just so…tired," he slurred, his eyes glazed.

I let him pull me down and cradle me against his chest. *Safe.* I was safe. Perhaps I could stay here. It would be so easy to close my eyes and drift to sleep. I could leave another night. Luka yawned into my hair. *Squeeze…Tap. I'm here, I'm with you.* "I won't let them hurt you again." His voice was thick with sleep.

If I stayed, they had won. All the death and pain would be

for nothing.

"I know," I whispered into the dark.

"Did you know your parents were part of the rebellion?" His voice trailed off at the end, muffled against my hair.

I turned to face him, his eyes were closed. I shook him, trying to rouse him.

"What? Luka, what about my parents?"

It was no use, the plan had worked too well. He was asleep. Nothing would wake him now.

Chapter Twenty-Two

I forced myself out of the bed. I didn't have much time. I flicked on the lamp, rolled up the tracksuit pants, pulled the shirt back over my head, and went hunting for a weapon. It was cold outside of the bed. I looked back at Luka's sleeping form. It would be so easy to slide back under the covers and sleep, but I had slept enough.

There were two swords hanging on the wall. Luka wouldn't have an ornamental sword in his room. I slid one out of its sheath. It was heavy but balanced perfectly when I rested it in the palm of my hand. A smile stretched the papery skin of my face. I searched the rest of the room. I needed something else. If I had to access my Magic I couldn't use the sword. I would cut my arm clean off. His room was sparse and there were not many hiding places. I opened his closet and found rows and rows of black uniforms. I pushed them aside searching the bottom of the wardrobe. Nothing but shoes. I didn't bother fixing anything up.

I moved to the grey ottoman at the end of his bed and felt the gritty timber underneath. My hands came across the smooth hilt of a dagger.

Bingo.

I ripped it out and admired it in the moonlight. It was achingly familiar. I steadied myself and hardened my heart. Luka was laying on the bed with the sheets draped over his waist. His muscled torso looked deadly even at rest.

This is my enemy.

He was the Elect. If by some miracle I made it out alive Luka would hunt me to the ends of the earth. This man had betrayed me. He had betrayed my friends. The Hunter had brought the Elect down on the rebellion. I had to banish the fallacy of *my* Luka and the Hunter—they were one and the same. A familiar rage begun to build within me. I clung to the feeling. This was the man that had dragged me to be tortured night after night. He had committed numerous atrocities in the name of his masters.

I passed the dagger to my good palm. My Magic purred and curled around me as it recognised my violent intentions. I crawled onto the bed and straddled his waist again.

It was hard to resist the urge to lay down on his chest and inhale the sweet scent of his power. He looked so much younger when he was asleep, so peaceful. There was no hardness behind his eyes, no snarl that curled his lip. The anger would keep me safe.

I pulled the memory of him pressing a dagger to my throat to the forefront of my mind. How he had held me against his car and threatened me with the paralysis potion. The memory was at odds with the way his Magic now protectively wrapped around me. The tendrils of his power caressed my waist, leaving behind a trail of goosebumps. I gritted my teeth.

It doesn't matter.

I dragged the sharp blade across my palm. The blood dripped through my closed fist and onto his chest. My power built within me, the warmth thrumming pleasantly through me until it reached the ends of my hair and my eyes flickered black.

I am the bringer of death. I am ruthless and merciless, a born killer. With each breath I pushed my soft, traitorous emotions down. My time in Ka had made me weak, but two years wouldn't erase my past.

The Hunter needed to die.

I knew hesitation was weakness, but still, I kept my Magic wound tightly in my chest. My hand shook as the blood pooled on his golden skin before rolling off his chest and onto the mattress.

He needs to die.

Salty tears ran down my cheeks and over my lips. I bit down on my bottom lip, letting the pain clear my mind. *I hate him. I hate him!*

But I couldn't bring myself to plunge my Magic into his

skin, or even to spill his blood. What I wanted to kill was much deeper.

You idiot.

I fled the room and Luka's sleeping body.

I'd be dead soon anyway.

In the next blink I found myself in the middle of a corridor. The hall was brightly lit and deadly silent. The Elect was too cocky to have enforcers roaming their inner sanctum. My body was tense as I moved silently through the winding halls. All remnants of Luka's power had disappeared from my system and I felt considerably weaker away from his presence. If I didn't concentrate on my bare feet moving over the cold tiles, I feared my mind would fracture again. I needed to find Judas.

My doubts were interrupted by a set of footsteps hurrying down the hallway. My heart thundered in my chest. *Had I been found?* Magic flooded my veins, racing to my fingertips and filling the emptiness inside my chest. My vengeance turned hot.

I hovered behind the corner, peering around slowly.

Two figures marched down the hall, stiff-legged and rushing. They were unarmed. For a moment it was if the world had turned warm and golden. My vision was enhanced, like I was seeing high definition for the first time. The Magic continued to build. It coursed through my body like champagne bubbles. I could revel in the feeling forever. Hatred filled me, it was acidic on my tongue.

I emerged from my hiding place. When they spotted me, they didn't hesitate.

Icy wind speared toward me, but I was too fast. I sliced my thigh and wrapped my power in a thick bubble around me. The attack rebounded harmlessly from my shield. I stalked toward my prey. I could see the whites of their eyes. The one on the left had been one of my jailers. He had particularly enjoyed watching me cry.

With a flick of my wrist I released the hold on my power and let the deadly tendrils fly. My power ravaged his body, consuming his Magic as his eyes bulged in his skull. The other enforcer tried to strike out at me with more wind but my shield held steady. When I finished toying with my prey, he crumbled to the floor his life force snuffed out. I killed the other one much faster, my Magic consuming him in a black noxious smoke.

"Stop! By order of the Elect!" a booming male voice sounded from behind me. I shouldn't have been so indulgent. It had given them time to scream.

It didn't matter now. Soon enforcers would flood the corridors and I would kill them all. I spun on my heel. A familiar battle rage rose within me. I had felt it every time I had stepped into the arena or killed a mark.

This was who I was, who I was meant to be.

Once I had taken my revenge I would finally know peace.

The skinny enforcer was swallowed by my Magic before he could launch an attack. Droves of soldiers began to escape from their rooms and swarm me. I couldn't fight them in the tight quarters. I sprinted toward the smallest group and, with a flick of my wrist, they died. I came to a large dining area and backed up against the far wall. The battle rage quieted and a tendril of fear slid up my back. I clamped down on the feeling, I couldn't allow any weakness now. My fingers coiled around the hilt of Luka's blade. My other hand cramped painfully in response. I didn't have much time to dwell on the pain. In the next moment a group of enforcers stormed me. With a slice of my blade, my blood begun to run freely down my thigh. I drew the Magic from deep within myself and unleashed it on my enemies. An alarm sounded.

I had never fought a group before. In the arena I fought with weapons and the occasional burst of fire. My time as a mercenary had been spent killing from the shadows. This was different. The darkness filled me and instead of reigning it in I let it rain down.

Everything fell away, and the only thing that mattered was the enemy in front of me. My power moved across the dining room like a storm rolling in. It devoured everything in its path, suffocating any magical attack before it could materialise. Some screamed in pain, but most crumbled silently under the weight of my power.

Enforcers continued to spill into the room in an endless stream. The tips of my fingers had begun to go numb and the cold was slowly spreading up my arms. My once-endless supply of power was suddenly fallible.

Stella had been wrong.

Some of the enforcers pushed past my line of black noxious power and sprinted toward me, swords drawn. I yanked my power back into myself, not wasting more energy. I fortified my shield. My concentration faltered as someone threw themself at me. I swung my weapon too late, their blade bit into my shoulder. My skin split open and my blood poured down my arm making the grip on my weapon slippery. The pain cleared my mind and my Magic came roaring back. I swung and cut through the enforcer. Luka's weapon was a thing of beauty.

My muscles burned and shook as I fought off four enforcers with my blade. I was outnumbered. Still I continued to stab and slash. It was only through years of ruthless practice that I able to keep going. Magical attacks continued to rain down on my shield. I struggled to keep standing. I swiped downward with the blade, a long gash opened up across the midsection of the enforcer in front of me and deep red blood coated my bare feet. He stumbled to his knees and I swung my blade down across his neck, his severed head fell to the floor with a thud.

Upon seeing his fellow swordsmen decapitated, one enforcer snarled at me and threw a vicious kick to my side. I dodged too slow and the wind was knocked from my lungs. I faltered for a moment too long. My blood-covered sword was kicked from my hand and it clattered to the ground.

The enforcer lunged at me with her sword. My adrenaline surged and my Magic followed, involuntarily burying through her veins. She collapsed to the floor, bleeding from her mouth.

My power faltered. Instead of fire, ice shot through my veins. My limbs grew heavy and I shook with the effort it took to keep standing. I would die here.

The crowd hesitated. Their eyes flicked between themselves and the pile of dead bodies in front of me. They didn't know how weak I was. If they did, they would have attacked already. The scent of blood hung in the air and my body was slick with it.

I took a deep breath and pushed the adrenaline down. Crouching, I lifted my sword and a wild snarl filled the quiet space between us. I finally looked like the monster I was. My body was scarred, my eyes like endless black voids and my hair mattered.

I would haunt their nightmares.

My muscles tensed and I was ready to launch into another attack.

A wall of blue flames rose in front of me, cutting me off from the group. Vanilla overpowered the scent of death that had filled the room and I whipped around looking for the cause.

The Hunter emerged from an unseen corridor beside me. I swung around, readying my weapon. I had been foolish enough to show mercy once. The mistake would not be made again.

For the first time in a long time I saw genuine fear flash behind his eyes. It was well placed. Finally he saw me for the monster I truly was. A bead of sweat rolled down my back.

I stepped closer to him and away from the suffocating heat. My back straightened and my shredded t-shirt slipped from my shoulder. His gaze shifted to my uncovered skin and his eyes raked my body. The Hunter's power licked at exposed skin. The heat from his Magic replaced some of the iciness that had weighted down my limbs. I sauntered toward him. He sashayed away, keeping his distance. I could hear the screams of the enforcers as they attempted to breach the Hunter's wall of flames.

"Rina, we need to get out of here."

I licked my lips, remembering the feel of his mouth as it trailed down my neck.

"You have to leave now or they'll kill you."

"I don't care. I want Judas."

Revenge would bring me peace or it would bring me death.

"He's not here. He left a month ago."

Liar. I flung the last remnants of my power toward him. He brought his hand up to shield his face, the black smokey tendrils parted and dispersed into the air like they were no more than smoke on the breeze.

No.

He looked as surprised as I felt. I grabbed the dagger from the waistband of my pants and crossed toward him. It seemed wrong to attack a man with his own blade. Good thing I had never had any honour. Before I could slash at him he threw a ball of flames toward me. I jumped out of the way, but the Hunter wasn't aiming for my chest so I misjudged the distance. The ball of fiery Magic smashed into my stomach. I waited for the pain, for the unbearable heat to spread across my chest, but it never came. Instead, his delicious, tingling power filled me. Sending pleasant shivers up my spine.

The fire replaced some of the Magic I had lost.

Like lightening, he rushed me. I kicked him hard in the chest. The Hunter didn't stumble back. Instead he grabbed my arm and tried to drag me away from his flames.

"We have to go now."

I struggled violently from his grip, screaming like a banshee. He was going to take me back to the cells. With my body as weak as it was there was no way I could beat him in a fight. I scratched at his face and bit his hand. His skin gave way under my teeth and his blood filled my mouth.

He swore and pushed me to the ground, pressing my wrists into the ground.

"Please," I moaned, trying to buck him off. "Kill me."

Panic overtook me. My breathing became rapid and shallow. My heart pounded in my chest and my vision threatened to go dark. I had thought my sanity had returned, but it was slipping through my fingers like sand. I felt like I was drowning with no hope of being saved. Painful memories began to spread through my mind and take me back to places that I never wanted to revisit. I strained my palms toward my ears and tried to block out the haunted screams, but it didn't work. They grew louder and louder and I desperately wished them away. Before I was lost for good, a golden thread of Magic cut through the dark. I was guided back to reality by the feel of a warm hand cradling my cheek. The screams finally began to quieten.

"Cut it out! I can't hold them off much longer." He forced me to make eye contact. If I looked away, the last threads of my sanity would float off.

"I won't go back."

"You idiot. I'm as much a traitor as you. We have to leave this place now."

He hauled me to my feet and dragged me through the corridors. Without warning we exploded onto the street.

The night air seared my lungs. There were no shouts coming from behind me or stray Magic being shot at our back. We were free.

I burst through the doors and kept running. The Hunter grabbed my wrist and turned me around to face the Elect headquarters. The building seemed small. It was all smoked glass and steel. It didn't look like it housed a rat's nest of horrors behind the clean facade. It was like everything the Elect built. The beautiful exterior hid the atrocity that lurked beneath. He presented me with the hilt of his dagger.

"Burn it."

"I don't have any Magic left." He flicked his wrist and the dagger disappeared.

There was a thin line of blood on the heel of his palm that he reached out and curled his fingers around mine. "Use mine."

I arched a brow toward him. "It doesn't work that way."

"Trust me." The Hunter kept glancing toward the building, waiting for the enforcers to burst from the doors. We didn't have much time.

I closed my eyes and stretched my awareness. Luka's hand grew warm in mine, but my skin did not blister. My power roared to life in a heady mix of vanilla and ash. My eyes flashed open and I stared at the Hunter.

"Quickly," he said.

There was too much glass and steel. It would take more

Magic than either of us had to burn it. I wove a golden rune in my mind's eye. I drew on Luka's power and felt it snake up my arm and settle beneath my breastbone. It was hot and light, so unlike my own. I bundled it together with the scraps of my own Magic. They melded into something stronger than either on their own. The rune clicked into place and I threw my good arm toward the building. The ground beneath us groaned. I dragged more and more Magic from the connection. My skin was on fire, but I ignored the pain. His grip stayed firm on my hand. The only thing that mattered was the feel of his calloused hand against mine. *Squeeze. Tap.* The stones beneath our feet begun to shake and a giant split formed and chased toward the building. The first glass panel shattering snapped me to the present.

Luka had taken a knee, and his eyes were half-lidded.

"Where are we going?" I shouted over the sounds of shattering glass. The building would fall soon. Luka caught his weight and lolled his head back to look at me. "Luka! Where are we going?" I tried to pull him to his feet, but he was too heavy. His eyes were glazed. I looped my arms under his armpits and pulled. He managed to get his feet under him enough to stand mostly on his own.

"Square…The Square." He pointed toward a corridor.

"Come on," I groaned and shouldered most of his weight. The building behind us began to scream as steel beams twisted and protested against the Magic. We stumbled toward the dais and I prayed to whatever God was listening that the collapse of the Headquarters had killed the enforcers chasing us and everyone else within it.

We stumbled toward the Square, but the dais where I had watched a young Blood Mage be slaughtered only a year ago was no more. The only things that remained was a pile of rubble and eleven mannequins hanging by their neck from a noose. I halted and Luka collapsed to his knees. Each mannequin was clothed in white rags and the sigil of the rebellion drawn in red, dripping paint across their chests.

Useless, futile hope welled in my chest. The rebellion had been dealt a blow, but they would survive. Luka motioned toward the pile of rubble and I dragged us toward it. Our travels were achingly slow and I resisted the urge to turn back toward the Elect's building. We reached the old stage and I saw where Luka was taking us. There was a small opening that looked like it had once been under the stage. I shoved the twisted steel and debris out of the way. There was a ladder that I couldn't see the bottom of.

"Can you climb down?" I asked the Hunter. He grunted in some sort of assent. It would have to be good enough. "I'll go first."

It was stupid to think I could save him if he fell. The only thing I would be was a trophy he collected before we both smashed onto the ground. I still went down first. My hands were slick with blood and I hung onto the rungs with all my strength. Luka's grunts of agony echoed through the shaft as he started his descent. After what felt like hours, my boots finally touched solid ground. The passage was pitch black, but my Magic still hadn't returned enough to be of any help.

Luka had stopped grunting, but his breathing was fast and laboured when he touched down a few minutes later.

"Rina?" he wheezed out.

"I'm here," I said, grabbing for him. "Where are we going?"

"There's a passage up ahead. It's just a little further and then we can rest." It sounded like he was convincing himself more than me. I threw his muscled arm over my shoulders and grabbed in the darkness until I found the tunnel. Luka had to duck his head to get through.

"On the left."

Just as he said it, the wall disappeared. I turned us around and we both stumbled over a large threshold. My hands and knees hit soft bedding. Luka cursed.

A match was lit and the tiny space was revealed under the warm light of a lantern. It was mostly taken up by the mattress, but supplies were squirrelled away in the nooks and crevices in the walls. Luka collapsed onto the bedding. Almost all of his olive skin was coated in blood. I grabbed some bandages and began yanking them from their packages. He let me wrap the the wounds without complaint. There was no potions in the poorly put together first-aid kit. They wouldn't have kept well underground. When I had completed the dressings, I lay back onto the mattress. My head ached with the beginnings of power backlash. Blood caked my whole body and dried in my hair. My borrowed clothes were soaked and heavy against my skin.

"I need a drink."

Luka's rumbling laugh bounced off the walls.

"We can rest here until morning. Loral and the others are hiding out in Kirkland. They will meet us outside the city in a few days."

For a moment his words didn't compute, and all I could do was stare uselessly at the ceiling. "I can't go back."

"They knew I was getting you out. You put a wrench in the plans, performing your avenging angel ploy. But it'll still work."

"You...You were talking to the others?" I couldn't even manage to push any heat into my accusation.

"Of course," he said the words as if I was the fool.

"I'm not going with you." I said the words with force.

"Why?" He pushed himself into a seated potion, genuinely puzzled.

"I betrayed them. I don't deserve to be..." My voice cracked. "...apart of anything."

"I told them everything. It's okay, Rina. We can go back."

"I won't." I shouted too loudly. His face fell. I rolled over and faced the wall, curling in on myself. My chest felt too exposed. I could feel the cold air ripping through my internal cavities. I blinked back tears. It was shame that snapped the invisible wounds shut. The slick emotion reminded me of my malignant Magic. I shuddered. It welled within my chest, coating my insides with oil. I squeezed my eyes shut, but it did nothing to soothe me. The Hunter did not attempt to offer any comfort, for which I was grateful.

After a few hours of terse silence, his breathing evened out. My tears had long since dried. I crawled out of the hole and back toward the direction of the ladder. The underground was suffocating.

Chapter Twenty-Three

I stood outside the gates of Lucia's compound.

The heavily-warded perimeter was at least ten-feet tall. The top was lined by poisoned barbed wire, enough to keep even the most adventurous of thieves out. The gates groaned as they opened. The barracks looked achingly familiar. The wooden building stood like an abandoned barn.

I slipped inside the gate before it had a time to completely open. Most of the fighters preferred to train outside in the night time air. They didn't stop when I came in. Lucia would have their hide if they did. She would be seated in her room at the top of the barracks overlooking training, occasionally screaming out commands. I eyed the fighters wondering if I would see anyone that knew me.

The dirt underneath my feet felt familiar.

For most of my life this had been my home, the place I had cured my grief and tendered to the worst parts of myself. It was the only place I belonged. I had thought that revenge would bring me peace, how many enforcers lay dead at my feet?

Fifty?

One-hundred?

It didn't matter. My mind was like a raging storm. If vengeance wouldn't heal my soul, I would return to the only place that had ever felt like home.

Arina Bluebell was no longer. She was the girl left rotting in the Elect cells.

Lucia came toward me, her fangs peeking out from her full lips.

"Welcome back Imelda."

Fantastic Books
Great Authors

darkstroke is
an imprint of
Crooked Cat Books

- Gripping Thrillers
- Cosy Mysteries
- Romantic Chick-Lit
- Fascinating Historicals
- Exciting Fantasy
- Young Adult
- Non-Fiction

Discover us online
www.darkstroke.com

Find us on instagram:
www.instagram.com/darkstrokebooks

Made in the USA
Las Vegas, NV
24 December 2020